"You're differe

Colin drew out the words, then added, "Compelling. In a way I've never known before."

In a stunningly simple black short shift that was sexier for what it covered, not for what it left uncovered, she could have stepped out of a fashion magazine.

And those lips—so artfully painted—glistened with promise.

"You did hear me say that when I'm done with my book I have to return to New York?"

"I heard."

"And you're okay with that?" The worry in her gaze hit him harder than the kiss waiting on her lips. She cared, too.

"Yes," he told her. She'd been honest. If, in the future, they needed to work out something... then they'd work it out.

Two nights ago his life had changed. He'd changed.

And it didn't seem as if there was a lot he could do about that.

Except to see where it was all going to lead...

Dear Reader,

What can I tell you about Chantel Harris that will make you want to read this book? Whatever it is, please imagine me saying it. Chantel is the best friend...but has few friends. Her closest friend, a female cop, was killed on duty. Chantel was the first responder.

She never expects things for herself, she only asks how she can help others. She's the kind of friend we all want.

If you haven't read previous Where Secrets are Safe books, relax, you don't need to. You won't feel left behind. For those of you who have, you'll have seen Chantel once before in book three, *Husband by Choice*, when she visited Santa Raquel to help her best friend's widower after his second wife goes missing.

Now a member of the Santa Raquel High Risk Team, she goes undercover to ensure the safety of a boy and his mother and ends up finding something horrible going on in the society she infiltrates. I didn't know, when I started this book, what was going to happen. I didn't know until the end how it was going to end. I didn't even know if the bad guy was bad. Chantel took care of it all. She took care of me. And she'll take care of you, too, if you give her a chance!

I love to interact with my readers. You can find me on Facebook at facebook.com/tarataylorquinn and on Twitter, @tarataylorquinn.

Or join my open Friendship board on Pinterest! Pinterest.com/TaraTaylorQuinn/Friendship

All the best,

Tara

USA TODAY Bestselling Author

TARA TAYLOR QUINN

——

Love by Association

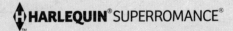

Recycling programs
for this product may
not exist in your area.

ISBN-13: 978-0-373-60949-9

Love by Association

HARLEQUIN®

™ www.Harlequin.com

Printed in U.S.A.

An author of more than seventy novels, **Tara Taylor Quinn** is a *USA TODAY* bestselling author with more than seven million copies sold. She is known for delivering emotional and psychologically astute novels of suspense and romance. Tara is a past president of Romance Writers of America. She has won a Readers' Choice Award and is a five-time finalist for an RWA RITA® Award, a finalist for a Reviewer's Choice Award and a Booksellers' Best Award. She has also appeared on TV across the country, including *CBS Sunday Morning*. She supports the National Domestic Violence Hotline. If you or someone you know might be a victim of domestic violence in the United States, please contact 1-800-799-7233.

Books by Tara Taylor Quinn

HARLEQUIN SUPERROMANCE

Where Secrets are Safe

Wife by Design
Once a Family
Husband by Choice
Child by Chance
Mother by Fate
The Good Father

Shelter Valley Stories

Sophie's Secret
Full Contact
It's Never Too Late
Second Time's the Charm
The Moment of Truth

It Happened in Comfort Cove

A Son's Tale

A Daughter's Story
The Truth About Comfort Cove

HARLEQUIN HEARTWARMING

The Historic Arapahoe

Once Upon a Friendship
Once Upon a Marriage

MIRA BOOKS

Street Smart
In Plain Sight
The Second Lie
The Third Secret
The Fourth Victim
The Friendship Pact

Visit the Author Profile page at Harlequin.com for more titles.

For Lynda Kachurek, who started out
as a fan and became a friend.
I am very thankful you sought me out...

CHAPTER ONE

IT FELT WEIRD being in an interrogation room out of uniform. Not that thirty-two-year-old Chantel Harris spent much time interrogating suspects. She was a street cop, not a detective. But in the twelve years she'd been a cop, she'd been called in to sit with suspects on occasion and to help with questioning a time or two.

Even worse than being out of uniform was entering the room on stiletto heels, with makeup on her face and with her blond hair, which usually lived in a ponytail, cascading down her back in artfully curled waves.

"Excuse me, miss, but… *Chantel*?"

She almost turned and walked right back out as Detective Wayne Stanton—a friend from academy days—whooped. And grinned.

"Impressive, Wayne," Chantel said, trying not to become too fond of the way the silk lining of her pants slid along her legs as she sat. Cops couldn't afford Italian-made silk-lined clothes. Shrugging out of the matching slate blue jacket, she drummed her blunt-cut fingernails on the table. "Let's get through this."

"Actually, you're the impressive one," Captain Reagan said, coming in behind her and closing the door. "You clean up nice, Harris."

"Thank you, sir." The undercover assignment had been her idea. Hers and Wayne's. She had no doubts about her ability to do the job. Or her desire to catch the rich scumbag who thought his money and power gave him the right to knock his wife around.

"I might make one suggestion, though." The captain was holding back a smile.

"What's that, sir?"

"Before you go to the fundraiser tonight, stop off at one of those walk-in nail salons—I believe there's one on the corner of Dunbar and First. Get yourself some acrylic nails. No rich society woman's going to show up with fingers that look ready and able to pull a trigger."

He had a point. "Yes, sir."

"The money you received was enough to buy you the clothes and things you need to see you through a six-week stint?"

Six weeks had been the operation's initial approval window. Chantel hoped she could either get proof in that time or enough evidence to warrant an extension on the assignment.

"Yes, sir. I found a secondhand shop in LA that sells high-end designer clothes."

"So just to be clear—" the captain looked at her and Wayne "—you'll work your regular tour, with pay. For this operation you have your project budget, but your time spent is on a volunteer basis."

"Yes, sir."

"Yes, sir," Wayne echoed. While the detective wouldn't be undercover, he was not only going to be the person to whom she reported, but he would also be doing follow-up, including information dissemination.

The captain shook his head. "You're both really committed to this High Risk team."

"Yes, sir," they said in unison. By bringing together members from all professions that came in contact with victims of domestic violence, creating an information pool that ensured that doctors and schools and legal aid and child protective services were all on the same page, the team was preventing domestic-violence deaths. Chantel had seen firsthand evidence...

The captain sat back. "You know, when I first read the memo on this team, I thought the folks in charge were nuts."

Chantel's jaw tightened as she bit back the ready defense that sprang to her lips.

"But I have to admit...domestic violence statistics, even here in Santa Raquel, are down remarkably."

She relaxed.

"And you." He nodded toward Chantel. "You know better than most..."

"Yes, sir."

She'd first visited Santa Raquel from San Diego two years before, as a favor to a friend who believed his wife had been taken by her abusive ex-husband. Wayne, who'd been a member of the Santa Raquel police force, had helped her—also on his own time—and they'd saved a woman's life.

As far as anyone knew, it had been Chantel's first personal experience with domestic violence. And while she'd always known that what had happened with her stepfather had been a crime, she'd only in the past months begun to realize just how hideous his treatment of her had been. Helping Max and Meri Bennet had changed her in a lot of ways. Not only in how she viewed love. Through them she'd found her calling, found a way to put her own past to good use. To make lemonade out of her lemons. She was *meant* to help other women who, though they may have the strength of Hercules, couldn't always fight their battles on their own. Innocent women who'd been betrayed in the vilest ways by the one person they were supposed to be able to trust above all others.

She'd applied for a position on the Santa Raquel police force, as well as with the High Risk team developed by The Lemonade Stand—a unique women's shelter right there in Santa Raquel. The place where Meri Bennet—wife to Chantel's close friend, Max Bennet—had run when her ex-husband, a Las Vegas police detective, had threatened the lives of her husband and young son.

In the time since Meri's rescue from the hands of a madman, Chantel had not only grown to know her, but to consider her one of her closest friends.

When she thought about what would have happened to her if Max hadn't been so adamant that his wife was in trouble…if Chantel hadn't loved him enough to have enlisted Wayne's help…

The captain tapped the table. "So, I've read the reports. We're all on the same page here, and unless I hear from Stanton that we have a problem, I'll expect normal reports on this sting until otherwise noted."

"Yes, sir." As a beat cop, Chantel wasn't used to sitting down for one-on-one conversations with a department captain.

She wasn't used to hobnobbing with the rich and famous, either. She hoped, during her debut that evening at the auction being hosted to benefit some art foundation, that she wasn't as tongue-tied and awkward as she felt right then.

The captain seemed to have dismissed them, but he was still sitting there. And until he stood, she couldn't. "I just have one question…"

"Yes, sir?" Wayne answered for the two of them.

"This collage thing… You don't think this is overkill? The department's money, going undercover, working your ass off for no compensation because some kid pasted pictures on a board during art class?"

"The boy's father has a sealed juvenile record,

sir," Wayne said, immediately pointing out the information they'd found when they'd started asking questions about the wealthy, respected and well-known Morrison family, who lived just a few miles from them in nearby Santa Barbara.

"I understand. He hit his younger brother with a baseball bat."

"The boy died."

"That was more than forty years ago. Plus, as we've already said, the record was sealed."

"Hospital records show that Mrs. Morrison is accident-prone." Wayne was all business as, in his suit and tie—daily attire for him now—he sat forward, facing the captain.

"I understand. She's not the only woman who appears to suffer from the malady. Believe me, I want domestic violence to stop. I don't want anyone to suffer abuse at the hands of loved ones. I'm just trying to understand, between you and me, why we're going to all this trouble because of a collage."

Wayne looked at her, and Chantel found her tongue.

"The artist who works in the schools doing collages with students, Talia Paulson, volunteers at The Lemonade Stand, sir. She has now had formal training in domestic violence counseling. She works with all students, but part of her purpose is to read the collages, as a way to pinpoint problems students might be having that the adults in their lives are either unaware of or not tending to.

"Anger issues, self-concept issues, grief… It all comes out not only in the photos these kids choose, but in organization and color expression, too."

She had Captain Reagan's full attention now. And though she felt like a bug under his microscope, she respected the man and needed his buy-in.

Not to do the job. The project was already approved. But for her own sense of…she didn't know what.

"Ryder Morrison is a straight-A student in a well-touted private school. He also used to be a star swimmer and was damned good at surfing, too. In the past year, he's become withdrawn. Never wanting to leave home, or seemingly leave his mother's side. Talia was called in. What she saw in Ryder's collage alarmed her to the point that she called the High Risk team immediately."

"I read the report," Reagan said. "What was *in* the collage? That's what I'm asking."

"Baseball bats. A series of them, hidden among a collection of surfboards, sticking out of the leg of a pair of swim trunks, as a tattoo on a businessman's arm. The bats were all small, and all black. The other thing that stood out was a collection of ads—all women selling house-cleaning supplies like furniture polish and floor wax. They also were spread throughout the other clear interest groupings. All of those were rimmed in red and purple. Colors that typically signify love and blood. Bruising. There were other things, but those were the most standout. Talia was alarmed and called us. Wayne checked it out and found not only that Mrs. Morrison was prone to being hurt—bruised—but that Mr. Morrison had had an episode with a baseball bat…"

"Did anyone think about asking the kid about any of this?" Reagan asked. "I didn't see anything about it in the report."

"His parents refused to let him speak with us," Wayne dutifully reported.

Chantel looked at Captain Reagan and made a split-second decision to trust him. He was a powerful man in the small police force. She wanted to know they had him on their side.

"Talia spoke with Ryder," she said. "He told her that he'd overheard something, but that when he'd asked his mother about it she'd told him he'd misunderstood. We don't know what he was referring to. But that had been his reply when Talia had asked him about the significance of the baseball bats. He said they were black to represent misunderstanding."

"A bit deep for an eleven-year-old."

"Kids who are forced to grow up quickly tend to be that way." Chantel knew.

Reagan frowned. "So you think what this kid overheard was something about his father killing his little brother?"

Wayne's head tilted a bit as he said, "Stands to

reason. It's pretty clear that whether it's something he overheard, or something going on in his home, Ryder has had a complete personality change in the past year and neither of his parents are acknowledging it."

Chantel added, "They say his behavior changes are no more than a phase, due to his burgeoning adolescence. And because there are no signs of physical abuse against him, no sign that he's being mistreated at all, there's no more we can do to gain entrance through a front-door approach."

"That family is in danger, sir," Wayne told him. "The boy is clearly afraid."

"I'm willing to work triple shifts without pay if need be to prevent Mr. Morrison from hurting his son. I wouldn't be able to live with myself if Ryder ended up hurt or, God forbid, dead because we did nothing."

"Not to mention Mrs. Morrison," Wayne added. "Her life is clearly even more in the balance than her son's since she's already exhibiting signs of having been abused. According to hospital records, she's had a broken arm, a broken collarbone, multiple contusions on the back of her head and ribs broken in her back. Those are the injuries she sought medical help for. We have no idea how many others there have been. As you saw in the report, we've had three doctor notifications of suspected abuse over the past several years, but each time, both parties deny any wrongdoing. It's clear she's not going to press charges. Or even stand up for her son. She won't let him talk to us."

While it was true that Leslie Morrison had refused police access to her son, Chantel wasn't as certain as Wayne that the woman wouldn't stand up for him. She believed it was more a case of the woman keeping her son safe by covering for her husband—and taking his abuse herself.

Reagan shook his head, picking up his folder. "So, she won't press charges against the bastard."

The statement hung there between the three of them. Questions choking them with their lack of answers.

Until it became clear that the only way any of them were going to find the peace they sought was by getting back to work.

"You be careful out there," Reagan said to Chantel as she walked down the hall of the station like she'd been born in fashionable heels. She'd been practicing in her apartment all week.

"I will, sir."

"This man, if he's guilty of all that we suspect—he's dangerous."

"I know, sir. Which is why we need a cop in there keeping an eye on things. Don't worry. I'll have my gun with me at all times."

He nodded as he left them. Then it was just her and Wayne, standing by the back door.

"You got me on speed dial?" he asked.

"Of course."

"Then go get them, Chantel. You're born to do this job. If anyone can pull it off, you can."

She hoped so.

Going against bad guys didn't give her pause. Drug dealers. Thieves. Rapists. She was trained to take them down.

But act all girlie and glamorous? A woman who could laugh in all the right places and move like she wanted every man in the place to look at her?

That wasn't her style at all.

CHAPTER TWO

"COME, ON, JULES, you know how much I hate going to these things by myself." Thirty-one-year-old Colin Fairbanks stood outside his twenty-seven-year-old sister's suite on the north end of the estate home they shared, talking to her through the door she'd just refused to open.

"Not tonight, Col." Her voice was strong. Determined.

She wasn't crying, didn't sound damaged…tonight. Still…

Her door opened, and she stood, looking beautiful and…normal, in jeans and a sweater that matched the blue in her eyes. "I'm in the middle of a project," she told him.

He could see the artist's lamp lit over the table, the stool that she'd obviously been perched on. Paper and pencils were spread across the tilted surface.

A project. Writing and illustrating children's stories that she wouldn't send out to agents or publishers. The collection was building. Colin had had a friend of his print some up for her to see—thinking that if she saw them as real books she'd be driven to find a publisher.

"I asked you two weeks ago to accompany me tonight," he told her. "You know way more about art than I do. And…"

"I told you I would think about it. I never said I'd go."

In ten years' time he'd managed to cajole, beg and probably guilt her into attending a handful of functions with him. Ten years of her life she'd never get back.

"Come on, Jules. A few hours out of your Thursday night is all I'm asking." The law firm of Fairbanks and Fairbanks—named for his father and grandfather, both deceased—represented a good many of the contributors who would be attending this evening. It was expected that a Fairbanks be there.

He'd probably be instrumental in the closing of more than one deal that night. Which was fine with him. He liked the challenge afforded him by his job as sole owner of Santa Raquel's most powerful law firm.

"I know you want me to think you need me there because of the art." Julie nodded. "But you and I both know you're just there for the legal contract part, Colin, not the value designation. We also both know you don't have to go alone. Just put out the word that you want a date and you'll have your pick."

Her smile was almost reminiscent of the loving scoundrel Julie had been until her senior year of high school. But not quite. That shadow of perpetual resignation ruined the effect.

"And if I go alone, I'm going to spend what parts of the evening I'm not overseeing potential negotiations fending off whatever women manage to get to me first."

Her eyes shone with sympathy, and a hint of the old mischief.

"Amber Winslow's going to be there," he told her. The woman—a classmate of his from the private high school they'd both attended—was a leech. And newly divorced.

In the olden days Julie would have been all over protecting him from that particular worm.

"So are the Smyths."

He hadn't heard, or he wouldn't have asked Julie to accompany him. He was surprised actually. Smyth wasn't a big supporter of the arts.

But that was that. As desperately as Colin wished his little sister could move on, he also understood why she couldn't. In the ten years since David Smyth had gotten away with brutally raping her at a party, Julie had not seen him. Even from a distance. She'd refused to be anywhere that either David Jr. or his father, David Sr.—owner of one of the last family banks in the state—were in attendance.

In spite of the fact that that meant she was cut

off from much of the social circle in which she'd grown up and thrived.

Not to mention losing the close relationship she'd had with Margaret Smyth, David Jr.'s mother.

With David Sr. being their father Michael's closest friend, they'd all grown up together. When Colin and Julie's mother had died, Margaret Smyth had been like a mother to them…

"Jaime told me they were on the confirmed guest list."

Julie's friend from grade school who'd moved to New York before high school, Jaime Mendonthol, had a couple of paintings in the evening's fundraising auction. She was in town, and the two women had met for lunch the day before.

Jaime had been the reason Colin had been so hopeful that his sister would agree to the night out. Missing Jaime's local show would be hard on her.

"I knew, anyway. Leslie Morrison sent me the guest list."

Leslie Morrison, wife of James Morrison, owner and CEO of Morrison Textiles—a third-generation company that had been using Fairbanks and Fairbanks as lead counsel for more than seventy-five years—was, as far as Colin knew, the only person in their circle who knew what had happened to Julie the night that David Smyth slipped a drug into her drink and then proceeded to sexually violate her in every way possible.

Most people knew of, or had heard rumor of, a

liaison gone bad between the two of them. But word among "friends" was that their sexual relations the night of the party had been consensual.

"Friends" including Santa Raquel's esteemed police commissioner.

When it had become clear that Julie wasn't going to get justice—due in large part to a law enforcement system that was willing to look away if the right money was involved—she'd begged Colin to keep the incident a secret. To preserve as much of the life she'd led as she could. He'd wanted to move, leave the country, even. Start over in Italy or someplace else beautiful enough to distract his little sister from the horror she wasn't ever going to completely escape.

Julie was the one who'd convinced him they needed to stay home. Pointing out, rightly so, that a lot of people depended on Fairbanks and Fairbanks, trusted them, in a world where having an attorney in business was an absolute must. Pointing out, as well, that if he closed the firm, they'd not only put a couple dozen attorneys and more than a hundred support staff out of jobs, but they'd lose the income necessary to keep their family home on the California coast—a home their grandfather had built from scratch.

Why Leslie Morrison kept the secret, Colin didn't know. Nor did he know, for sure, how she'd known what had happened. He'd just come home from law school one day, shortly after that horrible night, a twenty-one-year-old kid trying to raise his sister after their father's heart attack the year before and their mother's death from hepatitis the year before that, and found Leslie and Julie sitting on the couch.

Not all that unusual, seeing that Leslie chaired the county's Pet Adoption and Rescue Fund, a charitable fund that raised much of the money that helped support more than twenty shelters and neutering programs in a thirty-mile radius along the coast. Julie had run for and won election to junior chair of the fund her sophomore year in high school.

She'd been sitting on the committee's board ever since. Now with a college degree in finance, Julie was also part of the Sunshine Children's League—which raised funds for children without families, providing funding for basic necessities but also some scholarships to California state universities.

She attended luncheons and organized fundraisers. She shopped at the stores she loved and occasionally went to dinner with a girlfriend or two.

But she didn't date. She never frequented dinner establishments where she might run into a Smyth. She hadn't been back to Santa Barbara—home to the Smyth mansion where the rape had taken place—in ten years.

And she almost never attended evening social functions.

Colin gave up trying to change her mind that night.

FROM THE MINUTE she walked into the glitzy ball-room Thursday night, Chantel changed. As though she'd been born to wealth, her persona slid over her, oozing a confidence that surprised her as she entered the elegant party in the five-star resort on the Pacific coastline.

For that night she was a woman of privilege. And she was a woman on the prowl. Not unlike most of the unattached—and probably some of the attached, as well—women there. But unlike the rest of her unlikely peers, Chantel, while prowling for a man, wasn't there for personal gain. She wanted to pick up a man as badly as any of them. Maybe worse.

But she wasn't hoping he'd take her home. To the contrary. She wanted him locked up in an eight-by-eight cell, where she knew he'd never be able to hurt his wife again. Picturing the key to the cell flying through the air and landing in the ocean beyond the wall of windows at one end of the elegantly appointed room, Chantel sent a silent promise to Ryder Morrison that he wasn't going to spend the next several years watching his father beat up his mother. Or living in fear that his father would someday come after him with a baseball bat as he had his own little brother so many years before.

Not that arresting the man would guarantee that. They needed to build a case against him, find ample enough proof that no matter who came to the powerful man's rescue, the prosecutor could still win a conviction.

It wouldn't be easy. James Morrison was a respected and very rich man who'd funded many of the seated politicians in California's congress. He probably had blackmail goods on others.

And that was where she came in. With her blond hair curling over her breasts, the ample cleavage that was visible in the V of the black, figure-hugging and glittering gown she'd worn for her debut evening as the daughter of an East Coast millionaire newly settling in California, Chantel remembered the mantra that Wayne had been repeating almost hourly the week since they'd won approval for this sting.

Patience.

"Undercover work isn't about going in and getting it done," he'd told her. "It's about taking the time to become intimate with the life you're infiltrating."

Used to being the one who bulldozed ahead and made things happen, Chantel paused just inside the door of the richly decorated room. She'd passed her first test—handing off her invitation at the door.

Gleaned from the police commissioner himself. A man she'd never met, a man who wouldn't be acknowledging her presence that night—though he would surely be there, even if just to put in an appearance.

He'd agreed to the sting, wanted her to get Morrison if he turned out to be guilty of beating up his wife.

But he was expecting Chantel to clear the textile magnate's name. Morrison and Commissioner Paul Reynolds were golf buddies. They went way back.

Or so she'd been told.

Still, she couldn't know the commissioner. Not newly arrived from upstate New York as she was.

And she wasn't about to get cozy with James Morrison, either. No, her job was to infiltrate the community. Become friendly with those who knew Morrison. People who could let things drop that a police officer might be able to use to find the dirt on him. The truth about him.

Her job was to find out the man's deepest secrets, and if those secrets involved raising even a little finger to his wife or son, to expose him for the criminal that he was. She was there to get the proof...

COLIN WORKED THE room as his father had taught him, making time for each and every one of the firm's clients. Shaking hands. Being available to anyone who might need advice on the spot.

And making certain that Fairbanks and Fairbanks's top-grade lawyers, all in their tuxes and sipping on nothing more lethal than club soda, were ready to step into any situation that required more complicated legal machinations.

Though Colin was certainly as skilled and capable as the best of them, his job as the rainmaker, and CEO, of Fairbanks and Fairbanks required that he know about every single deal his firm handled. Which meant that he couldn't possibly give his wealthy clients the time and attention they required for drawing up complicated contracts with all t's crossed and i's dotted.

Colin handled the beginning and the end. The handshakes. Occasionally, on cases that took unexpected turns, he'd be in the middle, too.

His self-appointed job—his purpose in life—was to make certain that integrity was at the root of everything touched by a Fairbanks. He owed that to Julie.

And to the parents who'd died young and counted on him to protect her. He was a lawyer—educated at Stanford, graduated from the top of his class—and he'd been unable to bring his sister justice.

He'd learned young—and the hard way—that integrity was rare, and he couldn't count on it from anyone but Julie. Ever.

He hadn't seen Jaime yet—she was busy behind the scenes getting ready for the opening of the curtain that would highlight all of the night's top auction pieces on the revolving stage that had been set up in the middle of the room—but he hoped to be able to say hello. To invite Julie's friend to dine with them one night before she left town, to hear what Jaime thought of the Julie she'd seen that week.

Not that he'd gossip about his sister. But Jaime had known Julie before the incident. She'd gotten into trouble with her a time or two. Like the time they'd climbed to the top of the water tower to hold up a sign, a piece of artwork, really, made by Jaime, protesting the fact that they'd been told they couldn't pray in school.

Catching sight of the police commissioner, he made a sharp turn and a beeline for the bar, where he ordered a Scotch and water. The water in deference to the fact that he was driving. He kept his back to the room. Commissioner Reynolds didn't stay long at these things—usually leaving his deputy commissioner to the public relations duties required by the office he held—but with the Smyths in attendance, it was no surprise the commissioner had shown, as well. And if Colin turned around to look, he was sure he'd see Smyth, too. They were always together.

He hadn't seen either of the David Smyths that evening. But it wouldn't have mattered if he had. He'd faced them down many times, with polite indifference. Each and every time they were the first to look away.

He took some small measure of satisfaction in that. Not nearly enough to even hope to heal his sister's wounds, the damage they'd done to his family, but it allowed him to walk among them.

Julie was determined that people like the Smyths—people who bought police commissioners off rather than being accountable to their actions—would not chase out of town the people with integrity, namely the Fairbankses.

And that was the strongest reason Colin hung around. Because it was what Julie needed.

He could be a good lawyer anywhere and might even be better suited at finding a woman who didn't bore him if he weren't still living in the same small society in which he'd grown up. Or at least find one that he trusted to like him for the man he was inside, not for the man who happened to have a few million in his bank account.

One thing was for certain. While there were ample numbers of women here who would be eager to wear his ring, not one of them was willing to sign a prenuptial agreement.

He knew. He'd made quite a reputation for himself a few years back when he'd been on the brink of proposing and had brought up the prenuptial subject as a way of leading into the proposal. He'd actually thought love drove the liaison that time. That the woman in question understood that unless Julie married, Colin's inheritance would one day go to her.

He supposed it was lucky that he'd never made it to the proposal stage. He'd been saved from being married for his money. "A glass of Chateau Ste. Michelle Pinot, please?"

The voice, coming from just behind him on the left, seemed to pour over Colin's shoulder and down his body. Smooth and cultured, like she'd attended one of those finishing schools that always seemed to take anything natural and real out of women. And yet...with a hint of husky, too. A hint that maybe this particular woman hadn't been a complete success at that school.

He turned, expecting to see someone older, perhaps his mother's age. An art lover up from LA. Or one who'd flown in from the East Coast, like Jaime had...

Blond hair came into his vision, flowing over the most perfect breasts... The glass in his hand dropped to the bar with such force he was embarrassed. His mouth would have dropped, too, if he hadn't been so cultured himself.

She was most definitely not his mother's age.

"Hello," he said, making way for her to step up to the bar beside him.

"Hello." Her East Coast accent wasn't strong, but it was there. Another part of her the school couldn't quite ameliorate?

"I'm Colin Fairbanks," he said, holding out a hand to her.

He was a handshaker. It came with his job.

Her nails, conservatively longish and a sedate red, glistened as she returned his gesture. Her skin was surprisingly...not as soft as he'd expected, like she did her own gardening or, like Julie, had her hands in turpentine. Still, he wanted to hold on.

"I'm Chantel Johnson," she said, pulling her

hand back after a brief touch. And then, "Thank you," with what had to be a heart-stopping smile to the bartender as he slid her wine toward her.

She took a sip, those glossy red lips managing to caress the edge of the glass without leaving any residual red paint behind.

"You in town for the auction?" He asked the obvious because for once in his life he didn't have an interesting conversational tidbit to offer.

She turned that smile on him, and it was more potent than he'd imagined. The small shake of her head drew his gaze to where the blond curls were caressing her breasts.

Embarrassed, he immediately raised his gaze. She tilted her head. "Not much of a gentleman, are you, Colin Fairbanks?"

"I'm sorry." He was mortified. "I don't usually... Truth is, I haven't... You aren't in town for the auction, then?"

Some rainmaker he was.

More like opportunity-blower.

She shook her head again. His gaze stayed glued on hers.

"I'm here, tonight, for the auction, but I'm in town to stay. I've recently relocated."

Hot damn. Chances were, since she clearly had an invitation to the night's shindig, he'd be seeing more of her.

"Where are you staying?"

"In a hotel at the moment. Until I can find a place that suits me."

He asked her what kind of place suited her and found out that she wanted something with beachfront—and property—but didn't need anything overly large as she lived by herself.

Colin was grinning by that point.

"So what brings you to California?"

"I'm writing a book," she told him. "My family is in publishing, and I want the book to be published, or not, based on its merits. I plan to submit it like anyone else would have to do and, knowing me, it'll be easier if I'm not right there with everyone, having to make up stories about what I'm doing.

"Besides, until last week I had an office on the top floor—VP of marketing. If nothing else, that felt like a conflict of interest, though I can't really say why. Marketing and editorial are separate entities..."

Publishing. Julie's children's books.

This was getting better and better.

"You're from New York?" he asked, then said, "Publishing, and that little bit of an accent..."

"I was raised in upstate New York," she told him. Her wineglass was still full.

"So, since you're new here, I suppose you don't know many people."

"None, actually. A big black-tie charity event... if it's anything like home, I figured this was the way to get to know them."

He stood, almost full glass of Scotch in hand. "Will you allow me to introduce you around?"

He'd probably wake up in the morning and find out that he'd had one hell of a great dream.

"I don't know, Colin Fairbanks," she said, taking a step back and giving him a saucy grin. Yeah, that dream was getting better by the second. "If I'm seen with you, will it damage my reputation? For all I know, you could be Southern California society's bad boy."

For a brief moment, he wished he was. Because he had a feeling she'd like him that way.

"Sorry to disappoint you, Ms. Johnson. I'm the guy others don't like because I tend to see the world in black-and-white—and aim for the white every time."

"No shades of gray for you?" She ran her finger along the edge of her wineglass and then licked it.

He fought a very strong temptation to bring that finger to his lips but managed to simply shake his head.

"Disappointed?" he asked.

She sipped wine and studied him. "I'm not sure," she told him. "Can I get back to you on that?"

So she expected to see him again. "Anytime," he told her, one hand in his pocket.

His clients were probably watching him by now. Any other night, he'd have been out there with them—mingling, being seen, listening.

Appearing to enjoy himself.

Did it show that that night was the first time in a very long time that he actually *was* enjoying himself?

"What is it that you do?" she asked, still not moving on into the room.

"I'm an attorney. Owner of Fairbanks and Fairbanks."

"Hotshot corporate lawyer," she said. Her eyes might have darkened. He couldn't be sure.

"You've heard of us."

"Who travels in this circle and hasn't?"

She had him there.

She was welcome to him anywhere.

CHAPTER THREE

SHE WAS OVERDOING IT. She'd never be able to pull off the femme fatale flirtatiousness on a longer-term basis. Chantel took the sexy steps she'd practiced across the room at Colin Fairbanks's side, reminding herself that she had to be patient. To slow down. She was in this for the long haul.

As long as it took to build a strong enough case against James Morrison. Or to convince herself that, while the man had admitted to beating his little brother to death with a baseball bat, he really wasn't a wife and family beater.

She smiled, said hello and shook hands as Colin introduced her around. She'd seen pictures of the Morrisons but had yet to see either of them that night. She hoped Leslie's absence didn't mean she had new bruises that she couldn't bring out in public.

Always the cop, Chantel couldn't ever lose her awareness of the darker side of life. Not even in the midst of a life as beautiful as that glitzy ballroom with its linen chair covers and tablecloths, real crystal glasses and more diamonds than she'd ever seen in one place. The flower arrangements were real. She could smell the roses as she passed.

And felt the heat as Colin's tuxedoed arm brushed against the skin left bare by her halter-top gown.

"How long have you been in town?" he asked as they left a group of investors in conversation with a lawyer Colin had just discreetly motioned over.

"A week," she told him. Wayne had gone over her story with her umpteen times. She'd delivered it without a hitch. He'd come up with the idea of her living in a hotel. It was easy enough for her to get picked up and dropped off from a hotel lobby. To take the hotel's limousine service to functions and then to drive home in her older model Mustang to her small one-bedroom apartment across from the beach.

An added benefit to the plan was that Wayne had done a favor for the night manager at the hotel. If anyone asked about her using the hotel's car service, or asked about her hanging around, she'd have an alibi.

The writing…that had been her stroke of genius. A job she could "do" without anyone ever seeing her. She had a maternal aunt by marriage whose family was in the publishing business. And their name was Johnson.

She saw Commissioner Reynolds tipping glasses with another man almost straight ahead of them, close enough that she heard their laughter. Colin was going to lead her right to them.

An awkward moment she'd prefer to avoid...

"I'm getting a little warm. Do you mind if we step outside?" she asked, raising her glass to her lips at the same time to hide any telltale twinge at the side of her mouth.

"Of course." Colin sounded as pleased as she felt relieved; he took a right and led her to a pair of glass double doors that led to a balcony.

Thankfully, there were heaters out there. She'd freeze her tail off in this gown on what had turned out to be a forty-degree January night. Wishing she hadn't left the shawl she'd bought on her bed at home, she allowed herself to be led outdoors.

Colin went for the balcony rail. She could hear the ocean in the distance but got as close to the nearest heater as she could manage.

"I can tell you're from New York," he said, smiling down at her in a way that she found more than a little distracting.

While she'd had more than her share of admirers in her more than three decades of living, Chantel didn't usually find herself being viewed with tenderness.

She was a decorated cop. The men she worked with knew that. They respected her abilities to protect them as well as they'd protect one another.

She felt naked against the tiny white glittering

lights strung around a couple of potted trees on either side of them.

"My accent gives me away every time," she said, trying to tighten her mouth a little bit more around the words—instilling as much of her accented native tongue as she could. A sound she'd worked years to lose when, with her best friend, she'd migrated from upstate New York to LA right out of high school.

Neither of them had ever looked back.

"It's not just your accent," he told her. "Look around you."

She did. There were three older men, all in matching monkey suits, to her right, seeming to be hiding out from the activities going on around them. Another two, farther away, to their left, were smoking.

"I don't get it," she told her companion. What about these guys gave her away as being from New York?

"There are no women out here. Even with the heaters, it's far too cold. You're obviously acclimated to colder weather."

Nope. But she had tough skin.

She'd missed seeing herself as the "only woman." Probably because she was used to being the only female among men.

She was perfectly comfortable that way, but felt like she was quickly losing control of her cover.

Like maybe, just maybe, she couldn't do this.

"Well, perhaps I'm just counting on you to keep me warm," she said. She *would* do this. A memory of the picture she'd seen of Ryder Morrison, of the collage he'd made and she'd studied, had her straightening her backbone. The medical records she'd been privy to as part of a law-mandated notice sent from the hospital to the police department sprang to mind.

She pictured her friend Meri, thought of the scars she still wore so long after the brutal beating that had almost left her dead, of the way she'd been near death's door, mostly incoherent, and had still managed to get herself out to the street...

"You okay?" Colin leaned in toward her. She breathed in his musky scent.

"Of course I'm okay," she sputtered, covering another lapse with a small sip of wine that took a long time to swallow.

So she wasn't quite as good at this undercover thing as she wanted to be. It was her first night out. On her first gig.

And she cared more than she probably should about the ultimate outcome. But truthfully, what cop didn't?

She forced a chuckle. "Makes me wonder about you, though, that you'd think there's something wrong with me for counting on you to keep me warm."

He moved closer, put an arm around her and pulled her in close, shocking Chantel with just how good that felt. "It was your eyes, not your words, that made me wonder," he said softly, leaning his head down toward her ear. "You looked kind of lost for a second there."

She had a poker face. Almost always. But she took note to work on it in front of the mirror in "rich heiress" mode.

"It's all so new," she said now, speaking the complete truth. "All of this…it's nothing like my life in New York."

"You didn't live by the ocean, then?"

"No." Her family, the broken fragments of it, had mostly lived in a brick house that looked like every other brick house in the row of brick houses. "And I always had friends close by," she said, resuming character. One friend. Jill…

"I didn't realize it was going to be so hard… not knowing anyone. Truth be told, I was kind of looking forward to meeting a whole new group of people."

"Society life can be a little cloying, can't it?" Colin surprised her by saying. "You grow up with the same people, go through school with them, attend charity events with them…"

"Oh, the life of the rich and famous." She chuckled again but wondered at the very serious tone in his voice.

Initially she'd had him pegged as a privileged playboy, and then as an uptight, closed-minded, filled-with-his-own-importance type of guy.

She'd been profiling.

And he was proving her wrong.

She wasn't there for him to prove anything to her. He pulled her closer. She wondered if he was as good in bed as it felt like he would be.

"You're shivering."

"I'm not overheated anymore, that's for sure," she lied. A chance meeting with the commissioner might have been better than the balcony she'd traded it for.

"Colin?" The female voice behind them had Chantel spinning guiltily around.

What was she doing?

She had to get back inside and mingle. Clearly spending time with Colin Fairbanks wasn't going to be the "in" she'd hoped. Because "in bed" wasn't her goal.

"Leslie?" He turned, too, greeting the other woman with a warm tone. Chantel would have left, except that he didn't let go of her.

"I thought that I saw you out here," the other woman said. She was as beautiful as expected with a perfect figure and auburn hair that did all the right things, including tapering down to perfectly molded breasts. Probably due to inserts. "I've been looking for you." Her moist lips moved, but the smile didn't leave her face.

As she came closer in the dim lighting, Chantel got a better look at her.

She was a good ten years older than Chantel.

And probably Colin, as well, if she'd been right in assuming him to be about her age.

"Leslie Morrison, this is Chantel Johnson. She's new to town, and you're one of the people I wanted her to meet."

She reached out a hand, grappling with the twisted means of fate. *Leslie Morrison.* Her sexy, distracting, dangerous companion had just given her the means to speak with the woman Chantel was there to save.

Her meeting with Colin hadn't been a mistake or foolishness on her part. It had been preordained.

Chantel was going to use it for everything it had.

CHAPTER FOUR

"CHANTEL'S WRITING A BOOK." Colin spoke with bragging rights he couldn't possibly have earned in the space of an hour. He heard himself and stood there grinning, anyway.

He'd been the first to find her.

So he was staking his claim.

They were still with Leslie but had moved inside and had new drinks in their hands. They'd been joined by others, in ones and twos, who'd moved on in the same fashion.

Couldn't have high society looking like groupies. Or lose that slightly bored look in spite of the new flesh among them.

"A book?" Leslie's head dipped slightly, showing that she was impressed. In Leslie's case, Colin understood the gesture to be more than a show. While Leslie Morrison had grown up among the rich in Southern California and was considered old money, she also was one of the most genuine among them.

Which, along with the fact that the Morrisons and Fairbankses had been doing business together for almost a millennium, was probably why Julie felt so comfortable with the older woman.

With a bit of humility Chantel nodded a little shyly. He wondered what she hid behind the sip of wine she took.

Amusement?

Or real embarrassment.

He wanted to believe the latter but had ceased expecting the best from people—especially the people in his crowd—a long time ago.

"What kind of book are you writing?" Leslie asked.

Another bit of a pause from Chantel was followed by, "Women's fiction police procedural." She took another sip, and added, "It's a woman-in-jeopardy story told from the point of view of a female cop."

Not very ladylike material, which might explain her slight discomfort. But then she probably hadn't been in California long enough to know that she'd fit right in.

Leslie's eyes widened. "Oh, Colin." She reached out as though to touch his wrist and then pulled back. "You have to get her to help us with the library project," she said before turning to Chantel. "If you have time, that is…"

"Of course I have time," Chantel said. "My calendar is empty at the moment. What's the library project?" She looked at them, her gaze lingering a tad bit longer on Colin.

Pretty sure he wasn't imagining her interest, he took a step closer to her, intending to give her the short version, when Leslie said, "Colin, the two of you would be perfect for the lead roles!"

He'd agreed to help out—partially because his firm was handling the estate and resultant legal details, and partially because he wanted Julie to have more exposure in the book world—but his assistance was to have been only behind-the-scenes.

"What lead roles?" Chantel gave her head a little shake, but she was smiling through her confusion.

"Oh, we're hosting a decadent murder mystery dinner—at a thousand dollars a plate—to help purchase books for our own full-service library in Santa Raquel."

He'd hoped Julie would be a part of it, but so far, she'd refused to commit to anything other than helping Leslie with behind-the-scenes paperwork, guest lists and contacting people she knew with personal rare-book libraries who might be willing to donate a copy or two.

"Katie Estrada, a childless widow, willed her family's mansion to Santa Raquel with the caveat that it be used as a library," Colin said. "A trust was set up with money left in her estate to fund the salary of one librarian and to cover basic operating expenses for the first ten years," he added.

"Voters passed a one-time tax levy to fund the minimal renovations necessary to convert the first floor into usable library space," Leslie popped in. "But a similar levy to purchase books failed in November. Colin came up with the idea of the fundraiser. We're hosting it on-site, opening up the mansion for those on the guest list to have access to the upper floors and rooms, as well. The evening is based loosely on the children's game *Clue*, with built-in characters who will be seen in different rooms in the house and on the grounds. Attendees will be expected to speak with as many of those characters as possible throughout the evening and to ask fellow guests if they've seen or spoken to the characters, like investigators would question witnesses."

Chantel was following every word, grinning and nodding.

"My firm handles the trust and all estate matters." Colin explained his involvement.

"The idea is wonderful," Chantel told him. "And certainly not something they taught you in law school."

"It allows guests to feel some affinity with the home, to make a memory there." Leslie stole Chantel's gaze from him.

"The point of the format is to bring guests together in a feeling of mutual support, rather than in suspecting one another of 'murder,'" he added, not sure why he was promoting the event so heavily to this woman.

Because he wanted her to be his leading lady?

He wasn't even planning to play a part. Let alone a lead role.

Her approving nod gave him his answer. He was

trying to impress her. Might as well be honest with himself about that.

"We're hoping, of course, that attendees will pledge continued monetary support," Leslie added. "We'd like to be able to have the library open by summer. Colin and his sister, along with the rest of the committee, already have more than a hundred people confirmed for the event."

"I'd be happy to help in any way I can." Chantel didn't miss a beat. "I've been involved with library funding work in the past."

Of course she had. Her family was in publishing. He should have thought of inviting her to the event; he was sure he'd have gotten around to thinking of it.

Just as soon as he got his head out of his pants. Chantel Johnson was a beautiful woman and new to town. But she was also a person who'd piqued his interest.

He didn't just want to take her to bed—though there was no denying he wanted to do that—he also wanted to do it more than once.

Maybe even over a long period of time—if things continued as well as they'd started.

He'd been with her over an hour and she hadn't raised his defenses or said a single thing he'd found boring. Everything about her was unique. And everything about him was interested.

OH, BOY. She was in over her head.

Thanks to the family that had largely left her to

tread water in her formative years, Chantel was a good swimmer. Leslie leaned in, closing off their threesome from interruption from the rest of the room. "We have a basic script," she said. "But it's just that—basic. With the price we're charging, I've been a bit nervous that the evening would turn out to be too much of a been-there-done-that with this crowd."

Colin shifted. His arm brushed her bare shoulder again, but she was ready for the heat this time. She maintained the contact, her visible attention on the woman she'd hoped to meet that night.

But meeting Leslie Morrison wasn't even close to getting the job done. Chantel needed a lot more time in the woman's circle if she hoped to get the necessary evidence to save her life.

Or to gain her confidence enough to get her to press charges against her husband.

At the moment, Colin Fairbanks seemed like a fairly obvious godsend. He was her ticket to the circle—one that would not raise suspicion in anyone who might get nervous about Leslie suddenly having a new "friend."

Her job, she suddenly understood, was to make certain that she kept him interested enough to keep her around.

Leslie was still talking. "But if we can give attendees an evening to remember, something that's not easy to do with this bunch, we'll get donations commensurate with their enjoyment. Some of us out here on the West Coast might be hard to truly entertain, but probably because of that, we're very generous with our money when we do find ourselves having a good time."

She was speaking freely because she thought Chantel was "one of them." Chantel got that. It was up to her to keep Leslie and her crowd under that impression.

"So I'm thinking, with your writing skills...you could take the basic story and add twists and turns that will give them something they've never seen before, something unique."

Oh, what a tangled web we weave when first we practice to deceive. Her mother's voice, of all things, popped into her mind from many years before.

"I'd be happy to have a go at it," she said aloud, wondering how much it would cost the police department to hire a ghostwriter on short notice. One thing was for sure, her limited undercover budget wasn't going to cover it.

Her mother's brother's wife, whose family, the Johnsons, were in publishing in New York, had a small nonfiction publishing company. Her aunt and uncle had been at her high school graduation, and Chantel hadn't seen them since.

That contact probably wasn't going to be much help...here.

A couple passed behind Colin. He shifted, placing a hand at her back as he stepped closer. He left the hand there.

"You'll get a look at the lead parts, then," Leslie said. The slightly sly grin she gave Colin made it obvious she was working him. "Seriously, I think you two would be perfect for them."

"I'm not an actor." Colin's reminder was firm, but kind.

It would have stopped Chantel.

"Of course you are, my dear," Leslie said. "We all are. It's the only way to survive living among us all!" She chuckled.

And Chantel was chilled by the tragic truth she was certain she heard underneath the woman's polish.

"I'm not sure I understand why you think Colin and I would be perfect for the parts," Chantel said, an investigator, a high-society beauty and a writer all wrapped into one. While playing a part in the library's mystery-event evening could very well provide her with access to Leslie as well as giving her the excuse she needed to stick close to Colin, to use him as her cover as she attended functions over the next weeks, she didn't want him to have reason to avoid her.

Which he very well could if he didn't want to play the part.

She also didn't want to appear too eager. Was she adopting enough of the blasé attitude she'd ob-

served on so many of the videos of the rich and famous she'd watched over the past week?

His hand caressed her back. Whatever she was
doing, she had to keep doing it. She seemed to have
piqued his interest.

"The story is based on a couple who are newly
married and just moving into the mansion. They've
inherited it and a couple of staff from his uncle.
The day they move in, a couple of his uncle's close
friends stop by. They continue to check in. The
couple has only been there a few of days when
they discover a dead body that's been dragged behind a hidden door in the upstairs hall. The two
staff members, and everyone else who'd dropped
by, are suspects."

"But neither member of the lead couple is?"

"No." Leslie shook her head. "You see, that's
why you and Colin fit the parts so well…" She
had a little smile on her face, her eyes alight. And
no matter her age, she was really quite beautiful.

"Leslie." The one word was softly spoken, coming from just behind Leslie. A man had approached.

Chantel watched as Leslie's face became in-
stantly devoid of emotion and a split second later
was smiling again. "James." Leslie turned, taking
the man's hand and pulling him forward.

"James, good to see you." Colin reached to shake
the other man's hand. She didn't detect even a hint
of stiffening in the other man's presence.

Did he have any idea what James Morrison did to his wife behind closed doors?

God forbid, could Colin be part of the good-old-boy mentality that would cover up any hint of abuse with justification of one kind or another?

Or was the High Risk team wrong in their assessment of the situation?

"You're monopolizing Colin's time, my love," James said to his wife, a tender look on his face as he wrapped his arm around her lower back. "The auction is about to start."

Chantel zeroed in on the hand James had on his wife's hip. She was pretty sure, in spite of the room's elegantly soft lighting, that those fingertips had whitened with the application of pressure.

"No, I'm monopolizing her," Colin quickly asserted. He glanced at his watch. "We're making plans for the library. We've got another fifteen minutes or so before things get going. I promise to release her to you before then."

His easy tone matched his expression. James hesitated, but only for a second, before kissing his wife's cheek and telling her he'd meet her at their table.

"As I was saying…" Leslie was still with them, but the glow had gone from her eyes. "You and Colin just met—like the couple in our mystery just married. Embarking on the new, so to speak."

Colin lifted a hand to cover his mouth as he half coughed. "I don't know…"

"It's perfect because Colin is in charge of all the legal, technical aspects of the evening, and you'll be our creative administrator. You'll both need to be there, owners of the mansion for the evening."

Leslie smiled, and Chantel was fairly certain she saw a note of uncertainty on the other woman's face now. Maybe she was imagining it all—James's too-forceful squeezing of his wife's hip, her loss of positive energy.

And maybe she wasn't.

Maybe the woman's husband had just sucked the life out of her with his reminder of the harsh realities in her life.

"I'd be happy to play the lead female role," she burst out. And then glanced at Colin. In time to see his look of surprise.

An expression he quickly cloaked, leaving her with the brief thought to challenge him to a game of poker sometime.

"Then I accept, as well," he told Leslie. "I can't leave this lovely lady stranded without a hero in her first Santa Raquel story."

His words reminded Chantel that she was going to be expected to write that story, or at least appear as though she'd done so.

She'd feel more confident bursting into a bar, gun drawn, to break up a brawl. At least it was something she'd done before.

Accepting Colin's invitation to loop her arm through his and accompany him to the rows of seats up front to watch the auction, she promised herself a bowl of chocolate ice cream for breakfast.

Whatever it took to keep the panic at bay.

CHAPTER FIVE

"YOU'RE GRINNING."

"What?" A piece of whole wheat toast halfway to his mouth, Colin looked up from his tablet—he read the news every morning over breakfast—and focused on his sister.

"You're grinning," she said again. Dressed in light-colored pants and a long-sleeved T-shirt, with her long dark hair curling over her shoulders, Julie looked about sixteen. Spoon suspended above her grapefruit, she was watching him.

They took breakfast together every day in the small room with a wall of windows that overlooked the ocean.

"What's funny?" she asked now. In another half hour, she'd be leaving the dishes in the sink for their housekeeper and going up to shower. She had at least two meetings that he knew of that day—one in Los Angeles with executives from the Sunshine Children's League. She was hoping to get funds for the Santa Raquel hospital to hire a child-life specialist to work exclusively with patients without family visitors.

"Nothing's funny. I didn't realize I was smiling."

"You were staring at your tablet but haven't scrolled in at least five minutes."

She was exaggerating.

"I met the most marvelous woman last night."

"Oh?" Leaning toward him, she said, "Do tell."

"You can see for yourself," he said over his bite of toast. "She's agreed to help with the library project. She'll be at lunch tomorrow."

They were having it catered in what had been a dining room but was now a conference room at the Estrada mansion—giving the committee time to look around at the renovations that had been made since they'd last toured the place.

"You just met her and already roped her into helping us?"

He would have, if he'd thought of it first. "Leslie did."

"And that's how you met her? Leslie hooked you up?"

He might have been exasperated by his little sister's nosiness if he wasn't so damned glad to see the old teasing light in her eyes.

"No. I managed to make her acquaintance all on my own. She's new to town..." Did he bring up Chantel Johnson's publishing background now...or after Julie had a chance to meet—and like—her?

"And she was on the auction invitation list?"

"She's from New York. I'm assuming her family had connections." And if they hadn't, they'd just have needed to make a call or two to ease their daughter's introduction to LA society.

"Let me guess—she's slender, blond hair, big brown eyes and isn't quite as tall as you are, but she's not short. Oh, and last night she was wearing a black halter dress that she'd probably purchased last season."

Her grin had turned into a mischievous smile. She'd been messing with him. Lucky for her, he was in an unusually good mood.

"You've been talking to Jaime."

"She called as soon as the auction was over. I'd asked her to. I wanted to know how she did."

He'd have sought the woman out himself the night before, as he'd originally intended, but when he'd heard that Chantel had arrived in a hired car, he'd offered to see her back to her hotel.

"How'd she do?"

Julie named a figure that elicited a long whistle from Colin and then said, "So what's her story? This Chantel person. She must be something to have monopolized your time the entire evening."

Here's where he could tell her that Chantel was a writer, too. That maybe her family could take a look at Julie's series of children's stories.

He ate a couple of bites of melon from the crystal plate in front of him instead. "I'd rather you find out for yourself," he told her. "I'm interested in your opinion." True. And also prevarication.

"Ohhhh…" Julie's brows were raised, her lips

still tilted slightly upward. "You're looking for familial approval."

He could have firmly denied the accusation. Laughed her off. "I like her," he said instead.

Julie set her spoon down. "As in, you-want-to-see-her-again like her?"

Scrolling down on his tablet, he said, "I just met her last night." And then—partially because she was soon going to find out, anyway—he added, "We're going to be playing the leading roles in the murder mystery." He left out the part about Chantel juicing up the script.

"You agreed to play a part?" Her mouth hung open.

Looking her in the eye, Colin nodded. It had occurred to him that perhaps part of the reason his little sister didn't feel more of a drive to get out of the house and start really living again—as in looking for a relationship so she could start a family of her own—was because she was following his example.

It was one of his theories. Right along with the one where she'd go out with him, if he kept after her, because she felt safe with him. And once she started getting out more, she'd remember how much she'd enjoyed it. He'd been working off that one for more than a year...

"Wow. She must really be something if you're coming out of the background at a party."

He didn't know about that. But Julie's reaction did add to his suspicion that she held back more because he did. Could he help it that he took after their father? A man who preferred to observe and be aware? Julie had been more like their mother—the social one.

For a while, too long probably, he'd understood her reticence. But she was only three years from thirty. And hadn't been on a date since high school.

"Well, I think that since I'm going to be way out of my comfort zone on this one, you could join me in that state by at least attending the event."

She was still watching him. Her gaze more curious than guarded. She hadn't said no.

"Will you? Please?" It was still a month away. She could think about it. And say yes and then change her mind, too.

"Maybe."

"Maybe?" He raised an eyebrow at her, while inside he was hosting a minicelebration.

"I kind of want to watch you with your leading lady…" Her expression pointed, her tone wasn't filled with despondency. He took that as another small victory. "But it'll depend on the guest list." The last was issued with a matter-of-factness that had become a way of life.

It depended whether or not the Smyths were attending. He'd wanted to keep them off the list, but they both knew that he couldn't. Not while maintaining Julie's front of there being nothing egregiously wrong between the two high-society families. Because she didn't want it known how damaged she'd been. She wasn't going to let that family run her out of the town she'd been born to, raised in and loved.

Which was why, on rare occasions, she'd go to evening functions—to maintain her own status quo. But it was usually only when the Smyths were vacationing elsewhere.

And they weren't going to be this time. He'd heard the night before that they'd be attending the library event. It was turning out to be the event of the year. Everyone was going to be there.

Except his sweet sister, who was helping to put on the event?

Julie went back to her grapefruit and toast. Colin scrolled on his tablet and thought about the woman he'd met the night before. Thought about the fact that he was still thinking about her.

About ensuring that, aside from murder-mystery business, he'd be seeing her again. Soon.

"She really had an effect on you." He was deep in thought about him and Chantel on a yacht on the ocean—something about a private dinner at sunset—when Julie interrupted him.

Glancing up, he saw her studying him. This time minus the grin. "Who?"

But he knew who.

"You were grinning again," she told him. "And not scrolling."

Did Julie spend every morning watching him scroll, for God's sake? Making a note to read his

news before or after he got to the breakfast table—
to spend those few minutes every morning paying more attention to his sister—he said, "There's
something different about her, Jules. She's not like
the rest of the women I know. I'm eager for you to
meet her."

Julie did smile then. "And I'm getting more and
more curious."

He hoped so. He wanted Julie to like Chantel.
Not just because he did and hoped the woman
would be around awhile, but because her publishing experience, her own drive as a writer, could
help Julie take enough of a step out of her shell to
submit some of her work for publication.

Maybe she'd even be able to help him convince
Julie to attend the murder mystery gala. It would
be a miracle.

But who knew? Colin being preoccupied by a
woman was a bit of a miracle, too.

CHAPTER SIX

ON DUTY AT four on Friday, Chantel finished off a pint of chocolate ice cream for breakfast and lunch at a computer at the precinct, looking up names from the party the night before. Pulling police reports for any that had them. She already had everything there was to have on the Morrisons. Today she was looking at the others on the guest list.

A break-in, never solved. Several traffic incidents. A couple of DUIs.

First and foremost, she'd gone straight to the Fairbankses. And hadn't been surprised to find not one single reference to them in the police database. You didn't run a law firm as successful as Fairbanks, most particularly not with the types of clients they represented, if you were prone to mischief.

Still, a girl could never be too careful. If she was going to pretend an interest in the rainmaking attorney—and she was most definitely going to if she could persuade him to pursue her—she needed to be certain that he was going to help her case, not hurt it.

After brunch, already in uniform, she stopped to give the captain her report and then headed out in her car, driving by Max and Meri's house—completely unnecessarily, given that the man who'd tortured Meri was in prison for life in Nevada, but it was something she still did several times a week, just the same. And she took a drive by The Lemonade Stand, too, going around the block twice, just watching. She was glad to see that the shops that fronted the unique women's shelter were conducting business as usual. There was no reason for them not to be.

But the women who were fighting for their lives inside those shops, fighting for fresh starts, striving to live without violence, deserved to be watched over.

Then she went to the beach, to sit on a bench and watch the ocean. To clear her mind, relax a bit, so that she'd be prepared and focused when she hit the streets that evening.

What she saw, as she sat there, was an empty beach with an inner vision of her and Colin Fairbanks transposed onto the sand. They were walking, hand in hand.

And there the vision stopped. Even when she'd been in a serious relationship, Chantel hadn't been the type who held hands on the beach. Or had her doors opened for her, either.

But boy, if ever she had been, a hand like Colin's wouldn't have been horrible to hold...

Giving herself a mental shake, she thought

about Leslie Morrison and replayed their meeting the night before over and over. Making note of the "tells" the other woman had given her. There'd been too many to ignore.

Even accounting for the fact that Chantel had been specifically looking and could have made something out of nothing a time or two, she hadn't imagined Leslie's completely changed manner after her husband had joined them.

Whatever Chantel thought, personally, of Colin Fairbanks, whatever strange and possibly delicious feelings he'd raised in her undercover persona were irrelevant. If, indeed, he was presenting her with the perfect alibi for spending more time in his circle than a few charity events would afford, she was going to use him for all he was worth.

Because saving a woman and her son from brutality was far more important than Chantel's social life.

She'd just have to make certain that Colin understood, from the beginning, that their time together had nothing to do with any real caring between them. She couldn't let things develop beyond enjoying each other's company. Maybe she'd have to change her story a bit—maybe she was only in California until she finished her story. Maybe the family would need her back in her publishing position as soon as her book was done. She was out to save a life—not to be cruel.

COLIN FELT LIKE a schoolboy as he pulled into the recently poured parking lot of Santa Raquel's first and impressive full-service library just before noon on Saturday.

In business attire, minus the jacket, he perused the parking lot, wondering if she was there yet.

"You see her car?" Julie asked from the seat beside him. Guiding his Lincoln Continental to a stop beside a silver Mercedes—a birthday gift to Leslie Morrison from her husband—he shrugged.

"I have no idea what she drives. She was dropped off by the hotel's limousine the other night." And then he realized that he'd fallen into Julie's trap. She'd never named whose car he might have been seeking.

Yes, he'd been thinking about Chantel Johnson. Looking forward to seeing her. It may also have occurred to him that she'd change her mind and not show.

After all, what did he really know about her? Except that she was beautiful and had made one hell of a first impression on him. She could be a total flake. Lord knew, there were enough of them in their set. There were people, young women in his set among them, who did exactly as they said they would do, too.

A long black limousine pulled into the grand entrance in front of the historic mansion.

"Is that her?" Julie asked, looking beautiful in tight black pants, and a long, figure-hugging black-and-white silk top with a black silk scarf tied loosely around her neck. She handled her three-inch spiked heels like they were tennis shoes as she shut the door of the Lincoln behind her. "She's beautiful, Colin."

"Yeah, that's her." Reminding himself to wait for his sister, Colin approached the front entrance, getting turned on as one long leg followed another out of the car. In a fitted blue dress that ended just above the knee, the blonde woman with her perfectly manicured nails and sleek makeup could be stepping out of the pages of a fashion magazine.

Except that she looked far too elegant to ever parade herself for hours in front of a camera.

"Chantel!" He greeted her just outside the massive front door. "Good to see you again." She couldn't be blamed for thinking he was stalking her—appearing just at the exact moment that she arrived. "I'd like you to meet my sister." He drew Julie closer. "Julie Fairbanks, Chantel Johnson."

Two slender hands met. And, if he wasn't mistaken, the two women sized each other up. Julie's interest he understood. But Chantel's? Could it be that she really was as interested in him as he was in her? That the instant attraction between them was mutual?

Only way to find out was to pursue her. And so he would.

Holding the door, Colin followed both of the women inside.

THE LIBRARY COMMITTEE consisted of six members. Seven including Chantel. Each member of the committee was in charge of an aspect of the project—from catering to marketing—and each had people working with them. As they sat over lunch—a sample from the three top caterers in the running to provide the mystery dinner on gala night—one by one they reported on their progress.

Leslie, who was the committee's head, ran the meeting. To her right, at a table set for eight in what had once been a dining room and was soon going to be one of several conference rooms in the Santa Raquel Public Library, sat Emily Longfellow, a thirtysomething woman whose plain features were accentuated with beautiful jewelry. Emily was in charge of arranging the mansion for the evening's entertainment—including all furnishings necessary not only to accommodate dinner seating for a couple of hundred people, but for any necessary accoutrements for the mystery that would be unfolding throughout the night. Next to Emily was a little woman who must be at least seventy, Martha something or other, who was responsible for floral arrangements.

John Duncan, next to Emily, was a man Chantel had met the other night at the auction. He was a young attorney in Colin's office who, having just recently passed the bar exam, was on the committee but was there to oversee any work that Colin determined was legally necessary. John's father,

Clemency Duncan, was chief of neurosurgery at Stanford Hospital.

And then, opposite John, was Colin. Chantel was in between him and Julie, who sat directly to Leslie's left.

When Chantel was introduced as their artistic director, everyone smiled and welcomed her. She had a feeling every one of them had already known everything there was to know about her. What she'd led everyone to believe about her, she amended the thought as she smiled and greeted everyone before taking a stab at the salad in front of her. It had walnuts in it. And cranberries.

"Chantel's going to be beefing up the script for us, but since I am giving it to her only this afternoon, she hasn't had a chance to read it yet." Leslie continued and then moved on to Julie, in charge of invitations and marketing, who reported that their guest count was closing in on the two hundred mark.

Obviously in her element, Leslie Morrison appeared to be exactly what everyone thought she was—confident, healthy, in control, in charge. There was nothing about her that even hinted at any kind of unrest at home. She asked for the committee members' opinions as to whether or not they should raise the guest cap on the function in the event that response continued to be so positive. Leslie took a vote and the cap was raised by fifty.

Conversations broke out at that point, Leslie leaned over to say something for Julie's ears only and Chantel relaxed for just a moment. Long enough to feel the brush of Colin's thigh against hers beneath the table. He was engaged in conversation with John, and at first she thought the contact had been accidental.

Until his hand dropped to his lap, disappeared under the crisp white linen tablecloth and ended up on her leg.

He was taking a hell of a lot for granted, based on one night's meeting. Or was simply being bold, telling her in the only way he could in that moment that he was interested.

His fingers didn't slide up her leg. Or toward her inner leg. He wasn't being a creep. Or disrespectful, either. He just held on.

And Chantel liked it.

"Do you have some experience with scriptwriting?" Julie was trying the spinach quiche Chantel had shied away from, and, finished with whatever she and Leslie had been discussing, she was addressing Chantel while she ate. Her smile was warm and friendly, reminding Chantel of Jill—the best friend she'd had since grade school and lost to a crook's bullet several years before.

"None," Chantel admitted, breathing through the memory. And then, remembering her cover, said, "I'm a writer, though." You didn't have to be published to be a writer.

"Oh? What do you write? Anything I might have read?" Colin's hand moved from her leg, leaving a cold place.

"Hardly." She grinned and almost forgot to soften the edge of street life from her voice. "I'm not published. Yet," she added to give the impression that she was serious about her pursuit.

"Do you have an agent?"

Did she? Trying to remember anything she might have heard about her aunt's business, and the story she'd told Colin about her own publishing position, she decided on, "Yes." And hoped she wasn't digging a grave before she was ready to bury Chantel Johnson. She'd be doing publishing and agent research later that night.

"So what are you writing?"

"Women's fiction. Suspense. It's a woman-in-jeopardy story." And before she saw any of these people again, she better have some kind of plot fleshed out. She'd go through her case files. Find an interesting arrest that had converted to charges and then a conviction.

Colin's hand was back. Chantel's body responded with a small feeling between her legs. She didn't dare look at him. But she did notice that he was no longer speaking with John.

She assumed he was listening to her and Julie. So she slipped her hand under the table, leaving it on her lap. "My family's in publishing," she said, telling Julie that she'd left behind a position of VP of marketing. Colin's hand slid over hers.

When her libido leaped in response, Chantel took a sip of water and then added, "I'm going to go back to it, though. I talked to my folks last night. They agreed to give me as much time as I need to finish the book, as long as I would return to the family business when it's done. In the meantime, they're going to be sending work my way. Things they want my decisions on."

There. Cleared up a bunch of issues. Namely, any chance that Colin Fairbanks would think there was any future in a relationship between them. It also negated any need for her to be in the market for a permanent residence. Something she had a feeling this friendly and powerful bunch would be glad to help with.

His hand didn't leave her lap. Julie didn't respond, either. She was looking at her brother and was no longer smiling.

Did she know what Colin was doing to Chantel under the table? And she disapproved? She'd gotten the impression earlier that Julie had been pleased to meet her...

"What do you all think?" Leslie's voice raised as she addressed the table, halting private conversations. In that first second Chantel froze, heat rising up her neck and face. Did everyone know how her body was responding to the chaste touch of a man's hand?

"Did everyone get a chance to try everything?" Leslie followed her first question with a second.

Chantel hadn't had any quiche. Everyone else nodded.

"We need to make a choice today." The caterers weren't being mentioned by name. A had provided the quiche. B was the salad and bread assortments. C had brought some kind of grilled chicken that, in spite of the fact that it was chicken, the meat that was served at every banquet Chantel had ever attended, was delicious. Leslie passed around menus provided by all three caterers minus any kind of identifying determiner.

Discussion ensued. Chantel listened. Agreeing with Julie on every point she brought up—the flavors that, while gourmet, wouldn't please as wide a range of palette as others. The need for a variety of options for those who couldn't tolerate rich food but yet preventing the dreaded "bland" moniker being slapped on the evening. Colin opted for the meat and potatoes option over fondue and finger foods, his fingers leaving little caresses just above her knee.

As conversation died down, Leslie called for a show of hands in favor of A, followed by B and C. C had the job unanimously.

And Colin leaned over to ask her if he and Julie could drop her off at her hotel after their tour of the mansion, preventing the need for her to call and then wait for a ride.

Her announcement that she wasn't going to be around for long hadn't seemed to slow him down a bit. He was knowingly embarking on a short-time flirtation.

Which made him fair game.

She accepted his offer of a lift.

CHAPTER SEVEN

COLIN WAS READY to take the tour and go. Julie's gaze had bruised him a bit. His little sister was pissed at him for keeping Chantel's publishing background from her. He'd known she would be. But if he'd told her right up front, she'd probably have refused to meet her with an open mind.

Ever since the rape, she'd been slowly becoming more closed-minded. Stubborn.

Could he be blamed for caring enough to try to help her?

And Chantel…maybe she'd be free to have dinner with him that night. Just the two of them…

As Leslie was concluding the business portion of the day, the outer door of the library sounded. Someone had just come in.

"Ladies and gentlemen, dessert has arrived," Leslie said, smiling, as a couple of white-coated women came into the room, each carrying a large brown box. And right behind them was…Patricia Reynolds—Commissioner Paul Reynolds's wife.

Colin stiffened. What in hell the police commissioner's wife was doing there he didn't know. And he wouldn't have cared, if not for the fact that Julie was sitting just a few feet away from him.

This was why she didn't go out much. To avoid unexpected appearances...

"Now that the catering decision has been made, I can tell you that Patricia Reynolds has volunteered to handle the catering details for the mystery gala. As you all know, her daughter and son-in-law own Beachside Catering and, to avoid a potential conflict of interest, Patricia didn't want to take on her duties until our choice had been made."

Patricia smiled, including everyone in her greeting. The woman gave endlessly to the community. Volunteering everyplace she could. Providing companionship and guidance through a youth program she'd helped develop to young women who'd gone astray. If not for the fact that she was married to a man who could be bought, Colin would have liked the woman.

"Regardless of who we chose, Beachside Catering was providing our dessert today. But now I can tell you that caterer C, your unanimous choice, is none other than Beachside Catering." Leslie smiled as Patricia nodded toward the two women who were standing by a counter in the back of the room.

Crème de menthe parfaits were being passed around by the time Patricia settled into the empty seat at the end of the table between John and Colin, as far away from Julie as she could be while still being seated at the same table. Colin supposed Leslie was responsible for that.

But he had to wonder why the other woman had gone along with a plan to include Patricia on the committee at all. Leslie Morrison, the one person in their crowd who knew the details of Julie's rape, was usually the one who ran interference for his sister, to avoid exactly the kind of situation they now faced.

Bad enough that Patricia was on the committee, but to have blindsided Julie...

He was going to have a word with Leslie.

Later.

CHANTEL HAD NEVER been in a home, free to wander in and out of every single room, as magnificent as the Estrada-mansion-turned-library. If she hadn't been conscious of Colin's time, and the fact that Julie didn't seem to be feeling very well after lunch, she could have spent hours exploring the nooks and crannies of the place.

She couldn't imagine ever living there, however. Seemed like a lonely existence to her, having so much space to separate family members. And the idea of having to dust the place...

Julie didn't say much as they issued their farewells and made their way to Colin's town car. She slid into the backseat before Chantel could offer to do so, forcing Chantel to sit up front with Colin.

Not a bad thing. Just a little awkward at the moment, considering that ever since he'd had his hand on her knee, she'd been half-turned-on.

She knew that when cops went under they had to do a lot of things to protect their cover—take drugs, even—but having sex for the sake of the job was not something she'd ever do. Or have the department expect her to do.

She'd be fine. She just needed a few minutes back in her own environment to process what had happened. She wanted out of the heels.

And to scrub her face. She remembered why she eschewed makeup. It made her skin itch.

"If you don't mind, I'd like to run Julie home first," Colin said as he started the car. "I'm heading to the office, and the resort is in between."

"That's fine," she said, and tried to ignore the tingle she felt at the realization that she was going to be completely alone with him for the first time.

Would he fill the time with small talk? Or try to get personal?

She needed him to get personal. To take the next step in making them an item. A temporary one. A spring fling.

Problem was, she wanted it, too…

"You okay with that?" Colin was looking in the rearview mirror, obviously addressing his sister.

"Of course," Julie said and nothing else. Colin didn't ask her if she felt okay or if anything was wrong. It wasn't Chantel's business, but…

"Did something at lunch not agree with you?"

she asked, turning to look at the other woman. In her experience, guys didn't always pick up on the obvious. And if Julie, who'd been so friendly earlier, was unwell, someone should notice.

"What?" Julie asked and then said, "Oh, I'm fine. I feel fine."

Chantel didn't need to be a cop to detect the lie. But she figured she'd been put in her place—a stranger who needed to mind her own business—and turned back around.

Colin glanced in the mirror again, his expression softening, but still said nothing.

He turned out into the street, drove half a mile and turned again. The silence in the car might not be bothering anyone else, but in Chantel's world, it was weird—to have something lying there under the surface and not being addressed. But whatever. Must be how the rich and famous dealt with life.

Ignoring the messy parts.

Colin glanced in the rearview mirror again. For the fourth time.

"You want to come into the office with me?" Colin asked five minutes into the drive. "The preliminary child-life specialist contract should be drawn up. If you go over it today, we could have it vetted and ready to present as early as Monday."

"Next Friday, as we originally agreed, is fine," Julie said. "I'm not meeting with the Sunshine committee until then."

Another couple of minutes passed. Chantel

thought about chattering, except that she wasn't a chatterer. There were questions she could ask about the ocean in the distance, the weather she could expect during spring in California, about places to eat and things to see. But when in Rome…and she definitely needed them to think she was in Rome.

"I'm fine, Colin." The voice in the back of the seat didn't sound sickly.

He glanced at his sister again.

"I really am."

Another glance.

"I'm angry more than anything else."

Okay, this probably wasn't a conversation she needed to be hearing. Now that she knew Julie wasn't coming down with food poisoning. Or the flu.

"I'm going to speak with Leslie." Colin's voice was firm. His jaw tight.

Chantel went high into cop mode. Why would Julie be angry with Leslie? What had she missed back there?

And to do with her subject?

"Why?" Julie's question was sharp. "This has nothing to do with Leslie."

"She should have given you a heads-up."

"I never told her who he'd…" She broke off right when things were finally getting good.

Whether all eyes were on her or not, Chantel felt as though they were. In her world, she'd have turned around and asked what was going on. She'd have risked being told it was none of her business, but she'd have asked.

Her crash course in polite society hadn't prepared her for this moment.

"I'm sorry," she said. "I feel as though I shouldn't be here, and yet I can't politely exit a moving car." She spoke softly in character with Chantel Johnson, gentling her voice. But the Chantel Harris in her hadn't been able to keep her mouth shut.

"No, I'm sorry," Julie told her. "I've behaved horribly, letting my personal feelings put a damper on what was a really nice afternoon…"

"Your personal feelings matter," Chantel said. Just as Leslie Morrison's personal feelings mattered. People got upset for good reason. "Clearly you need to speak with your brother…" And she needed to keep her mouth shut.

Colin had glanced in the mirror a couple more times but was otherwise driving with his attention seemingly on the road.

"It's just… Patricia Reynolds…"

Not Leslie Morrison? Chantel waited.

"She's following me."

What?

"She's not following you, Jules." Colin was stopped at a light and turned toward his sister.

"Yes, she is, Colin. She's the police commissioner's wife," Julie said to Chantel, who'd also turned around. Chantel continued to face backward as the light changed and Colin was driving once again.

She'd known, of course, exactly who the woman was. Knew, too, as soon as she'd appeared in the room, that the woman had made an excuse for joining the committee late so that she could watch over Chantel. Either to report back to the commissioner on how his undercover rookie was doing in case she was screwing up and he needed to intervene or to provide inside support in what was a very sensitive investigation.

A question she'd intended to ask Captain Reagan first thing Monday morning.

"You think the police commissioner's wife is following you," she said now. Curious.

"I know she is."

And the obvious response to that, in any society, had to be, "Why?"

"I'm on four committees, and she's managed to somehow be involved in all four projects."

"Our circle isn't all that big," Colin said. "Patricia has been heavily involved in volunteer projects since before she married Paul. You know that."

Paul. To him. Commissioner Reynolds to everyone in Chantel's circle.

"Yes, but over the past several months, she's joined each project I'm involved with, and they didn't just all start up," Julie said. "I know I'm right on this one, Colin. She's spying on me."

With a mental step back, Chantel faced front but had to ask again, "Why would she spy on you?"

It would be weird if she didn't ask. Right?

"I was…involved…in something. Years ago. And recently, another woman we all know had a situation…something that came out through her son at school…and Patricia, I'm sure at Paul's behest, is watching me."

"Why?"

Colin glanced at her then. "They want her to stay quiet."

"About what she was involved in years ago? Or what happened recently?"

"Nothing happened recently," Colin said. "It was just a misunderstanding stemming from the wrong interpretation of a harmless school project. But Julie's friends with the woman. She thinks that Commissioner Reynolds is nervous that she'll try to bring up old grievances."

"I know he is. And it's not just that I'm friends with…the woman. The things they're saying… there's something in it similar to my situation. And we know mine is true."

Colin didn't respond to Julie's remark. This time Chantel followed his lead.

Heart pumping, she made a mental note to check Julie Fairbanks again. She'd already run a check on the family, the night after she'd met Colin. But maybe she'd missed something?

She had to find a way to get Colin to explain to

her why he didn't have much faith in his sister's judgment on the matter. And why the commissioner would send his wife to spy on her for being friends with someone.

Maybe, if she got lucky, he'd even tell her what the matter was.

In the meantime, she'd gained an important piece of information for her case. The woman Julie had just mentioned—the one who'd appeared to have a similar problem, but didn't—had to be Leslie Morrison. Surely there weren't two kids with school projects that had been interpreted to mean trouble in their admittedly small circle.

That would be too much of a coincidence. And as a cop, Chantel didn't put a lot of stock in coincidence.

CHAPTER EIGHT

WHILE JULIE'S SUSPICIONS had put a definite damper on the mood in the car that afternoon, Colin found that the changed atmosphere didn't dim the flame of his desire to see Chantel again. As quickly as possible.

Because that was a first—him feeling driven from within to pursue something non–Julie related when his sister was obviously upset—the urge grew in intensity. That Chantel was attracted to him, too, wasn't a huge surprise to him.

But even the possibility that she could be like most of the women who made their attraction to him obvious—after him for his money as much as anything else—didn't put a damper on his fervency.

So he asked her to dinner. She accepted. And as he went on with his day, he had a smile on his face.

IN JEANS, a button-down shirt and over-the-ankle hiking boots, Chantel spent a couple of hours at the precinct Saturday afternoon. She checked in with Captain Reagan. Filled Wayne in on lunch. And told him that she'd be having dinner with Colin Fairbanks again that evening.

"Didn't take you long to find an 'in,'" Wayne said, studying her.

Chin up, Chantel withstood his visual interrogation without as much as a held breath. "I'm good at my job," she told him. Married to it, was more like it.

"You *are* good at your job," Wayne said, pulling out an empty chair at the table where she sat with a department-issue laptop in front of her. "Maybe too good."

"What's that supposed to mean?"

"You put the job above everything else."

"Lots of guys do." And she was one of the guys. They had one another's backs.

He looked away. "And many of those who do also spend some of their off time in strip clubs."

"You think I should go to strip clubs?"

"I think you're a healthy, three-dimensional human being who is living a two-dimensional life. Eventually, that's going to catch up with you. I just don't want it to be now."

She wanted to continue to pretend ignorance. Recognizing it as a weak ploy, she said, "You're thinking that I might fall for Colin Fairbanks?"

"The thought has crossed my mind."

"Because he's rich?"

"Because you're out of your element." He was being a good friend, telling her what he thought she needed to hear, not what she wanted to hear. She took offense, anyway.

"You don't think I'm up to running with the rich folks?" She was keeping her emotions in check. It was what she was trained to do. You had to when you were on the job.

"I'm more concerned with the part you're playing," Wayne said. "You're hot as hell, Chantel. You play it down here—like now, your hair pulled back tight, no makeup, loose clothes and those hiking shoe things you seem to wear night and day, even at the company picnic in the middle of summer…"

He broke off, as though realizing what he was revealing—the fact that he'd not only noticed how she was dressed last summer at the picnic, and all the time, but that he remembered in such detail.

Still smarting from his insinuation that she wasn't up to this assignment, Chantel let him swim in his own stew.

Leaning forward, his elbows on his knees, he seemed about to tell her something confidential. In a lowered voice, he said, "When I saw you the other day, in character…"

He'd just turned up the heat on his pot. Chantel smiled.

"Sounds to me like you're the one with issues here, Wayne," she told him. Because, after all, friends said what the other needed to hear, not what they wanted to hear. "Maybe you should be the one visiting a strip club."

The statement was mean. She knew the second it hit its mark and felt bad. She and Wayne were such close friends because, when they'd been trainees together many years before, his wife, Maria, had caught him out in a bar with a stripper and Chantel had stepped in and helped saved his marriage.

"You get prickly when you're feeling defensive."

"That's right. You had no business implying that I can't do my job."

"It's not your job I'm worried about," he said, still leaning close. He rubbed his hands together. "I don't think there's doubt in anyone's mind that you're the best man for the job. That's not what I'm talking about. And I think you know that."

Okay, yeah, she'd known. But...

"You work so hard to be an equal here, Chantel, that you go overboard. You seem to forget that you're a woman. Like it's a bad thing, so you pretend that part of you doesn't exist."

"I'm not a woman at work. I'm a cop."

"And when you're not at work?"

She thought about work. Or ate chocolate ice cream. Or went to the gym to keep in shape for work.

"I hang out with Meri and Max," she said. Wayne knew them both. He'd been instrumental in saving Meri from her fiend of an ex-husband. He also knew that Max had once been married to Chantel's best friend, Jill. And that Jill had died on the job, saving another cop. "The baby's over a year old now, and Caleb's four. I watch them at least once a week so Max and Meri have time to enjoy each other."

Because she'd never seen a love like the one they shared.

Wayne was still watching her, his glance more focused than she liked. He was a great detective.

Partially because, when he looked, he could see things most people missed. Uncomfortable with that eye turned on her, she shored up her defenses again.

An instinctive maneuver, not a conscious choice.

"I'm a woman, Wayne. I love children and nurture them. I have friends. I go to the beach..."

"Have you been out on even one date since you've been here?"

Chantel thought back. Had it really been over a year since she'd moved from Las Sendas up to Santa Raquel?

"I've been busy finding a place to live, setting it up, spending time with Max and Meri, staying in shape, getting up to speed on the High Risk team. It's not like I've had a lot of spare time."

"You're thirty-two years old. If you're going to have a family, you should start thinking about doing so..."

"You and Maria don't have kids."

His head dropped enough that she couldn't see his expression. "We're trying," he said, leaving her to wonder if they were having problems conceiving.

"You're human, Chantel," Wayne said, lifting that

gaze up to pierce her again. "Young and healthy. It stands to reason that at some point…"

"Hold it right there." Her voice hard as rocks, it was her turn to stare down. "Before you say something we'll both regret…"

But why shouldn't he express his concerns? She wanted to be one of the guys, and guys talked about sex all the time.

If she weren't the cop in question, if they were talking about someone else, she might even share his concerns.

"Look." She softened her tone. Remembered that she was talking to her friend. And recognized that he had a point. She'd proved it for him with her less-than-stellar behavior. "I admit that the idea of having someone to go out with is…not unpleasant. I'll even go so far as to admit that Colin Fairbanks is extremely…easy…to be with. I like him. But you have nothing to worry about."

"Forgive me, but those statements give rise to concern rather than alleviate it. And you know as well as I do that telling me not to worry raises more concern because I have to wonder if you're in denial."

Calm now, Chantel nodded. "I know. But I'm not. Listen, Wayne, like you said, I'm thirty-two years old. And yes, I'm healthy, of course I have sexual feelings, and maybe it would be easier if I could visit a male strip club now and then, but I'm just not into that." She grinned, and then, serious again, said, "I'm thirty-two, not twenty-two. I've had relationships. And painful breakups, too. Life experiences teach us things, and I've learned some things along the way. Two of them…"

She stopped. Feeling a little stupid, sitting there ready to share her innermost thoughts with another cop.

"You're going to tell me what they are, right? We're just waiting for you to get there?"

Guy talk, Harris, she reminded herself. And was struck with the thought that she was hiding behind it. Which was ludicrous.

It bothered her—that she'd think such a thing. She loved her job. And really liked having male friends…

"I'm assuming one of the broken relationships, and lessons learned, had to do with Max?"

"What? No! Why would you think that?"

"Don't insult me or cheapen our friendship, Chantel. Either be honest or tell me to go to hell. But don't sit there and lie to me."

"I learned something from Max, yes, but not one of the two things I was talking about. And there was no breakup. That's the honest-to-God truth."

She couldn't lose Wayne's respect. It was one of her most valued assets. Clasping her hands together, she faced him fully. "You're half-right. I did think I was in love with him. But it started long before Meri's disappearance last year. I fell in love with him when Jill did. And when I saw her putting the job before him, risking her life unnecessarily while he was at home trusting her to keep herself safe…it was the one time I really had a problem with her. I'm not saying that what she did…saving that rookie's life… It was the right thing to do. I'd have done the same. So would you have and any officer worth his salt. But there were times… I don't know, it was just like Jill thought she was invincible or something…"

Picturing her friend, in uniform, with a grin on her face and a gun in her hand—just after shooting practice when Jill had hit three bull's-eyes—Chantel's gut clenched with a longing that nearly killed her. Like when Jill had first died.

Would she and Max have ended up together if Chantel hadn't been too lost in her grief to pursue him?

"Anyway, so, yeah…when I came up here to help him last year, the old feelings…they were still there. But seeing him with Meri, or rather, *not* with her, seeing how much he believed she was in serious trouble, when all of us were certain that she'd left him of her own free will, seeing how hard she fought to stay alive, to get out of that house when she should have been passed out on the floor—I'd never felt anything like that. But I knew, then and there, that I wanted it and that I couldn't accept anything less. I'm not going to date a man until I feel something more for him than a desire to not be alone."

She looked at him, expecting derision, and instead met the serious expression on his face.

"You think I'm nuts, don't you?"

"No, honestly, I feel sad for you."

"Because I've never been in love?"

"Because you didn't even recognize what love is."

"You're telling me that you believe in being in love?"

"Of course I do. Why do you think I was ready to jump off a roof when I thought I'd lost Maria all those years ago? And why do you think she took me back?"

"Because I was pretty damned persuasive?"

"Probably." He grinned. "But also because she's in love with me as much as I'm in love with her."

Damn. So it happened more than once in a blue moon. Who'd have guessed?

"Jill wasn't in love with Max like that." Jill had been turned on by Max. She'd loved him. But she hadn't been *in* love. Chantel, as her most trusted confidante, was certain on that score.

So, well, she had hope, then. Maybe someday...

"You were going to tell me about the two things you'd learned."

Right. *Thanks for the reminder, Stanton.* She didn't have a hell of a lot of hope. Maybe someday... Not. Maybe when hell froze over.

"First, I'm attracted to alpha men. You know,

the strong, protective types. The ones who rule the world."

"Aren't all women?"

She didn't think so. Since there were men who weren't so filled with testosterone that they'd fight first and ask questions later. Not all men were aggressive go-getters. And yet, there were women who loved and needed them.

She just wasn't ever going to be one of them. More the shame.

"I guess I wouldn't know," she told Wayne. "Jill was. I am. Meri is. That's pretty much the sum total of my experience. And it doesn't really matter," she said. "Because the second thing I've learned is that aggressive men don't like aggressive women, unless it's in their beds, and then only when they want it that way. Protective men like to protect. They don't want a woman who says, 'Stay down. I've got this,' while facing the bogeyman alone with a gun in her hand. Near as I can tell, it emasculates them. Or, at the very least, makes them feel incompetent."

Wayne's silence wasn't a surprise. Because he was one of those protective guys.

He knew she was right. The upside was, he left her alone after that so she could pursue the work she'd stopped in to do.

To no avail.

No matter how she searched, either as victim or perpetrator, Julie Fairbanks was not in the system.

Keeping an eye over her shoulder, lest someone see what she was doing and wonder why she was looking at the commissioner's wife, she tried to find what she could about Patricia Reynolds. It took her two seconds to discover that the woman didn't have a police record. No real surprise there.

The society pages were filled with her. The queen of philanthropy, she'd been an advocate for the downtrodden since high school, using the influence of being the daughter of a senator—before she'd married Paul Reynolds—to draw attention to matters that bothered her.

She and the commissioner had no children—due, one article said, to her own infertility. She sat on the boards of three different infertility clinics as fundraising chairperson.

And there Chantel had it. Too bad "it" wasn't anything she could use.

CHAPTER NINE

COLIN WAS TOO practical to believe in love at first sight. He wasn't even sure he truly believed in falling in love at all. You loved your parents and siblings, the people you were born to and who were born to you. If you were lucky, you'd feel a strong fondness for a friend or two along the way.

And when you married, if you were a smart man, you chose a woman you liked spending time with. A woman you trusted. Someone you cared for deeply. One who'd be a good mother to any children you might have. One who enjoyed at least some of the same things you did. And, of course, one who turned you on.

He'd yet to find that woman. He'd thought he had, once. Until she'd left him because he was leaving his inheritance to his sister. He'd thought maybe he was close another time or two. But with his parents dying so young, one after the other—necessitating him taking over the business long before he'd expected—with Julie's attack and resultant internal battles, time had passed, taking his twenties with it.

And now here he was, just two nights after the

evening he'd gone to a dreaded art auction, sitting across from Chantel Johnson and feeling as though he'd known her since before he was born.

Or something equally as foolish.

They'd had gourmet food for lunch. He'd decided on fondue for dinner because the restaurant he had in mind had quiet, rounded, high-back dimly lit booths that secluded each party and provided excellent views of the ocean in the distance. And because cooking each course at your table made for a long dinner.

He ordered a bottle of wine, poured them each a glass and discussed the various menu choices with her. They had to make meat selections, choose vegetables, and items for their dessert tray. It didn't even surprise him that they went for the same things.

"To you." He raised his glass of wine and tipped it to hers.

"To you," she said, and when she added, "To my good luck," it was like the words slid right inside of him.

"Your good luck?" he asked, but he knew what she'd meant. He wanted to prolong the conversation.

"I go to my first public function in a state that is completely new to me, knowing not a single soul, and the first person I meet is you."

The sincerity shining from her gaze hit him harder than the wine.

"So I'm not alone in this…strange feeling…that's been accompanying me the past couple of days?" He heard the sex in his voice but couldn't have changed it if he'd wanted to.

He wanted her.

And not just for sex.

He was drawn to her. Suddenly more alive because she existed.

Her smile was sweet. Loaded with invitation—though maybe not intentionally. "You care to define that feeling? I like to know what I'm agreeing to before I commit myself."

His first thought was to ask her to commit herself to his bed. That night. And for the foreseeable future. Thank God he was mature enough to stop himself from actually acting on the thought.

"You're different," he said, watching her over their glasses of wine lit by candlelight. He drew out the words. His voice purposely "bedroom," liking the foreplay. "Compelling. In a way I've never known before."

Eyes glistening, she didn't shy away from his boldness. "I can commit to that," she said.

In a stunningly simple black short shift that was sexier for what it covered, not for what it left uncovered, she could have stepped out of a fashion magazine. Again. He wondered who did her hair. The color was so natural looking he couldn't stop watching it. Wondering how it would feel to run his fingers through it. To have it falling around his body, tickling his chest…

And those lips—so artfully painted—they glistened with promise.

"But…"

When her eyes shadowed, he brought himself back to dinner. To what was, in reality, a first date.

"But?" he asked.

"You did hear me say that when I'm done with my book I have decided to return to New York, after all? My family misses me more than I thought. I've promised that I will resume my former position within the company."

He'd heard. But he knew that so much could happen in just two days, let alone the months and months it must take to write an entire book. After that, who knew? If parents could die in the prime of their lives, then equally good miracles could happen, too, right?

Like maybe a move to New York?

Or, at the very least, frequent flights…

"I heard."

"And you're okay with that?" The worry in her gaze hit him harder than the kiss waiting on her lips. She cared, too.

"Yes," he told her. She'd been honest. If, in the future, they needed to work out something, then they'd work it out.

He spent his days borrowing trouble—looking to the future for any potential pitfalls so that he could protect his clients ahead of time. He'd spent his life doing the same—looking to be used before he looked to be liked.

But not this time.

Two nights ago his life had changed. He'd changed.

And it didn't seem like there was a lot he could do about that.

Except to see where it was all going to lead.

THE CHEESE FONDUE appetizer was phenomenal. Chantel, a woman whose appetite was voracious enough to go along with the adrenaline it took to be a beat cop on the streets of California, had to hold herself back to stay in character. But boy, it was good.

Not half as good as the company, though. If all undercover jobs were like this, she'd sign on for life.

Still on her first glass of wine—she couldn't forget that she was on the job—she sat back while he dipped the last cube of bread into the cheese. Watched a drop of cheese hit his lower lip. And followed his tongue as he cleaned it off.

Attention to detail was her job.

She had no idea how a guy could look so damned sexy cleaning gooey cheese off his lip. She gave herself a little shake, remembering why she was there, and said, "Is Julie feeling better?"

Replacing cheese with a sip of wine, he returned his glass to the table. "I haven't seen her."

"She was already gone when you got home?" It was a natural assumption with it being Saturday night and her being twenty-seven.

"No." He looked toward the ocean. As though some answer was out there, waiting for him to find it.

His sister had been home when he'd stopped there to change, but he hadn't seen her? Hadn't he gone to find her, knowing that when he'd dropped her off she'd been upset? They lived in a large house, a mansion by the looks of things. It would be easy for two people to live there and never see each other. But...

Chantel wasn't a detective yet—mostly because she'd turned down the promotion the first time it had been offered—but she knew a lot about getting information out of subjects. Sometimes you played rough. And sometimes you didn't say anything at all.

He watched the horizon. She watched him. Wondered at the battle that seemed to be going on within him. He'd been jovial until she'd mentioned Julie.

But he didn't seem angry. More contemplative.

A whole minute had passed. She took another small sip of wine. Just in case he'd forgotten she was there.

"My sister... I don't talk about her. Ever."

"I understand," she said. When, of course, she didn't. How could she? She had no idea why a brother wouldn't talk about his sister. Unless she'd really pissed him off. That clearly wasn't the case here.

His gaze pierced her. Off balance, she told herself, *No more wine.* "I want to tell you about her," he said.

Chantel wanted more wine.

"Okay."

"I'm not really at liberty to do so. And at the moment, I'm a bit unnerved that I even want to."

She was beginning to see his problem. "You don't have to tell me anything." But the problem lay there between them. He wanted to. And she wanted him to.

She also might need him to, depending on what it was he had to say.

"Julie likes you."

"She told you that?" She'd been in the car when they'd dropped the other woman off. And he'd just told her he hadn't seen her since. Didn't mean they couldn't have talked, but he'd said he didn't know how Julie was doing. If he'd talked to her, he'd have had an idea and...

Chantel never quit looking for the lie in everything. She had to be prepared for danger around every corner. It was how she protected lives. Including her own.

"She didn't have to tell me. In ten years' time, she's never...ever...opened up in front of anyone like she did in the car today. You have no idea."

No…but she was bursting with wanting to. She had to remember she was playing a part. The slightly bored, well-to-do woman on a date. Would she be bored with talk of his sister?

Deciding that if she would be, she was going to change right then and there, Chantel Harris gave him a small smile. "I liked her, too. A lot."

He nodded and knocked his knuckles on the table. "She's the one who opened the door," he said, his gaze meeting hers in the candlelight. Intimately. "Julie is a bit of a recluse…"

Was he trying to tell her Julie was agoraphobic? She tried to imagine that…

His struggle—what to say, what not to say, talking about his sister at all—touched her. She couldn't help it. So she jumped in to help. "She seemed fine today…until the end there." Maybe Julie was only mildly agoraphobic. Maybe with help…

"She *is* fine, more than fine, pretty much all the time. My sister's a strong, independent woman who not only knows her own mind, but has little problem expressing it. She's also generous almost to a fault and loves helping people."

Relief flooded her. And she didn't really even know these people. Nor was she going to be a real or significant part of their lives.

He topped off her wine. Drawing an imaginary line on the glass, marking how much he added, she knew she had to leave that much. One glass and that was it.

Not because the captain, or the job, said so. Undercovers did all kinds of things—joined in where they had to in order to not blow their cover. It had just been her own rule, laid down strictly to herself earlier that evening while she'd been donning the attire for the job.

She wished she had more cheese. Might even have been tempted to run her finger along the edges of the pot—to hell with the burn—if it had still been there. They'd removed it, returning with a different kind of pot filled with oil, which was presumably heating to a temperature that would sear meat.

Distraction was what she needed. Not more of those sincerely heart-stopping blue eyes giving her their full attention. She wasn't as great as that look was making her feel.

"Julie sits on a couple of charitable boards and some committees. She attends meetings. It's not that she has a problem with going out. She has a problem with who she might run into."

Chantel sat up straight.

"Like Patricia Reynolds?"

Tilting his head for a second, he shrugged. "That was a new one."

"So she has…like…hallucinations?" That wasn't good. Probably worse than agoraphobia.

"No!" He gave her a twisted smile, then shook his head. "I'm trying so hard to be careful here, to protect her privacy, and instead I'm making it sound worse than it is."

There were times when a cop needed to help her subject give her the information she needed.

And she needed to know about Julie now. She just did. Running the tip of her tongue over her bottom lip, she lifted her glass and at the last minute remembered to soften her voice. "So why not just tell me what's going on? As you said, she opened the door…"

He nodded. Appraised her. If he gave her a genuine precious-metal test, she'd fail. And be miserable. Lifting her chin, she looked him straight in the eye. Intending to keep her silent promise to protect whatever he told her. To protect his sister. At all cost.

That was her job. To protect others.

"Ten years ago Julie was brutally raped."

The quick intake of breath, the gasp, Chantel let loose was not ladylike. A passing waitress looked over at her.

She knew she was in over her head.

She also knew she had to learn fast how to swim. There was no other choice.

CHAPTER TEN

EVERY NERVE IN Chantel's body stood up.

Leslie Morrison, probable victim of abuse, was friends with Julie.

Julie was certain the commissioner's wife had been sent to watch over her because of a correlation being drawn between something that had happened to her and the recent revelation regarding Ryder and Leslie Morrison.

Whether that last was true or not, Chantel drew a correlation. Because Julie, who knew facts of both situations, had drawn her own.

Would finding out more about Julie lead her to the evidence she needed to save Leslie and Ryder Morrison from further harm?

It should. If she was connecting her dots right...

And what about sweet Julie? Colin's baby sister?

Having some idea of what a girl felt like after she'd been morally and physically abused, Chantel wanted to cry for the woman she'd just met but cared about already.

"I don't know what to say." The words, Chantel Harris speaking for Chantel Johnson, were completely authentic. As was the pain in her voice.

Colin swallowed, appearing to do so with difficulty. The tightness in his jaw told the rest of the story.

"Did they catch the guy?" Could she have given them enough determiners? Did they get a good enough composite sketch? Was he convicted?

Thinking of Leslie, of Julie's conviction that someone didn't want her speaking about the past in relation to the rumors regarding Ryder Morrison's collage, Chantel had a really bad feeling about the whole thing.

"They didn't have to catch him. He was right where everyone knew he would be—home in bed. Julie knew him. They were at a party together. She was his date."

Oh. This was going to be bad.

"I'll leave any details to her to tell, if she ever needs or wants to tell you. But in order for you to understand yesterday, and the door Julie opened... the guy is a member of our social circle. Julie told me what had happened as soon as she got home that night. I took her to the hospital. A report was made. I stayed on top of it by the minute. But the case stayed hushed behind closed doors. A couple of days later, the story was that the sex had been consensual, that when Julie found out that sex was all it was, that the guy wasn't interested in a relationship, she made the accusation of abuse out of bitterness and hurt. No charges were ever filed, and as far as we know, no one in our circle even knows they were ever even considered. It was said that the secrecy was to protect Julie from any possible embarrassment or repercussion for making a false report."

The commissioner had to hear about this. Chantel was going to tell him. There was no other choice.

"Who was it?"

His gaze dropped, but only for a second. "I can't tell you that."

"The doctor's report…did you see it? Medical reports are pretty specific. The doctor would have said if there'd been any…" She'd almost said *tearing*, but realized Chantel Harris's dinner conversation could not come out of Chantel Johnson's mouth.

Pushing her glass of wine farther away, she bowed her head. She had to be careful here. More so now than ever.

"I'm sorry," she said, looking back up at him. "I just… This is so upsetting. I don't really know what a medical report would say…just what I see on television, and I know how naive it sounds of me to think that in real life…"

He shook his head, his look all intimate again. "No, you're absolutely right," he told her. "They can tell if there was…force. And, well, let's just say it was obvious. But what I was told was that rough sex is not all that uncommon these days. It was very clear that Julie and I were going to get no help. Either we agreed to be quiet about the matter, or she would be charged with false accusation and sued for slander. I told her I would proceed, that I would stop at nothing to get her the representation she needed to win her case. But she said no. It would be her word against his, and the family is prominent. And well liked. Julie and I had only each other, and I was still in law school. It was somewhat known that Julie had had a thing for the guy. She'd agreed to attend the party with him. Had arrived with him. We had money to buy the best of the best, but so did her opponent."

"I wish she'd fought, anyway."

"I know. But I agreed with her decision to let it go. She was right—her chances of getting a winning judgment against the powers on the other side weren't good."

"The powers? You're telling me that a judge was involved?"

"I'm neither confirming nor denying that. Powerful people in prominent positions need only to have one highly appointed, respected confidant to make things disappear. It shouldn't be that way, but you know as well as I do that in our world that's how it happens."

Just like all Chantel Johnson knew about cop work was what she'd seen on TV, all Chantel Harris knew about his world was what she'd either seen on TV or read about in the past weeks. So she took his word for it and nodded. "You didn't have a higher higher-up you could grease," she guessed.

She hated the idea of living in such a world. And hearing her cop radar buzz over and over.

Julie had refused to press charges, to fight the beast who'd hurt her, because she knew she couldn't win. Leslie Morrison was refusing to press charges, denying any crime had been committed against her. Because she knew she couldn't win?

Judging by Leslie's hospital records, Morrison's abuse of her—if it was real—had been going on for some time. Which meant Leslie had been hiding the truth for a long time. Hiding her pain, living without justice.

Was that what the two women had in common?

And this "higher-up" with greased palms—was he the same, too? Was that why Julie was certain that people wanted to keep her quiet?

"The Fairbankses don't grease palms." Colin's expression had firmed, losing the warm touch.

And Chantel realized that she'd made another blunder. A big one.

She nodded. And then grinned. A quiet, classy grin...she hoped. In a lowered voice, she said, with complete and utter honesty, "I can't tell you how glad I am to hear that, Colin." And then added, "Because neither do the Johnsons, and as you say, in our world you only know who's who when you've lived among them for a while. Being new here..."

She broke off, hoping he'd get her point. "Anyway, I'm sorry if I offended you."

"I'm finding it difficult to believe I took offense,"

Colin told her with a slightly boyish grin. He sipped his wine, watching her as he did so. "I've always been the guy who could let boulders roll off his back without cracking a sweat. I don't know what it is about you that has me acting so out of character..."

"Well, I hope you'll understand, then, that I'm struggling with the same malaise..." She'd heard a woman use the word in one of the documentaries she'd watched about the rich and famous and had had to go look it up. "Please forgive anything I do that might appear out of character—it's because I don't quite know how to handle myself around you. I'm feeling a mixture of giddy excitement and complete discomfort all rolled into one." Total honesty on that one. And a perfect cover for her, too.

COLIN WASN'T SURE if the blow to his head was figurative or if he'd somehow been in an accident that had been so severe he'd forgotten about it. Of course, as soon as he had the thought, he knew how ridiculous it was. Ludicrous, really. There was nothing wrong with his head.

It was something else that was out of kilter. Unbalanced.

"You're knocking at walls that are miles thick," he said aloud. And immediately wanted the words back. He was coming across like some kind of needy lecher who'd never been exposed to a beautiful woman before.

Like a man who didn't know the ropes. Or how to respect boundaries.

"I'm sorry," he said before she could respond. "I'm embarrassed by my behavior. Please, can we go back to the part where I pick you up from the hotel lobby, tell you you look beautiful and ask if you like fondue? I swear, I've been on a date before and do know the proper etiquette. Which I will show you if you'll give me the chance."

He was going to kiss her. Soon. Maybe within seconds. Before she agreed to go back…

Or…he'd kiss her good-night.

Either way, he was going to kiss her.

"Are you looking for an honest answer?"

The woman took his breath away. "Always."

Anyone he'd ever been out with, *everyone* he'd ever been out with, would have taken this opportunity to escape speaking of embarrassing emotions, or getting too emotionally personal and moved on.

"Then no, I'd rather not go back."

He had no idea what to do with that. The situation was becoming disturbingly familiar.

And delightfully different, too.

"My sister tells me that I'm known, among our female set, as a fun companion as long as my dates always wear sweaters."

Her frown was cute. And drew attention to eyebrows that didn't look fake. Neither drawn on, nor artfully waxed. They were shaped. Beautiful. But… unusual, now that he noticed them.

Striking. Like everything else about her.

He had a feeling that he could spend a lifetime with her and still not see all of the unique things about her...

"I don't understand," she said, drawing him back to the conversation.

"I'm apparently considered to be emotionally cold." Slow to trust, he'd take that label. But cold? Not true at all. Still, the reputation served its purpose.

Until now.

"You are?" If she was playing with him, she was more of a master than anyone in his circle.

"I've actually been proud of that fact," he admitted. "I'm rich and single. Which makes me an obvious choice for anyone looking for a husband. For herself. Or, in many cases, her daughter. Again, as I'm sure you know, business deals are made in the form of marriage. And a woman who's grown up never having to lift a finger unless she chooses to is pretty driven to find a way to continue that lifestyle into adulthood. In order to do so, she has to find a husband rich enough to support her in the manner in which she wants to be kept."

What in the hell was he doing? Saying?

It was to Chantel's credit, a sign of the most elite and respectable upbringing, that she still appeared to be listening to him. And looked interested, too. It was an art, Julie had once said, a woman's ability to look interested while bored to tears. She'd been speaking to their mother about their mother's ability to always appear interested, when the best Julie could manage sometimes was to stay awake enough to keep her forehead out of her soup bowl.

"Go on," she said now. "Why'd you stop?"

"Because I sound like an asshole." Not dinner conversation with a lady—at least not in his parents' day.

He sounded exactly like what he was. A man with trust issues.

"You sound like a man who feels hounded by members of his own clan." She was staring at his face, her gaze roaming over it, and he felt as though her fingers had caressed him. It left him wanting more.

"If I'm going to be used, I want to know about it," he said slowly. "And I don't want to care. Emotions are messy. They cause mistakes."

Which explained the mess he was making of what could have been the best night of his adult life.

He was not making it easy for himself to get to where he really wanted the evening to go—his lips on hers.

"Emotions are most definitely unreliable," she agreed. He watched her mouth move.

"So we build walls around ourselves…" His arm slid along the back of the booth behind them; his hand dropped to touch her bare shoulder.

"Thick ones." Her husky voice could only be heard if he leaned in toward her.

"I pride myself on not trusting anyone until their trustworthiness has been tangibly proven to me."

Her lips were inches away now.

She licked them. "How does one tangibly prove their trustworthiness to you?"

He was going to kiss her. Right then. Right there. Protocol be damned.

"Okay, your oil should be hot enough..."

Oh, God, the fantasy was gaining momentum and getting out of control.

"I'll get your meat right out. Would either of you like more wine? Or a bottle of water?"

Their waitress had come around the corner. Colin hadn't kissed Chantel.

Yet.

THEIR ASSORTED BITE-SIZE pieces of meat arrived on a large china platter. Chantel listened to instructions Colin had clearly heard before as he jumped into clarify a couple of times. Or demonstrate how to handle her fork in hot oil without losing her dinner to the bottom of the pot or getting burned.

When they were once again alone, and their first pieces of meat were bubbling side by side in the pot, Chantel tried to figure out how to get the conversation back on topic. On Julie. And hopefully Leslie, too.

How to make certain it never got as personal as it just had. Fate had intervened in the form of their waitress. Chantel was certain it had been fate. The timing had been too critical. Saving her from blowing what could turn out to be the biggest job of her life. By forgetting she was Chantel Johnson and letting Chantel Harris fall for her subject.

She'd almost kissed him. Right there in the restaurant. She, who'd never, ever felt comfortable with public displays of affection.

She didn't believe in coincidences, so yes, fate was on her side...

Colin adjusted their forks so that his wasn't beneath hers, lifting her meat out of the oil.

"I just need to say one more thing about Julie, and then we can put difficult topics aside and enjoy our evening together," he said, as though he knew she'd been trying to find a way back. She and this man who was way out of her league were *sympatico*. Chantel wished she was surprised by that.

She also wished she didn't find the fact quite so delicious. She just needed to eat. She was starving. She should have had more cheese.

"You don't have to entertain me, Colin. I'm happy to talk about, or listen to, anything you need or want to share."

Surely people in his circle shared real conversations when they were out alone among themselves, in personal settings. She had to get the information she needed out of him.

And then find a way to keep herself cool while she pretended to date him for as long as it took her to find out the truth—with usable proof—about Leslie and James Morrison.

To find out who'd raped Julie Fairbanks and bring him to justice.

His look thoughtful, he nodded. "The reason Julie didn't want to pursue charges back then..."

She raised her brow and nodded, trying to show compassion but not avariciousness in her need to know. And felt like she was on the edge of her chair.

She had to stay on track.

The more information she could take to the commissioner, the better chance they had at finding the mole in the department. Because there was no record of Julie Fairbanks ever having made a complaint against anyone, for anything.

No official record of a medical report, either.

Which meant that someone in the Santa Raquel Police Department was guilty of a cover-up. She was going to have to find out who the rapist was. And track possible connections and associations from there. Both in the police department and in the court system...

And something told her that when she did that, she'd also find out who or what was keeping Leslie Morrison quiet. Talking to the woman wasn't going to net her what she needed. If conversation could get Leslie to turn her husband in, Chantel wouldn't be undercover.

But if she could find out the truth—through Julie—and help both women at once…

"Santa Raquel is our home. Julie loves it here. We're living in an ancestral home that's been in the Fairbanks family for more than a hundred years. She doesn't want to leave. And neither could she bear the idea of being looked on with either scorn or pity from members of our social circle. Some of the kids knew she hooked up that night. The story that went around was the breakup soon afterward was mutual."

"Surely people know…"

"No one knows. That was part of the deal we struck," Colin said. "If anyone from either side speaks of the incident, the other side has means for pressing charges…"

"Which is why you aren't telling me who it was."

"That. And because the details aren't mine to tell. I just needed you to understand how important this is."

To know that his sister wasn't on the verge of crazy.

"So, this other incident Julie mentioned today— the one where she thinks there's a possible link— was there suspicion of another rape?" If it was

Leslie Morrison they were talking about, that answer would be no.

And the abuser wouldn't be the same, either, as Julie's rapist would have been someone close to her own age. Which completely ruled out James Morrison.

"No. It really was nothing. Even Julie realizes that." Colin, thank God, was keeping to his corner of the rounded booth they were sharing.

"Is she just being paranoid, then? Thinking she's being looked at because of it? You didn't seem to buy in to her theory that Patricia Reynolds is spying on her." Purposely choosing Julie's word—*spying*—because she didn't know how Chantel Johnson would ask the question, she took a sip of her wine.

His frown made him look…studious. Dependable and trustworthy and…

He was a subject. Not a man for her to find likable. And more.

"With good reason, Julie doesn't trust many people. She's suspicious because she's been taught she has to be."

"But you know the truth. The facts. You were there, too. And you don't think Patricia Reynolds is spying on her."

"I don't."

Chantel Johnson nodded. Chantel Harris wasn't so sure Colin was right.

Still, for now, until she had more than gut to

go on, her report to the commissioner was going to be nice and clean. And her first piece of meat was done.

But her fact-finding had only just begun.

CHAPTER ELEVEN

As FATE WOULD have it, Colin didn't kiss Chantel Johnson Saturday night. He didn't even finish the dessert they'd ordered. He'd had a call—one he couldn't not take—and had to take his date home and go to work. At ten o'clock on a Saturday night.

A billion-dollar business deal that one of his clients had been trying to put together in Japan was on the brink of being waylaid, and Colin had had to pack a bag and hop on a chartered jet to Asia. Signed deal in hand, he returned to the United States, along with a very happy client, early Monday morning. Exhausted, disoriented and eager for a shower.

Before bed, though, he was going to call Chantel.

He'd texted her from Japan.

She hadn't responded.

On the plane, on the way home, with a good internet connection and his mind not staying as focused as he wanted, he did some surfing. Because he was uncomfortable. Afraid he was getting in too deep. How did he know whether or not Chantel Johnson was really who she said she was?

So, right, her invitation to the auction Thursday

night was a pretty good determiner. Due to the value of the property being auctioned, the guest list had been exclusive. She wouldn't have been in the room if she hadn't been carefully vetted.

Feeling a bit dirty, like someone Smyth might like, he searched public records for Johnsons in New York. And found seven Chantels. Two of which fit her age group. Making note of their latest known addresses, he went to a map website, one that he'd used before. It gave him bird's-eye views of the neighborhoods. One of the two was upscale.

As was the case with a lot of people of substantial wealth, there was little else to find. At least for someone with his limited access.

And he was ashamed of himself. Hated the idea that Chantel could ever know he'd done such a thing. Turning off his tablet, he closed his eyes. Told himself to rest. And half an hour later he had it back on again.

Searching for a New York boutique publisher by the name of Johnson.

When it took all of two minutes to find it and find out that a Pamela Johnson was CEO, Colin wiped out his search history, turned off the tablet and put it away. He'd guess her mother's name was Pamela.

But he was going to wait for her to tell him that before he'd know for sure. He'd verified enough.

For the first time in too long, he was going to

accept someone on faith. At least, he was going to give it his best shot.

Because Chantel Johnson was different. Though he had no explanation for it, in a world of lies, she inspired truth.

FATE WAS ON her side. Chantel was meant to be doing this job. Not only had fate intervened in the form of the waitress when Chantel might have started making out in a restaurant with a subject. But she'd come to the rescue a second time, before Chantel had given in to more of a temptation than the chocolate fondue they'd ordered would have offered.

Chantel didn't need to be hit over the head to know that fate, in the form of an important client, had whisked temptation away. All the way across the globe. Probably because the sweet knowing force had recognized the danger Colin Fairbanks had been presenting that night.

A danger that had been on the winning side of a seasoned, capable and loyal cop. By the time they'd finished feeding each other meat, devouring each other with their eyes the entire time, she'd been weak in more than the knees.

If he'd asked to come up to her hotel room that night, she might have invited him. If she'd actually had a room to go to.

But no more. She'd spent Sunday on the job. Arresting a perp for shoplifting. And answering a call that had her stumbling upon a portable meth lab in a big-box store bathroom. When a call had come in late for a missing older woman who was suffering from memory loss, she stayed late, joined the search and was outside the home, helping with crowd dispersement when the woman was brought safely back just before midnight.

By Monday she was rested and firmly committed to her assignments. Period. She'd continue to see Colin. He was the most expedient means—possibly the only means at the moment—of successfully preventing another domestic-violence death. Time was of the essence in the Morrison case. She couldn't risk hurting Colin's feelings, thereby necessitating that she start over in finding a means to infiltrate Leslie Morrison's life without drawing attention to the fact that she was doing so.

He was also now a victim, and an invaluable source, in the unresolved, officially unreported rape of his sister. Chantel had been sleepless most of Saturday night, appalled at what she'd heard. A young woman had suffered a horrible crime and then suffered again when nothing was done about it. And more—if what Colin said was true, and she had no reason to believe it wasn't—there was corruption someplace in the Santa Raquel Police Department.

And she couldn't rid herself of the idea that the same corruption was putting a gag in Leslie Morrison's mouth.

She had to find the source in order to help either woman.

Just to make certain that she didn't tempt fate, she didn't respond when he texted her on Chantel Johnson's police-issue cell phone. And when she didn't keep checking to see if he'd texted a second time, she knew she was good.

Yes, she had it all under control. Which was what she told Wayne when he asked her about the case over lunch Monday at an innocuous diner not far from the station house.

They were facing each other in a red plastic-padded booth, and he needed to get beyond any worry about her and Colin. She had much bigger news to talk about.

"How many quarts of chocolate ice cream did you consume this weekend?" Grease dripped onto his chin as he took a bite of his patty melt.

"None." Not since Friday.

His eyebrow raised.

Afraid someone they knew might walk in, interrupt the little bit of time they had together before she started her shift and he went home to his wife, she pushed aside the second half of her second burrito and leaned toward him. "I've stumbled onto something, Wayne," she said, her voice low. Not soft, like Johnson's, just hushed.

"You got something on Morrison already?" He looked impressed, which took a lot of doing.

Chantel shook her head. "I mean, yes, I think I

do, but there's more. I don't have anything more than a conversation to go on, but I'm as certain as I can be that a cover-up from ten years ago has something to do with Leslie Morrison's refusal to admit her husband has been abusing her."

Otherwise, why would Julie think the questions recently raised by Ryder Morrison's art project would have an impact on what had happened to her ten years before?

She told him about Julie Fairbanks's rape. About Colin being in law school. About the charges that disappeared.

"Are you sure they made an official complaint?" Wayne asked, eating as they talked.

"Colin was already working in the family law firm, doing paralegal work, before he ever started college. He said Julie made a formal report that night, right after they left the hospital. He's as certain that the report was filed as he is that a couple of days later it disappeared and charges were never filed."

A French fry followed another bite of patty melt into Wayne's mouth. "Probably wasn't enough evidence to get a conviction and charges were dropped."

She'd thought of that, too, of course. But Colin had given her enough information to know that that hadn't been the case. "There was a medical report, Wayne. She went straight to the hospital. According to the doctor, there was evidence of rape."

Wayne stopped chewing. "Colin saw this medical report?"

"Yes."

"And he's sure it was in the police file?"

"Yes."

"So they know who did it."

"Yes. Unequivocally."

"You checked for the report." He wasn't actually asking now; he'd know that she had.

"Yes. There is no Julie Fairbanks, or Colin, either, in police record."

Wiping his mouth, Wayne lowered his voice as he asked, "Who was the officer on record?"

Gary Bartlett. Chantel gave him the name Colin had given her when she'd asked as he was dropping her off Saturday night. He'd been apologizing for spending the first half of the evening on such a serious topic and then bailing out on the second half.

She'd assured him that it wouldn't have a negative impact on his chances of seeing her again. She'd then jumped on the chance he'd given her to get back to the topic she most needed to discuss with him—Julie's rape.

"I've never heard of him," she said now. "But then I've only been up a year and a half. What do you know of him? Or what happened to him? Did he retire?"

"I never met him," Wayne said, "but I know the name. He transferred out of state shortly after I started here."

"Was he a detective? Or higher up?" How bad was the news going to be when she took it to the commissioner?

"He was higher up."

Wayne did't look any happier than she felt.

"We can hope that if indeed there was corruption, and I agree with you it certainly sounds that way, that it ended with Barlett's departure."

She wanted to believe that. In the worst way. Bad enough going to the commissioner with news of an injustice that was going to make the Santa Raquel Police Department look bad, but to have to tell him that it wasn't an isolated incident…

"I'm not sure it did," she said now, a theory that had been building all weekend coming to the forefront. She'd kind of been hoping that talking things over with Wayne might put things in a different perspective, give her reason not to be as concerned, send her down another path. Something.

"Why do you say that?" he asked, lowering his head as well as his voice.

"Because Julie Fairbanks was certain that what happened to her has some connection to the Morrisons. Since there's been no history, evidence, claim or even mention of sexual assault at the Morrison home, she could only have been referring to the way wrongdoing disappears as though it never happened."

"You're saying that James Morrison is getting

away with beating up his wife because someone in the department is allowing it to happen?"

"I don't know what I'm saying." She didn't want it to be true. But… "We have to go to the commissioner, Wayne. This might be bigger than either of us can handle. We at least need another ear in on this. Other eyes watching…"

He was shaking his head before she was halfway through talking.

"What?"

"Nothing."

"Wayne." Her tone spoke warning. She wasn't going to be brushed off. "Don't you find it odd that Bartlett got the call from the hospital? That he was the policeman contacted?"

"A beat cop would have gotten the initial call. Or a detective."

"Exactly. So who was that? And where is he or she now?"

"We have to find out who that was. Unless…do you think the doctor was in on it, too?"

"The thought crossed my mind, but if he had been, the simplest way to make the whole thing go away would be to just not make the report. Or to say that, in his opinion, there was no evidence of rape. Why tell the victim that he'll corroborate her story, file a report and then put in a call to someone on the department who would make it go away?

"Unless he didn't know who the alleged perpetrator was at that point…" She broke off, shaking her head. "No, Colin said that the doctor followed up with him. He would have gone to court for them if Julie had opted to file civil charges."

"You need to see if Colin Fairbanks knows who took the initial call."

Nodding, she sat there in her uniform and focused, playing all facts through her mind again. And again.

"Speaking of which, I'm still a little worried about him seeing you out and about like this. Or anyone else from that group seeing you, for that matter."

She laughed. "You didn't even recognize me at first when you saw Chantel Johnson."

"True."

"In the rare chance that anyone from that crowd would happen to be in the lowly places Chantel Harris inhabits, they're going to see a beat cop in uniform and pass right on by. Or, if I'm off, a woman in jeans and hiking shoes who doesn't know the first thing about hair, makeup or class. But you know as well as I do, in the time I've been here, the times I'm in public out of uniform are pretty rare."

"I know. Maybe I can pay a visit to the doctor who saw Julie that night. And since we have no records, I'd need you to get his name for me, too."

"I'm sure I can do that." She felt better already. The world wasn't sitting completely on her shoulders. It never was. She just had a bad habit of trying to hold it there, anyway.

"You've got to be careful, Chantel. You can't do any police work on this Julie thing—other than having Chantel Johnson ferreting out any information she can. Let me do all of the legwork. We can't have Fairbanks getting suspicious about you. It would blow your cover and then the whole Morrison assignment is blown."

And her career right along with it. Not that her career mattered one whit in comparison to Leslie's and Ryder Morrison's lives.

"So…you want to go with me when I talk to the commissioner?"

A waitress came to ask if she could remove any dirty dishes or bring drink refills. Wayne waved her away, his expression dead serious. "I don't think we should go to the commissioner just yet."

Shocked, she felt sick all over again. Wayne? Above anyone else, she'd trust him with her life. Which was saying a lot.

And then she shivered and started to sweat. "You don't trust the commissioner," she whispered. Then she told him about Patricia Reynolds's new appointment to the library committee.

She started to breathe freely again when Wayne said, "I trust the commissioner. And I'd bet my life's savings that Mrs. Reynolds is on the committee in case you need help. She's a financial supporter of The Lemonade Stand and was a proponent of the police being involved with the High Risk team from the very beginning."

Okay. Good. Chantel's world righted itself again. Facing down a gun she could do. Finding corruption in the man who was a god to her and all of the men and women who served with her wasn't something she wanted to think about.

Not that she wanted to believe that any of the men and women who were part of the Santa Raquel police force could be bought.

"We don't have enough to take him yet," Wayne continued. "When we do this, we have to be careful. Very careful. We have no idea who might have been involved. Who might still be involved. No idea what careers we might jeopardize, and I sure as hell don't want it to be my own. Or yours."

"You're thinking someone higher up might know about this already."

"It's a possibility we can't ignore. Which is another reason we can't get Fairbanks suspicious. You said you thought there might be some connection between Morrison and what happened before. And Fairbanks is friendly with Morrison. He might not know where the leak, if there is one, is coming from. If we're going to pursue this, we have to keep it strictly between you and me."

What he said made total sense. She didn't like it, but she knew he was right. "Okay, but we tell the captain, right?" He was their go-to on the assignment.

When Wayne shook his head one more time, Chantel realized just how deep this assignment had taken her.

She wasn't a member of a team right now. Not part of the brotherhood that had become her family. Except for Wayne, she was completely and totally on her own.

With no one to run to. And no one who had her back.

She had to call Max. Just in case.

CHAPTER TWELVE

As SOON AS his flight landed, when everyone around him was turning on cell phones, texting and calling their people, Colin thought about calling Chantel. He didn't, of course. They weren't at the text-as-soon-as-you-land point in their relationship. He'd never been at that point in a relationship.

But he was thinking about it now.

His plan was to call her on the way home. And then he'd text Julie. His sister would be in LA, having lunch with a couple people on the Sunshine committee—hoping to get their support for her child-life specialist project at the Santa Raquel Children's Hospital—but she always wanted to know when he was back in town, which she defined as back in Santa Raquel.

He didn't call Chantel on the way home. He returned a couple of business calls, texted his sister as soon as he was in the house. And then took a shower.

Twenty minutes later he was back out the door. She worked all day, she'd said. On her book, in her hotel room. But she had to break to eat, didn't she? Maybe, if he got lucky, she'd be ready for a late lunch. If she'd already eaten, at least he could say hello. Apologize, again, for his abrupt departure the other night.

Who was he kidding? He wanted to look her in the eye and get the feeling he got every single time she looked back.

Pulling into the resort, he left his car with the valet and went straight for the front desk. He wouldn't take up much of her time. Hell, he didn't have but a few minutes to give. Just enough to solidify another date.

Another chance to be alone with her.

She hadn't answered his text. If she wasn't interested in pursuing time with him, he'd know the minute he saw her and leave her in peace—of that he was certain. He was enchanted by her. He wasn't a stalker.

Rejection would be a new experience for him. Maybe one that he needed and should have had long ago.

Lord knew he was acting like a lovesick schoolboy. The whole thing would be humiliating except that for some god-awful reason she meant something to him. Enough that he was willing to face whatever came next.

"Can I help you, sir?" The black-suited gentleman behind the counter spoke in a way that instilled confidence.

"I'm here to see Chantel Johnson," he said. "She

doesn't know I'm coming, and I was hoping you could ring her room for me."

He could have called her cell phone, but the man behind the desk didn't know that.

This was probably a bad idea. One of his worst. He should have just called, had a casual conversation, then determined from there if she had any interest in furthering their association.

At least he hadn't come bearing flowers. Or chocolate...

"I'm sorry, sir, we have no Chantel Johnson staying here."

On a good day, Colin didn't have a lot of patience with inefficiency. With very little sleep and suffering from jet lag besides, he wasn't on a good day. "Could you check again, please? I know she's staying here. For an extended period," he said, keeping his tone even. "I dropped her off here myself on Saturday night. Walked her in and watched her get on the elevator." He spelled Chantel's name. Just as he'd seen it on the email Leslie had sent out to the library committee. Leslie had been formally introducing her before the lunch on Saturday.

He waited, glancing over the counter to the keyboard to see that the man typed the name correctly.

He did.

Good. Any minute now...

"I'm sorry." The man shook his head. "We have no one registered under that name. I can call a manager for you if you'd like."

Colin shook his head. He wasn't going to cause a scene. He'd just call her cell. "That's not necessary, thank you," he said, turning to leave.

"I'm sorry, sir," he heard as he retreated, head held high. Until that point, he'd figured he'd left some dignity intact.

But no. It was pretty obvious that the front desk clerk at a hotel he could probably afford to purchase had just pitied him.

CHANTEL AND HER current partner, Daniel Lewis, a gray-haired twenty-year veteran, didn't have a lot in common. They rode well together because they didn't get into each other's personal shit. Daniel, who'd acquired somewhat of a paunch, was the type of guy who went by the book, did his job well, but didn't do anything he didn't have to do. If the call didn't come to him, he didn't take it.

When it did, he was rock solid.

She could learn a thing or two from him, Wayne had said. Both good and bad. Monday's shift— a four-to-midnight crossover—was more good than bad. They'd had a domestic-violence call that turned out to be a vindictive girlfriend who'd tried to get her man in trouble and had confessed to the childishness three minutes after Daniel had sat down with her in her living room. He'd been taking her report, had shown compassion and, after looking at the clean apartment, the worried-looking boyfriend and the girl's unmarked skin, had gently explained to her how she could ruin someone's life if she made reports that were untrue.

This opened the door for Chantel to make clear to her that when she cried wolf, she made it more difficult for true victims to get the help they deserved, as people were less likely to believe them.

As they were leaving, Daniel, in an aside to the boyfriend, suggested that he might want to move on down the road.

They went from there to a bar fight, which resulted in an arrest that took far longer than it should have, as they had to wait for an interpreter.

They shooed a couple of hookers out of a hotel lobby where two thousand people were gathered for a pharmaceutical convention.

All in all, not a bad night. Until she was standing in front of her locker, freshly off shift, getting ready to change back into her jeans and head home. She'd left Chantel Johnson's cell phone in her locker. And had reached for it first thing.

She'd missed three calls. All from Colin Fairbanks.

He'd left three messages. The first one concerned. The second one worried. And the third one...final. Unless she got back to him. He didn't know what game she was playing, but since she wasn't returning his calls and he now knew she wasn't staying at the hotel she'd said she was at, the hotel he'd dropped her at on three different occasions, he was not going to call again. Before he hung up, he wished her well.

Chantel changed in thirty seconds flat, hurried out to her car and called Wayne.

Half an hour later, she was dialing Colin Fairbanks. He picked up on the third ring.

"Hello?" He'd clearly been asleep. Perhaps she should have waited. But...

"Colin, it's Chantel. I'm sorry to be calling so late, but I just got your messages and I feel awful. I know you've got meetings in the morning, but I couldn't leave things. You said you were done, and I don't want that. And..."

"Chantel?" His voice grew in stature and she knew she had his full attention. Pictured him sitting up in bed.

Then she closed her eyes as a vision of him sleeping naked sprang to mind. She'd yet to leave the precinct parking lot.

"Yes. Listen, I won't keep you. I just wanted you to know I've been out doing research today. My heroine runs a whale-watching business, and I'd been invited by a local company to shadow their resident expert oceanographer."

She named the company Wayne had told her to name: a small, two-boat, six-employee venture. His sister, Ann, owned it. Chantel was going to be spending two hours with her early the next morning.

"You were out on a whale boat?"

"Yes. And then spent the evening over a lovely fresh crab dinner, asking Ann, my heroine's counterpart, questions and talking about her life. I thoroughly enjoyed myself and had no idea how late it had gotten."

That explained her absence. Her lack of phone contact.

Now for the rest of it.

"I'm at the Landau Resort." A room had just been arranged, courtesy of the resort management, and would most likely be comped, as it was for official police business—details to be ironed out in the morning. Her budget wouldn't cover one night at the place. But Wayne knew the night manager. The guy owed him a favor. "I'd asked that the information not be given out," she said now, knowing she had to pull this off. "Not under any circumstances," she added. "A request from my father, and because it wasn't unreasonable or a huge inconvenience, I granted his request. You never know, in our position, who might try to find you and with my family being so far away…"

"You're at the Landau right now?"

Oh, hell. The way her luck was going with him, he'd be in the lobby bar, not home in bed like she was imagining.

A bar would be much better for her equilibrium than home in bed.

And she could always say she'd showered after

her day on the ocean and wasn't up to seeing anyone that night. "Yes, I'm here now. Room 12334."

"So I can call the resort, ask for your room number and you'll answer."

Shit.

"You don't trust me, Colin?" She put the same amount of disdain in her tone as she'd heard a woman do in a documentary she'd watched. "I just gave you my room number. Pick me up here tomorrow at noon. We can have lunch at the Beach Café. It's down by the water and really quite nice."

She'd taken a tour of the resort before going undercover. When Wayne had named his contact and suggested that they use the hotel as her cover's residence—as the place she'd use as Johnson's drop-off and pickup location.

"I know the place," he said. "And you're right. It's quite lovely. Tomorrow at noon?"

"If that works for you. Or any other time that's better. If you want to, that is. If not, that's fine, too. I just…" She'd pack some of her Chantel Johnson stuff in the morning. Arrange it around the room as Wayne had instructed.

"No. Noon's fine. I'll see you then." Warmth had returned to his tone.

"Room 12334."

"I've got it. And, Chantel…"

"Yes?"

"I'm glad you called."

She was glad, too. And drove home through the quiet Santa Raquel streets looking forward to a good night's sleep.

COLIN WAS TEMPTED to call the resort and ask for her room. Just to wish her good-night a second time.

Just to hear her answer the phone.

To check up on her story.

Which was unacceptable. He wasn't going to be that kind of man. That kind of person.

Don't you trust me, Colin?

At work, it was his job to doubt everyone and everything, to check up on every possibility, to prepare for the worst in order to protect his clients.

At work, sometimes being lied to was a part of life, depending on the case. Defendants weren't fond of admitting wrongdoing. Deny. Deny. Deny. That was the moniker at work.

Where Julie was concerned, he'd stop at nothing to protect her, only trusting as a last resort.

But in pursuit of an attractive woman? He couldn't give in to the temptation to prove to himself that she was trustworthy. Not at every turn.

She'd issued a very direct challenge to him— *Don't you trust me?* Mostly, he did. Which was extremely out of character.

But it was worth the discomfort of forcing himself to follow through on that trust with action. He'd see her in her room the next day at noon.

Until then, if he needed to reach her, he'd call her cell.

Like any well-adjusted, sane man would do.

For now, for a few hours, he'd allow himself to wallow in the pleasure of knowing that she'd called him back.

That she'd wanted to see him, again, too.

He wasn't on this crazy ride alone.

LUNCH ON TUESDAY couldn't have been better. Well, maybe it would have been if she hadn't been undercover and could have actually enjoyed the ambience and the food. And the company.

Chantel checked herself. *Ambience?* Not a Harris word.

What could have been tempting danger—opening her hotel room door to Colin Fairbanks—had turned out to be innocuous. He'd called up to her room from the lobby, and she'd answered. Proof that she did, indeed, have a room.

From there, the lobby, they walked to the café, chatting about the grounds. Over menus they talked about his trip to Japan.

He never touched her. Nor did she touch him. Gone was the intimacy of his hand on her leg at the library, the near-kiss over dinner.

Maybe he was touching her more intimately with his focused attention, with the look in his eyes, but she chose to brush that thought aside. Her inner critic trying to sabotage her ability to get the job done. She'd have none of it.

By the time her chicken Caesar salad arrived— she was lusting after the open-faced meat-loaf sandwich that had been delivered to the table next to them—she was firmly at work.

She had the name of the arresting officer from the night of Julie's rape. She'd told Colin she'd called the Santa Raquel Police Department, looking for some information pertaining to the case in her book. She'd been invited to visit the local precinct house. And wondered if the rogue cop was still there. Colin didn't know. But had told her the guy's name as he advised her to steer completely clear of him.

He didn't want anyone associated with him and Julie to have contact with the guy.

She'd played on his protective instincts, and the play had paid off.

The emergency room doctor's name was still a mystery to her. She'd been afraid to press her luck with another lie in such a short period of time.

On her way in to hook up with Daniel an hour later, she stopped off at Wayne's desk, giving him the name of the police officer who'd met Colin and Julie at the emergency room the night of her rape. She also had to admit to Wayne that the details of the rape, and the perp, were still unknown to her. She was going to have to get those straight from Julie, whom Colin hadn't seen since they'd dropped her off together after lunch on Saturday. With his trip to Japan, and then her being in LA until dinnertime on Monday and him having a dinner with clients, they'd conversed only through texts.

Apparently, she'd missed their usual breakfast together on Tuesday morning. Colin hadn't been sure why. And had seemed a bit bothered by the lapse.

Chantel made a mental note to try to call the woman—from Johnson's phone—if she had a break during her shift. She was going to keep the cell on her at all times in the future, to avoid another mishap like they'd narrowly escaped the day before.

While they could always come up with reasons why she wasn't available at a given time, and would if they had to, the best way to keep anyone from getting suspicious, Wayne had said, was to be easily accessible.

She and Daniel made a stop for a man driving with illegal plates on Tuesday afternoon and answered a call to a local dealership with a broken security gate and missing brand-new Mustang convertible—which they found, while out canvassing the area, nose down in a ditch a few miles away. There were no bodies in the car, no arrests to make, so they left the scene to the detectives, to see about a report of indecent exposure on the beach. She and Daniel were just pulling into the precinct house, a naked perp wrapped in a blanket in their backseat, when Johnson's cell phone rang.

Leaving Daniel to get the perp dressed and turned over to the jail, she took the call outside in the parking lot. Colin wanted to meet for breakfast.

And her heart leaped. Because he had breakfast with Julie every morning and she needed a chance to speak with his sister without library committee members present.

She accepted his invitation eagerly, and asked, "Will Julie be with you?"

"No."

Of course not. He was attempting to date her.

As aggressively as she was trying not to fall under his spell.

A small snag in her plan. An added challenge to the assignment. Not a road block.

"I just... You said you two have breakfast together every morning and she missed this morning, and I don't want to impinge on that time. I understand how important it is." She slowed herself to a more refined Johnson level. "I liked her, Colin. I just want you to know that I don't mind... if she joins us."

"Thank you." He gave her that intimate tone again. The one that slid through her ear and down to her toes. "But Julie's otherwise engaged in the morning."

"Again?"

"Apparently."

She frowned, leaning against the brick wall of the building, enjoying the cool night air. She

watched as another cruiser pulled in, and Dave
Butts, an officer she'd worked with a few times,
pulled a purple-haired teenager with a tattoo down
his neck out of the backseat.

"You still haven't seen her?"

"No. Which isn't all that unusual, except for
breakfast. When she's working, she locks herself
in her room and doesn't want to be disturbed."

"She has to eat."

"She has a refrigerator in her studio and a hot
plate—not that I've ever known her to use it for
anything but making tea."

"Her studio? I thought she was like Patricia
Reynolds. Occupied full-time by charitable work."

"She spends a lot of time with committee work,
but nothing like Patricia. Julie's actually quite
talented...with pencil drawings mostly. She has
an art degree from UCLA with a dual minor in
finance and early childhood development."

Smiling, Chantel put one booted foot up against
the wall. He sounded like a proud papa. And, she
supposed, in some ways he was one.

In that moment, he reminded her of Max. And
she told herself not to care. She was on the job.

"So you're certain she's okay?" she asked, getting back to breakfast the next morning. And the
possibility of him asking Julie to join them.

"Of course. I knock on her door. She tells me to
go away. I text. She answers."

"But breakfast...you said that was a given."

"I think she's avoiding me."

Dave Butts was back in his car. His partner had yet to return. Daniel would be back any minute. Her time was running short.

And all Chantel wanted to do was stand there and chat. "Why would she be avoiding you? Not because of that Patricia thing. Is it? Is she really that upset about it?"

"I don't think so."

"She hasn't told you?"

"No."

"Have you asked?"

"Of course."

"Do you want me to invite her to join us for breakfast?" she finally asked.

"That would please me very much. However, I think I need to have one more try at her myself. I just heard a scrape of a chair on the dining room tile. I should go."

"Text me if you want me to call her. I've got her number from the library committee roster."

"You got it. And, Chantel?"

"Yes?"

"Thank you."

"Of course. I'll see you in the morning."

It wasn't until after she'd hung up that she realized they hadn't said when or where.

CHAPTER THIRTEEN

JULIE WAS AT the dining room table—in colorful flannel pants and a cami top—a cup of tea and a plate of peanut butter toast in front of her. Colin stood back, watching her for a minute, missing his folks. They'd know more what to do with this shadow of the spirited child they'd raised—how to bring her fully back to life.

If his father had been alive, the rape would not have gone unpunished. Of that Colin felt certain.

"Mind if I join you?" he asked from the archway several feet behind her.

"I heard you leave your room, and I'm still here."

Helping himself to a shot of warm, perfectly aged whiskey from the sideboard, Colin took a sip and sat next to her.

"What did I do?"

Ironic, considering the thoughts he'd had when he'd first seen her sitting there, that the look she gave him was reminiscent of her pubescent years, when she'd been so certain that she knew every- thing and he was a dork.

"You aren't upset about Chantel, are you? You've been nagging me for years to open myself up to the possibility of a lasting relationship." Her words, not his.

But he knew that sometimes you had to be careful what you wished for. That when what you thought you wanted came along, you realized you didn't really want it at all.

Was she afraid he was going to move Chantel—or someone—into their home and obliterate the peace she'd found here?

Did she fear exposure? Guilt rose within him as he thought about what he'd already told Chantel about Julie.

Just the basics. The legal facts.

Far too much—when he considered the insular way he and Julie had decided to handle the situation.

"Do you dislike Chantel?" he asked. Trying to find his footing with her.

"To the contrary, I like her very much. She seems genuine. More down-to-earth than anyone else you've ever dated."

"So what's the problem?" She wouldn't be out there if she wasn't ready to talk.

"You." Her gaze pinned him.

"Me?" Colin took a sip of whiskey, wishing his old man was sitting in the chair he now occupied. "What did I do?"

Other than disagree that Patricia Reynolds was spying on her? That Julie even thought it was a possibility concerned him. She'd had occasional instances of paranoia since the rape, but fewer now and never anything that wasn't directly understandable.

Was Julie getting worse, not better? Was she starting to lose her grasp on reality?

"You disappointed me."

He knew she was struggling, but her words still penetrated. Deep enough to hurt. "How did I do that?" he asked, finding the patience that had always been within him when it came to her. He'd listen, and then he'd help her see that maybe, just maybe, Patricia Reynolds had an agenda other than Julie. Maybe she had an overactive conscience and was on every committee she could find as a means of giving back to the community commensurate with what her husband took from it.

Spying on them made no sense. Julie had to see that. The commissioner and Smyth had them over a barrel. They'd all signed statements. Julie wouldn't be charged with slander; there'd be no scandal and no behind-the-scenes or under-the-table innuendoes or backstabbing. Fairbanks and Fairbanks would not have a sudden depletion of clients. To the contrary, the firm would continue to stand strong regardless of the fact that the new CEO was so young—and Julie would never again accuse David Smyth Jr. of having raped her.

There was no way Julie could press rape charges at this point even if she wanted to.

"You say we're different. That we aren't users." The words came out of left field. Eyes narrowed,

Colin studied her, trying to read her mind. Which hadn't been easy even in easy days.

"We aren't."

"You're using Chantel Johnson, Colin. She's a decent woman. Sincere. And you're doing to her just what others have done to us."

Was this her way to justify the fact that she didn't like the idea of him pursuing a relationship, after all?

It didn't make sense. Julie might be reclusive, but just as he'd told Chantel, his sister was also savvy. Strong.

But then, it didn't make sense that Julie thought Patricia Reynolds was spying on her.

"If you want me to stop seeing her…" He wasn't sure he could at this point. He damned sure didn't want to. But if it was what she needed, he'd try to find a way to meet those needs. Somehow.

Or get them both some help.

"No, I don't want you to stop seeing her!" There was no mistaking the look of outrage in Julie's gaze. "I want you to admit that you're using her and apologize for it."

"What?" Frowning, he stared at her. He was a bit off his mark since meeting Chantel the previous week, but…

"Have you told her that I've written some children's books and that you're after me to get them published?"

Shit. "No."

"Have you told her that I'm a writer at all?"

He wanted a sip of whiskey in the worst way, but didn't dare take it. Not right then. She'd take it as an admission of guilt. "No."

"You didn't tell me she was in publishing, either, but you knew, didn't you? Before you introduced us on Saturday?"

He took that sip. "Yes."

"And when you first heard that she was in publishing, did you think, 'Now here's a plan. Introduce her to Julie and maybe she can help me convince her to publish her books…'" She mimicked him.

He sipped again.

"You weren't going to tell either one of us. You were just going to put us together and then manipulate the rest with little bugs in both of our ears. Let her know I write. Get her to ask me if she can see one of my books. She tells me they're really good and offers to help publish them."

"Would that be so awful, Jules? To give yourself a chance to succeed?"

The moisture in her eyes cut him. "I am a success, Colin. Can't you see that? Creation comes from within. You have to dig deep to hear the voices and see the visions. You have to access your core, open yourself and let what's inside out. That's what I do every single time I sit down in my room and go to work. Every day, I open up a little bit more. See a little more. Feel a little more. I'm not letting what happened lock me away. I'm finding ways to let myself fly."

He felt like an idiot.

"So maybe I only fly solo these days. When I'm by myself. But it's the way it is. For now. At least I'm flying."

"Why didn't you tell me this before?"

She gave him that quirky tilt of her head, accompanied by a wry grin that used to be commonplace with her. "Did you get the part about going solo?"

He got something else, too.

"You aren't solo right now."

She didn't blink. "I know."

"Why not?"

"I don't know the answer to that. Except…I'm angry with you, and couldn't keep it inside. I also feel a bit threatened. I don't want my work exposed, Colin. Not until I'm ready. You need to come clean with Chantel. Tell her that you purposely kept my writing from her and that you hoped she'd be able to help me get published. Then you need to tell her that I'm not interested and that you understand why. Get it out on the table and make it go away. I can't have this pressure, worrying about exposure. It's stifling my process."

Her words were filled with drama—but not the empty teenaged variety she'd exhibited so freely in high school. He felt the depths of her pain.

"Your writing is your therapy."

"Yes."

"It's what's helped you get more involved in your charity work. To branch out more."

"I think so."

"Will you accept my apology?"

"Yes, but it's not just me you have to apologize to. And it's not just this writing thing with Chantel. It's that you tried to manipulate us, Colin. How does that make you any different from the Smyths and Paul Reynolds?"

"Because I did it for good reason? To help you?"

"If I never publish a book, that's my right. If I never even try to do it, that's my right. And if Chantel finds out I'm writing a series of books and wants to help, or doesn't want to help, that's for the two of us to find out. Not for you to orchestrate." She shook her head. "I'm not even sure you see the difference anymore. You're living in their world, Colin. Making your high-powered deals because your clients expect it of you. And you're becoming more and more like them."

He wasn't. But he didn't blame her for thinking so.

"I'll come clean to Chantel in the morning," he said. "I'm meeting her for breakfast."

"Where?"

They'd never said. He'd heard Julie in the dining room and come running.

"I don't know yet. But I want you to know that I not only hear what you're saying, I understand and will make a conscious effort to tend to it. You know I'd never sell you out, Jules. Not ever. I was only trying to help."

"Trying to help is letting me know that you met someone with ties to the publishing world. Asking me if I want you to mention my writing to her. Not taking matters into your own hands."

"I know. And I'm sorry."

She nodded and grinned at him. "Good, then invite her here for breakfast. I'll cook. And then I get to listen to you confess your stupidity."

The imp was back.

Colin vowed not to disappoint her again.

PARKING HER NEWLY rented luxury sedan in the roundabout outside the ornate double doors of Colin's ancestral home Wednesday morning, Chantel noticed that one of her short but perfectly manicured acrylic nails was chipped.

Shit. Who had time to stop at a damned nail place?

How did women do this on a full-time basis? It had taken her an extra half hour to get ready that morning. Time she'd needed to attack the script she'd been given on Saturday and had yet to tend to.

Wayne had a copy and was in charge of finding someone to beef it up. But Chantel had to at least read it in its original form so she'd know what changes were made when she got the copy back.

And she was going to have to put gas in the car the department account had paid for her to rent.

With the clothes and shoes she'd purchased, the nails and hair treatment, she was down to less than a hundred dollars of her original budget.

In cream-colored pants and a black, tapered silky cotton button-up shirt, embellished with a floral border in black stitching, she swung one stiletto black heel out of the car before remembering to exit gracefully. Her second leg followed more slowly.

The walk she had down. Two steps from the front door, it opened.

"Welcome." Colin's greeting might have been formal, but the glance he gave her body—all the way down and back up again—was not.

He was a tornado in her life. Spinning in unexpectedly. She was in grave danger.

Taking the hand he offered, she let him lead her—a woman capable of taking him down—up the last step.

Suddenly he stopped and turned, causing her body to knock into his. Full front to full front.

"Julie's in the kitchen," he said, his lips only inches from hers. "She's serving quiche and fruit this morning and will be ready for us in about five minutes."

Step aside, Harris commanded.

The intense look in his blue eyes captured her. Rooting her. *Sounds good*. Johnson's thought couldn't quite make it from her head through her throat.

When he lowered his head, dropping his lips to

hers, caressing her mouth in the most spectacular way, she just kissed him right back. Fully. Open mouth to open mouth.

"Good morning." He was grinning at her.

"Good morning." Chantel didn't even want to know what the silly grin on her face looked like.

She shouldn't have kissed him.

But at least she'd stopped.

His hand still holding hers, he led her inside.

And she wished Chantel Johnson was real.

CHAPTER FOURTEEN

HE CONFESSED HIS SINS. Chantel looked pained in the brief second before she schooled her expression. He wouldn't have seen the pain at all if he hadn't been looking straight at her as he apologized for trying to manipulate her into helping his sister.

Julie teased him, and the moment passed. Breakfast was…reminiscent of the days when an entire family lived in that home and ate at that table.

The quiche was probably phenomenal, but Colin didn't remember much about the food.

"So…have you tried to get your series published?" Chantel's question came over coffee. She'd cleared her plate—not that she'd served herself all that much. He'd yet to meet a woman with a truly healthy appetite.

Still, he liked a woman who didn't pick over her food. And would probably be just as hot for a woman who did if that woman was Chantel.

He was still waiting for Julie to answer. His sister had gone completely still and was staring at the few pieces of remaining melon on her plate. This was his fault.

Julie took a bite of fruit. He ached for her and

hated feeling so helpless, so powerless to make things better for her.

He'd failed her. And, in so doing, had failed his parents, too.

Closing his eyes against the thought, Colin swore to himself that he would never again agree to settle for less than he knew was right. The papers he'd signed with Smyth ten years before had solidified the resolve in his professional life then and there. Which had probably gone a long way toward insuring the beyond-expectation success the firm had experienced over the past decade.

It was time to apply the same resolve to his personal life. No more settling. Never again was he going to be this powerless...

"It's okay." Chantel broke the deafening silence just before Colin broke his promise to his sister to let her handle things her own way by opening his mouth and butting in. "I know you don't want to use me," she told Julie, her voice soft and sweet and about the most beautiful thing he'd heard in a while. "I'm asking because I'm genuinely interested in the answer."

"No," Julie said. Her shoulders straightened. A prelude to picking up her dish and leaving the table. "As I explained to Colin when I figured out what he was doing, I don't want them published."

Chantel nodded, as though, in the publishing world from which she'd come, not wanting to be published was perfectly normal.

"At least…not yet," Julie said.

Colin almost spit out the sip of coffee he'd just taken. Both women looked over at him as he coughed. And covered his gaffe with another sip.

"Do you mind if I take a look at them?"

Chantel's next question, while a natural progression, considering her business, caused him to tense up all over again. He had to stop this. Now.

"Now's not a good time," he said. "Jules has to be in LA this morning. She's trying to get a proposal passed to fund a child-life position at the new Santa Raquel Children's Hospital for patients whose families can't be with them. Someone to work as an advocate for the families and their children. To spend quality time with the children, to be there to support them through procedures and to measure and capture age-appropriate development advancements…"

Mr. Rainmaker was putting both feet in his mouth at once.

"It's okay, Colin." Julie's interruption was not the least bit timid. She turned to Chantel. "I'd like to show them to you sometime. But not because I want your opinion on if they're publishable. I can't think of them in those terms. I'm afraid they'd lose their current purpose, and I can't afford to take that chance."

He sat completely still. Afraid to even move his glance from where it had been passing over the empty place mat across from Chantel, who was in between him and Julie at the round table in their breakfast room. The mat was handwoven off-white silk—he remembered Julie's excitement when she'd won the bid for the set at an auction the previous year.

"What's their current purpose?" Chantel sounded genuinely curious, but she wasn't prying. And again Jules had opened the door.

Twice now with this woman.

Was Julie noticing that there was something different about Chantel, too? Like she was an angel handpicked by their folks to save them from themselves?

He glanced at his sister as the thought occurred to him, then started to sweat anew. He hadn't told Julie yet that he'd told Chantel she'd been raped.

"I was raped ten years ago." The words dropped baldly into the room. Definitely not breakfast conversation, not that he gave one hoot about that. There wasn't so much as a tremor in Julie's voice.

It was the first time, since the night it had happened, that he'd heard Julie say the words.

Sitting forward, Chantel reached for Julie's hand, taking hold of her fingers lightly. Julie didn't pull back.

She always pulled back when she was touched. Most particularly by a stranger.

"After Saturday in the car...Colin told me that you'd been attacked at a party." Chantel's words were going to get him in serious trouble with his sister, not that she'd know that. He respected her for telling the truth, rather than pretending that she hadn't known.

Something his discerning and ultrasensitive sister might have seen through.

Julie nodded. Swallowed. Turned her hand over and clasped Chantel's fingers.

"The books... They're how I fight my way out of the darkness. I have to find the child within me to create them. To see the simple yet seemingly endless beauty in the world..."

"To view the world from a child's innocent and trusting eyes." Chantel's soft voice took up where Julie's dropped off.

"Yes," Julie said. She was smiling. And there were tears on her cheeks, too.

His sister's tears were nails in his heart.

But a miracle was happening.

He wouldn't have stopped it if he could.

CHANTEL WAS OFF work until Saturday, when she and Daniel had to work a special detail—a visiting dignitary who was traveling down the coast and would be stopping for a meal in Santa Raquel. The dignitary and the reason for his visit were unknown to lowly folk like her. The hours and the pay were good. A full shift's pay for six hours of her time.

Didn't much matter to her who it was. She'd make certain that her stretch of street stayed safe and bankroll the bucks. Babysitting was her least favorite part of the job.

Before she'd left his home after breakfast Wednesday morning, Colin had invited her to the theater Thursday night. She had to accept. But she suggested they meet in LA, rather than drive down together, as she had a friend of her mother's to meet for lunch. Total bullshit, of course, but she couldn't take a chance on the long drive home late at night becoming too intimate. He'd be dropping her at her hotel and…

Nope. She had to make that drive alone.

He tried to work out another solution, even to the extent of hiring someone to drive her car back for her, but in the bright morning sun, immediately following the emotional moments with Julie, she remained resolute.

She had a job to do—two of them now, Julie and Leslie together, two women who deserved justice— and she was not going to screw it up. Or screw him.

Whether she was free to fall for Colin Fairbanks or not, he was…everything she'd ever dreamed of finding in a man, minus the wealth that definitely wasn't her style. She'd be damned if she was going to hurt him.

Which was why she'd made certain that it was clear, right up front, that their…friendship…was only temporary.

Right. He knew that. They were fine. She was fine. But she made that call she'd been promising herself. To Max. Her best friend's husband. First Jill's, her lifetime best friend. And now Meri's, her only close female friend in the world. When he invited her for dinner, she accepted immediately. She spent the evening playing with four-year-old Caleb, in between holding and feeding fifteen-month-old Haley. She was honored when, as always, they offered to let her rock the baby to sleep; in the chair next to her in the nursery, Meri rocked Caleb. And the silence was truly golden.

She'd planned to leave as soon as the babies were in bed, but Max grabbed her shoulder, pulling her backward from the hall toward the living room. "Not so fast," he said.

Meri, standing beside him, grabbed her hand and led her to the couch. "Out with it," she said.

"I don't have to say anything." The retort felt even more childish than it sounded.

"No, you don't. But we'll all get more sleep if you do."

They worried about her. And she wasn't looking forward to facing the darkness that was waiting for her at home. She was too wound up to sleep. And had no valid reason to stop by the precinct.

"I'm going to stop at the gym." She came up with the idea on the spot. It was in the basement of the precinct house. If there was anything going on, she'd hear about it. "I'll be plenty tired enough to sleep when I get home."

"Good plan," Max said. "Now tell us what's going on."

"Nothing's going..." He saw them both look pointedly at her hands.

She'd taken some razing at work. Not from Daniel, who wouldn't have noticed anything as personal as her fingernails or have said anything if he had. But a couple of other guys had noticed the acrylic. Not the polish. She didn't wear that to work. And was actually getting the hang of putting it on and taking it off by herself.

She just hadn't taken the time to remove what she'd put on that morning before breakfast. She hadn't been going into work.

And couldn't go to the gym with her hands looking that way, either.

"Do you have any acetone-free polish remover?" she asked Meri.

"I do." Meri, who'd held on to a little of the weight she'd gained having Haley—enough so that she no longer looked emaciated—didn't move from her seat on the couch beside Max. "And I'll get it for you as soon as you tell us what's going on."

All over a little polish on some fake nails. Good thing she'd scrubbed off the makeup—when she'd gone home to change back into jeans and a T-shirt—and brushed out the curls in her hair and put it up.

What if she'd come in wearing her stilettos? They'd probably be calling in the armed guard.

After they picked themselves up off the floor seeing her sway so perfectly in them...

She'd left on the damned polish. Chantel was too good a cop, too good with details, too aware, to have done that by mistake.

"I'm working undercover."

The announcement wasn't anything earth-shattering. She was a cop. Cops went under sometimes.

Jill had. Once. For an evening. She'd posed as a waitress in a strip club. Max had shown up, plopped himself down as a client at a front table and got so drunk he'd had to be taken home in a cab.

He'd been furious with her for taking the assignment. She'd been furious with him for checking up on her, for thinking he had to guard her all night.

And Chantel had prayed that they'd start talking to each other again before any real damage had been done. They'd held out for two days, until Jill's next days off. Chantel only heard bits and pieces of the fight that had ensued. But they'd worked it all out...

When Max took another look at her nails and left the couch to go stand by the mantel—the one that held his favorite picture of Jill, along with a million photos of the babies and him and Meri—she realized that his mind had traveled the same road as hers.

"It's not what you're thinking, Max."

"What's he thinking?" Meri asked, looking be-

tween them. Beautiful, strong, peaceful Meri. She
worried like hell, but only about external dangers.
She didn't doubt Max's love for her, nor did she hold
back any of her adoration for him. Chantel, who'd
been largely instrumental in saving Meri's life and
getting her and the baby she was carrying—Haley—
back to him, was family to them, not a threat.

They'd made that very clear. Which was why
she was there.

"Jill went under once," Chantel said, "at a strip
club. Waitressing only, but it was still a strip club."

"She had men sticking bills in places that…"

"This isn't anything like that," Chantel inserted
quickly. Max was as protective of her as he had
been of Jill, though in a different way. And where
Max relaxed, Meri took up worrying.

She told them what she could—that she'd in-
filtrated the world of the rich and famous—and
nothing else. She couldn't talk about an ongoing
case. And couldn't mention her specific cover. So
there'd been no point in coming to them with polish on her nails.

"How are you doing with being two people at
once?" Meri's soft blue-gray gaze rested on her.

Then Chantel knew why she was there. "Sometimes, I've got it down pat," she said. And added,
"How did you do it, Meri? How did you keep up
the facade of being one person when your real heart
was so ripped up?" Through the years of running
from her abusive ex-husband, Meri had taken on

a number of different identities, but those had just been name changes. This last time, the time Chantel had been involved, she'd actually pretended to be someone she was not, leaving Max and Caleb and starting a different life in order to protect them from the danger following her.

Chantel's situation was not nearly as desperate. But at least one life—Leslie Morrison's—might depend on it. How did she keep her heart at the precinct when she went to work with Colin?

"I don't have an answer for you," Meri said. "I was desperate. And protecting Caleb and Max. I honestly didn't care if I lost my life as long as it saved theirs."

"You were shut down," Chantel guessed. "Like when I'm at work and it gets dangerous. You just do what you have to do."

Her statement was directed completely at Meri. Max didn't like hearing about her job. He'd hated being married to a cop. And didn't like that their closest friend was one.

"Exactly," Meri said.

When Max sat back down beside her, leaning forward with his elbows on his knees, his hands clasped, Chantel knew more was coming.

"I'm taking it that you're not confident about your ability to keep your cover separate from who you really are."

"Maybe."

"Then get out, Chantel. Now. Before someone is hurt."

"Before *I'm* hurt, you mean."

"Okay, yes. Before you're hurt. Don't be like Jill…thinking you're invincible. You don't have to take on every single challenge that comes your way. You don't have anything to prove."

Like Jill did. She heard his words and partially agreed with his assessment of her best friend. But only partially.

Jill and her…they'd been born to the job. Neither of them had realized it at first, but for some reason being cops had been something they'd both wanted to do.

"I can't get out," she said now, emphatic. "You're right that I'm not as solid as I'd like on my ability to keep myself out of the cover, but I'm here to figure out how to do that, if I can. I won't even consider getting out. It's not on the table." She'd been tough with Max before.

"What about the case?" he asked, looking fierce and unbending. And incredibly sweet in his need to protect. "If you get personally involved, you risk the case."

No, she solidified her cover. "The only thing that risks this case is blowing my cover. Or getting out. I'm not the one in danger, here, Max. And if I get out, chances are nothing else will be done until someone *is* in danger. Or a life is lost."

She was on the verge of saying too much. She

stood to go. She wasn't going to be waylaid a second time.

"Look, I'll figure this out," she told them as they rose to follow her to the door. "But…I just want you both to know—this might be a long assignment. Weeks or more. And no one on the job, other than Wayne and the captain, know about it."

"When you're dealing with money, or threatening to bring down someone who has a lot of it, you're in danger." Max wasn't letting this go.

"I'll be careful, Max."

"Just stay alive."

Chantel didn't know what to say to that, so she turned to Meri, gave her a hug and let herself out.

CHAPTER FIFTEEN

FAIRBANKS AND FAIRBANKS had class-A season tickets to Pantages Theater in Hollywood, where nationally touring casts performed the best of the best Broadway shows. He'd seen a lot of theater productions but had yet to see Woody Allen's *Bullets Over Broadway,* which was what was showing.

While he thoroughly enjoyed the comedy, he did so with only half of his attention. The woman next to him, lightly perfumed in a room full of overly scented beauties, outshone the bright lights.

Recognizing how corny his thoughts were getting, Colin grinned to himself. He'd waited a long time for Chantel Johnson to come into his life. He hadn't been looking, or expecting or even hoping. Yet, here she was.

The way Julie had taken to her was nothing short of amazing.

And Colin was ready to move to the next level.

From the moment he met up with Chantel in the parking lot of a well-known luxury hotel just outside the city, the place where she'd been meeting her mother's friend for lunch, he'd been touching her. A hand in the middle of her back. Shoulder to shoulder. Holding her hand. Thigh to thigh.

He'd barely kissed her, and he was ready for bed.

By the beginning of the first act, he was considering leaving his car at the resort, or better yet, talking her into staying there with him before driving back to Santa Raquel in the morning. He was mentally ordering champagne and chocolate for the room during the middle of the first act. And imagining sliding a silk robe around Chantel's shoulders for a midnight supper by the beginning of the second.

At the end of the play, she declined a nightcap, and when they reached the hotel, she already had her keys out of her purse and asked if he minded dropping her right at her car. She was eager to get the long drive over with.

But she also asked if he'd be following her back. She was clearly pleased when he told her that of course he wouldn't have her making the trip alone so late at night. It was, after all, almost ten.

She also agreed to attend Friday night's wine tasting with him. And they had another meeting of the library committee on Saturday.

He whistled a good bit of the way home.

WAYNE STOPPED BY Chantel's little one-bedroom apartment Friday morning before she'd made it to the shower, to drop off a copy of the rewritten script for her to take to the library meeting the next day. He told her the cop who'd been responsible for taking the original report on the night of Julie's rape was no longer in law enforcement—or even in California. He owned a small fishing boat in Florida. He suggested they not reach out to him just yet. They most definitely were not contacting the higher-up who'd taken the phone call from the hospital. Not until they put a trail together, connecting the players, so they'd know who not to tip off.

As soon as he left, she went straight out to the beach with the script and a cup of coffee.

Work was the panacea for anything that ailed her.

And if that didn't work, there was always chocolate ice cream.

CHANTEL LIKED WINE. A lot. And she knew a lot about it—where to get it the cheapest and which of the grocery store sale brands didn't give her a headache if she had more than one glass. She knew she liked dry better than sweet, white better than red and usually zinfandel was a nice compromise between the two.

She'd have bet her entire life savings, and that of her parents and heirs, that there was nothing akin to asparagus or bell pepper in sauvignon blanc. Even after smelling it with utmost concentration. It was still just fermented grapes.

But dressed in a simple, figure-hugging black dress with a panel of purple flowers running up the middle, Chantel Johnson smelled asparagus. Pepper. Cabbage. She'd even smell poppy if someone else did.

Making her way slowly around the room with Colin at her side, she sipped, rolled wine on her tongue and oh-so-delicately spit into a brass pot she'd been given to carry along with her. The best thing about the night, other than being with drop-dead-gorgeous Colin—which was also the worst part—was that she wasn't getting drunk.

Who knew that wine tasting didn't mean wine swallowing? At least, not for this group.

What she did know was that Colin Fairbanks expected to take their relationship to the next level. His looks, the offhand, seemingly causal touches—her side still tingled from the caress of his fingers—he was telling her quite clearly what he wanted. She wasn't going to be able to hold him off much longer.

Not without losing him.

One thing was for sure, men like Colin didn't hang around for brush-offs. They didn't need to.

The wine they were tasting wasn't helping matters. There were descriptive notes at every station. *Pardon My Body?* Okay, the cabernet sauvignon was substantial on the palate—apparently its jammy red and black fruit gave it body—but really? What was fate doing to her here? She was supposed to pardon her body for going nuts on her? Because there was no way in hell she could pardon his.

She was alone a couple of times, as Colin was

drawn off to discuss business with one client or another. But neither time lasted for long. Whatever else these society people might be, they were polite. And, at least on the surface, quite friendly with the new woman among them whom they considered one of their own.

She chatted some. But mostly she listened. And embarrassed herself with her seemingly obsessive need to keep an eye on Colin. Her only consolation there being that he was embarrassing himself, as well. Anytime she looked for him, looked *at* him, he was looking right back at her.

"It seems you've got his attention, but good." A woman in her mid-forties appeared at Chantel's left, reaching for the sip of wine the vintner poured as she approached his station. Having already swirled, smelled, sipped and spit, Chantel had been about to move on.

"Excuse me?" she said instead, softening the words with a smile. She'd like to think it was the generously fruity red blend that was bringing out the wildness in her. She'd have had to swallow it to even be able to pretend to believe that one.

"Colin," the woman said, sniffing, sipping and swallowing the wine in her glass. "I've known him his entire life, and I've never seen him as interested in anyone as he is in you…"

Heart aflutter—because she was getting too much into the Johnson part, she assured herself—

Chantel chuckled. "I'm sure you're imagining things."

"I'm equally certain that I'm not." The woman was smiling, too, in a friendly way. As Chantel moved away from the vintner's table, hoping to leave the idea of luscious flavors gliding across her palate like silk behind her, the woman stayed with her. "I'm Cora Ashbury," she said. "And don't mind me. I'm what everyone calls a busybody. You know, telegraph, tell Cora…" Her tone was dry. The sparkle in her eye was not.

"I'm Chantel—"

"—Johnson, from the New York publishing Johnsons. Yes, I know," Cora said. "It's really quite an anomaly that it's taken me this long to meet you," she continued. "My husband and I were away on a cruise, and when I got back and heard that we had someone new in our midst…well, I told Kenneth that we just had to be here tonight…"

The town busybody. A woman who prided herself on knowing everything about everyone and didn't seem to be remiss in sharing what she knew. Fate again stepping in to give Chantel a hand.

Forcing her gaze to stay away from the man she could feel in her blood even from across the room, she turned to face Cora fully.

"It's good to meet you, Cora," she said, holding out a hand and then wondering if society women shook hands. "I've only been in town a few weeks, so you didn't miss much. I'm afraid everything's pretty much still a blur to me at this point."

Cora's fingers were soft against hers, her grip light. "Yes, well, if there's anything you need to know, just call me. I'm always happy to help. We can be a tough bunch to get to know, but with Colin at your side, you'll be fine. He's a good man…"

She leaned in closer to add, "I've always felt bad for him, you know? His parents dying so young, back-to-back like they did, leaving him, not even out of law school to take over the firm, with a teenage sister to care for. You'd think that folks would have looked out for him, but no, everyone with a daughter anywhere near marrying age stepped in and tried to bring him into their families. And not out of any real regard for what was best for him or that sweet sister of his—though she is a bit of an odd one, isn't she? Shameful, really, the way he's been treated like an Arabian stallion on the auction block. It's kind of fun, seeing him hook up with someone none of them even know. Anyway, there I go again, carrying on and on. Kenneth says that I was born without a shutoff valve, but I do mean well…"

Apparently, society or no, there was one in every crowd. In her world, they called them informants.

Opening her small black clutch to pull out Johnson's cell phone, Chantel was about to ask for the woman's contact information when Cora, who also had a hand in her beaded clutch (real pearls, Chantel was sure), pulled out a card and held it out to her.

Colin was on the move. She'd caught his black-suited shoulders out of the corner of her eye. And tried to ignore another surge of hormonal overload where he was concerned.

As she reached the next station—where there was a chardonnay that apparently shied away from an oaky buttery style—Chantel didn't just swirl. She didn't spit. She swallowed.

If she thought there could be something—anything—between her and Colin, she was wrong. He wasn't personal.

Yes, she was with him. But only under pretense. It wasn't real. None of it was real.

Real was a boy crying for help in the only way he knew how—through artwork at school. A woman whose husband was probably beating her and had it in him to kill a family member. Real was Julie Fairbanks sitting at home alone because her rapist was most likely in the room with Chantel tonight, sipping wine.

"Seriously, if you find yourself at a loose end or just want to go out for lunch with someone who doesn't put as much weight in how other people feel about her as she does about how she feels about herself, give me a call." Cora had been speaking all along. Chantel wasn't sure she'd heard everything the woman said. "You can ask anyone—I talk a lot, but I'm harmless."

Taking the card Cora still held, Chantel smiled, made some appropriate—she hoped—reply and tucked the contact information securely into her clutch. Busybodies had a lot to say, but rarely was second- and third-hand information completely accurate. Still, if she reached a dead end in her investigation, if she got desperate, she could always call Cora.

She was on track. Working the room.

And working Colin Fairbanks, too.

Because he was her cover.

Cora Ashbury probably wouldn't be pleased if she knew.

He's a good man. Cora's words wouldn't get out of Chantel's head. Whether she was at his side or trying not to ogle him from across the room, she was aware of him every single second. Johnson's insides burned for him.

Harris, at the same time, just kept hearing Cora Ashbury's words. *He's a good man.* People had been using him, or attempting to do so, most of his life. And still, *He's a good man.* Standing among crooks. Manipulators. Power-hungry, powerful people. And other good men.

He joined her at a merlot booth and took her hand as they swirled, inhaled, sipped and spat side by side. Her skin burned from the inside out.

He's a good man.

It was ironic that a self-professed busybody— a woman people had probably long ago learned how to tune out—would have such an effect on one pretty-much-hardened cop.

At the next table, serving a merlot blend with, according to the three people already standing there having a haughty discussion on the complexities of the one sip they'd just poured across their palates, a tobacco component, Chantel had an attack of the guilts that practically consumed her.

Colin didn't do anything particularly heroic, just handed her a crystal wineglass containing a taste of burgundy-colored liquid. He picked up a glass for himself, clinked it against hers and, holding her gaze with a warmth that was more liquid than the wine in their glasses, sipped with her.

She swallowed. Again.

COLIN TOOK THE long way home—driving along the coast instead of through town, to the resort where he believed she was living. Most of Johnson's things were there, in the room that was being comped to the department. Whenever she had the time, Chantel was getting ready at the resort for her undercover assignment. It helped her to get into character.

And why waste a great room? It wasn't like she'd ever be able to stay in such luxury on her salary.

Because no matter what she wanted Colin Fairbanks to believe, she wasn't Chantel Johnson. She was Chantel Harris. A cop on duty.

A cop whose senses were tuned in to Leslie Morrison's absence that night.

"I looked for Leslie," she said, gazing out into the night. "I was going to tell her I finished a rough draft of the script."

She'd finished reading it and thought it was pretty damned good. Considering.

"Someone said that Ryder had the flu," Colin said. "I'll have Julie call to see if Leslie needs to have the meeting at her house instead of the library. There are few enough of us on the committee, so it shouldn't be a problem."

He was holding her hand in the car. Johnson's hand. She liked it. A lot.

Liked, too, that he seemed to be certain that Leslie would be holding the library committee meeting as scheduled the next day, even after news of Ryder's "flu" had broken.

Which meant that she couldn't be too obviously beaten up, if she'd been hurt at all. Kids did get the flu. Enough that it wouldn't be a coincidence to have it happen on a night his parents had been scheduled to go out. Especially considering the social schedule the Morrisons seemed to keep.

"I was reading up on some of the local charity boards today," she said, making herself focus on the job at hand. Not the man at the wheel. Or where they were headed. "There was one, The Lemonade Stand. Do you know of it?"

"Sounds familiar. It's a women's shelter, right?"

"Yes. Anyway, there's a doctor who's pretty closely associated with it—a woman who's made it her cause to support victims of domestic violence. She works at the Santa Raquel hospital and used to be in the emergency room. I wondered if maybe it was the same woman who helped Julie..." A bold-faced lie, and if she hadn't been desperate to help, she'd have been ashamed of herself.

"Was it Dr. Albertson? I could see her advocating for a women's shelter. She'd be perfect for it actually."

"Albertson?" Frowning, Chantel shook her head. "No, it was...Montoya, or Martin. Something like that."

"I'm not even sure Dr. Albertson is still around."

"You never heard from her after that night?"

"Once we signed the papers, I told Julie that we weren't to speak with anyone who had anything to do with the incident. I didn't want to risk the other side claiming that we were breaking the agreement."

"Better safe than sorry," she said. Itching to call Wayne. She had a name!

"I was already sorry," Colin said. "I just wanted to keep Julie safe." He looked over at her. "You're so serious all of a sudden. Didn't you have a good time tonight?" His smile sent her pulse racing again. Just when she had herself under control.

"I had a great time," she said before she could check herself. She couldn't have him thinking that they'd had a failed date. "Truly." She allowed herself to meet his gaze as he briefly turned his head. "More than I've enjoyed myself in a long time."

His clearly self-satisfied grin told her she'd missed another land mine.

All of the investigating in the world wasn't going to reach fruition if she lost her cover before she had her answers.

Content to be fully on alert at the library committee meeting the next day, when she could see Leslie without raising suspicion, Chantel tried to relax.

But she kept feeling those fingers threaded through hers. A foreign object integrating with part of her body. Her very lonely body...

"I enjoyed myself tonight, too." Colin's voice, soft and deep, fell into the quiet intimacy of his luxury sedan. It was just a little after ten, but there were very few cars on the road, very few headlights coming at them, illuminating his features.

Or hers.

"I'm glad."

She could hide in the darkness. Pretend, just for a few minutes, that she was on a real date.

That she was allowed to enjoy the man at her side.

A man who was so different from anyone she'd ever known. Compelling in a way she'd never experienced and couldn't explain.

At least, not to her satisfaction.

"You want to know the best part of the whole night?" he asked, glancing her way before returning his attention to the road.

She did. Badly. And she didn't. Unless it didn't have anything to do with her. And then she did. And she didn't. "Yes."

"Knowing you were there."

Yeah, she hadn't wanted to know that.

And she had.

"That's a new one for me," he continued, as though he'd already determined not to give her a chance to respond.

Saving her from herself. Not that he'd know that.

"I'm the guy who's always free to come and go. Who answers to no one. I've often been told and pretty much believed that I'm the envy of just about every other guy in attendance."

He would be again. Soon.

"But tonight I understood something. I'm not the lucky one. The guy with a woman who is looking for him while he's looking for her is the lucky one. The guy who has someone in the room who cares that he's there…"

He could be taking a lot for granted. Chantel needed that to be the case. But she feared that it wasn't.

"You bought a bottle of wine from that last guy," she said, sounding more like the lowly cop she was than some society beauty. But she kept thinking about that wine.

How Colin had looked at her when the vintner had told him that if he wanted to drink it that night, it would be good warm.

How that look had leaked a pool of desire between her legs that wasn't dissipating.

"I'm hoping to share it with you."

Throat dry, she ran her tongue along her lower lip. Saw him glance her way in time to catch the act. And wondered if his penis was growing in proportion to the wildness coursing through her.

"Where?"

They were heading toward her resort.

"Your choice. The beach. Or your room."

Oh, God. He wanted to have sex with her. Not that she hadn't already figured that one out. She wanted to have sex with him, too.

Something told her it would be the most incredible sex she'd ever had. Way better than any she'd fantasized about having before meeting him.

She was working. Working. Working.

"I told you, Colin, I'm...not here for long."

"You said until you finish your book."

"Right."

"How far along are you?"

What if he asked to see it? Or the laptop upon which she was supposedly writing it? She'd play the author-confidentiality card. And if that didn't exist, then the author-paranoia one.

"Further than I expected to be at this point, but I'm not putting a page or chapter count on the finished product. I'm just writing until the story is told, and then I'll go back and pay attention to particulars during the revision process."

She remembered listening to her aunt as a kid. She'd been editing a nonfiction self-help book. She'd been telling Chantel's mother that she understood the initial writing process but that the author had skipped the revision process.

His fingers were climbing up the inside of her arm.

"We might only have weeks."

Pulling into the resort lot, Colin parked and turned off the car. "Then I suggest we make the most of them," he said and leaned over, planting his lips firmly on hers.

CHAPTER SIXTEEN

THERE MIGHT HAVE been hesitancy in Chantel's words, but there was absolutely none in the kiss she gave him. Or in the fire in the tip of her tongue as she used it against his, luring him to travel with her to that compelling place they'd both been but never together.

"I say we skip the beach," he told her, breaking away long enough to look her in the eyes. "And yes, I'm fully aware that we might only have weeks together."

He wasn't going to borrow trouble. If they were meant to be more than burning embers, if the flame didn't fizzle out, they'd find a way to bridge the distance between New York and California. He was a millionaire. What better way to spend his money than to commute by air from work to home?

"I…" She broke off, confusion and…something else in her gaze.

He kissed her again. Long, tempting kisses. And then, with his lips barely apart from hers, he said, "We're consenting adults, long past adolescence," he told her. "Let's just go where this is taking us for tonight. And worry about the future tomorrow."

"You want to make love, no strings attached."

Not really. But for starters… "That's what I'm proposing."

He'd do it any way she wanted if he could just get his aching penis out of his pants and feel her body holding it. Binding them together. Making her as much a part of his life as any woman had ever been.

It occurred to him that he was rushing things. Lawyer that he was, he looked for the why. And didn't like the obvious answer.

If he was rushing things because he didn't trust himself to be able to trust *her* long enough to take things slowly, then that wasn't good. But if he was hurrying because their time was limited and he wanted to make the most of what they had?

"For tonight," he added. "That's what I'm proposing for tonight."

He could feel the struggle going on inside of her and waited. He *could* convince her to have sex with him. After the way she'd just kissed him, there was no doubt in his mind about that.

But he didn't want her to regret sleeping with him. Or to allow him into her body if she wasn't sure she wanted him there.

"Can we just take a walk on the beach?" she asked him. "Maybe bring a glass of wine with us?"

If she'd been any other woman he'd been hoping to get into bed, he might have been disappointed. "Of course. We can stop at the bar for a couple of glasses," he told her, reaching for the wine he'd purchased that evening.

Watching him, she nodded and slowly got out of the car.

A WOMAN COULDN'T walk on the beach in high heels. At least not one who'd only been practicing in them for a couple of weeks. Stupid of her to have made the suggestion.

Figuring barefoot was better than naked— which was what she could become if she took him upstairs—Chantel took off her heels and lost a couple of inches. She felt little next to Colin.

And...naked.

Until she'd taken on Johnson, Chantel didn't leave her house without hiking boots. "All the better to kick them with, my dear," she used to joke to Jill, purposely misquoting Little Red Riding Hood. A kid shouldn't have to be afraid of a wolf in a grandma's clothes.

Glass of wine in one hand and shoes in the other, she stepped forward and cool sand inserted itself between her toes, caressing her feet in a way that was invigorating. Not relaxing.

Colin slid his arm through hers. She could feel heat emanating from him in the cool night air. Making her think of his stomach against hers. Him lying on top of her. The hair on his chest. And...

All things that were awesome and sexy and natural and so not right.

"Where's Julie tonight?" She gulped her wine. When the glass was empty the walk would be done. The night would be over.

"Home. Where she usually is at night."

"I've been thinking about her a lot." Good, Chantel—both Chantels. Keep the focus where it needs to be. "I'd like to help her."

She was being completely sincere and also saying something bound to keep him interested in her.

But for how long, if she completely rejected his sexual advances?

Sex was a much easier commodity to come by these days. A guy like Colin could find it just about anywhere he wanted it.

She couldn't have sex for the job. Even *she* had boundaries.

"I'm open to any suggestions," he told her. But he said no more, asked no more. Walking with him on the deserted beach, their voices silent while life raged around them—the waves against the shore in tune with their heartbeats—Chantel fought the most dangerous battle of her life.

She wasn't going to sleep with him.

But she couldn't just send him off, either. Couldn't risk him losing interest. Not with beautiful, vibrant Julie passing her life at home alone. Not with Leslie and Ryder possibly running from a demon in their own home. And in their hearts. Not when, if what she suspected was right, the two cases were joined by the same wrongdoing. Not when by fixing one she could fix the other.

And what would have happened if neither Leslie nor Julie existed? That insidious inner voice taunted her.

Then she'd already be upstairs with him. The answer came swift and sure in the moonlight with a bit of wine in her.

An answer that allowed her to convince herself that she wasn't using him or whoring herself when she said, "You want to take the rest of the bottle upstairs?"

She wasn't going to have sex with him.

But they could play with fire for a little while. Until the wine was gone.

HE TRIED NOT to pay too much attention to her room. But he was interested in every single thing about the luxury space that said she'd been there—the desk chair pulled out slightly from the desk, the closet doors firmly closed after she'd accessed them to dress that evening.

The soft scent of whatever it was she wore on her skin. Nothing he was immediately familiar with. But something that drew him to her every time he got a whiff. More so than the finest wine.

Or the best steaks on the grill.

He was hungry for her in a way food and drink were never going to assuage.

She left the lights low, turning on only one, by

the couch and chairs that faced a sliding glass door. She'd pulled the sheers, but not before he'd seen the balcony beyond.

"You've got a beach view," he said. Because something had to be said. They'd been quiet for too long.

"Yes."

She didn't sit. Or fidget. She just stood there, her empty glass on the dresser beside her. Her hesitancy—and maybe a tiny lack of confidence— turned him on more than the cleavage showing at the top of that sexy black dress.

Something became quite clear to him then. Chantel Johnson was not a woman you hurried.

Or had casual sex with.

Even if their liaison only lasted weeks, it would mean something to her. It was his duty to be aware of that.

"Ready for another glass?" he asked. The one he'd had on the beach had been his first for the night. He could easily afford a couple more. Even if he found himself behind the wheel of his car before morning.

"Y-yes, I'd like that." Picking up her glass, she approached him, hips swaying like a model's as she traversed the carpet in the heels she'd put back on the moment they'd left the sand.

He was looking forward to taking them off again. And putting his tongue where the grains of sand had been.

First, though, with his own glass filled, he sat with her on the sofa, facing out to the ocean hiding in darkness.

He knew it was there, though. Living and breathing. Swelling. Rushing. Occasionally dancing. Grappling. And sometimes killing, too.

"Do you remember the first time you ever saw the ocean?" he asked, ready to be patient. Content to sit with her in the intimacy of her room. Learn more about her.

Her life was an aphrodisiac.

As were the blond curls that moved along her shoulders when she shook her head. "My family used to go to the ocean for holidays when I was little," she said. And then blinked as though she'd forgotten herself.

He wanted to know what she'd remembered, and why the memory seemed to cause her unrest.

"What about when you were older?"

Another shake of the head was his only response.

"What?" she asked, looking at him over the top of the wineglass at her lips.

"I didn't say anything." Not out loud at any rate. Did she have any idea how incredibly beautiful she was? And how different from every other woman he'd ever known?

"You had a look… You were frowning."

He smiled. "The way you answered my questions…made me wonder if you're growing-up years weren't as blessed as I'd assumed they were."

Her shrug told him more than she probably knew. "Money doesn't buy happiness," was all she said. But it was enough.

That left him certain that he wanted to make her happy.

Whatever it took.

SHE WASN'T DRUNK. Wasn't going to get drunk. She also wasn't driving home that night. She didn't work in the morning, but she had to be dressed as Johnson and at a committee meeting by noon the next day. She'd read the script.

She would see Leslie Morrison then, too.

Chantel took another sip of wine. Content that Colin seemed happy just to sit with her. This was nice. Sitting with someone who really seemed to like being with her. Someone she really liked.

Weird. Different.

"You're very neat." He was looking around them at the table and desktops that were devoid of clutter. Because Johnson wasn't real.

But he'd have seen much of the same in her little apartment, as well.

"I've always been that way," she told him, relieved to be able to share a bit of herself with him in complete honesty. "I think I was born neat. My mother used to tell everyone that, even as a toddler, I picked up all of my toys and put them all away."

"I expected to see a desk with a laptop in the

middle of it surrounded by papers and folders. Maybe even a research book or two."

He'd given her the perfect opening—the perfect explanation. Making a mental note to run home for her laptop, she shook her head with ease. "I clean up every day. More so here than I did at home." She felt free to expand now. "With the housekeeping staff in and out, I don't want to risk losing notes or having them reordered from being picked up for dusting."

His nod, the admiring glance he bounced off her chest, told her all was well.

The shields she normally wore around her—as well as the one she wore on her uniform every day—seemed to fade a little. Leaving her…a little exposed. But also…a little free.

"Would you like more wine?" he asked, holding up the bottle.

"Only if you'll split it with me." They both had a bit left in their glasses. She wondered if the place had a hot tub. And then, reminding herself that it had three, wished she'd thought to buy Johnson a swimsuit.

It was January. Hadn't dawned on her that she might need one.

"What are you thinking?" He was grinning at her.

"That a soak in hot jets would feel heavenly right now." Or damned good, depending on whether Johnson or Harris was doing the thinking.

"I have a hot tub on the patio off my bedroom." His gaze looked bedroom-esque. And she was picturing him naked.

He knew it, too. His sexy grin told her so. Or told her that he hoped she was picturing him naked.

Colin Fairbanks was clearly a man with confidence.

She was definitely a woman turned on by confident, powerful men.

Men who were generally turned off by buff, capable, strong women.

She wasn't that woman right now. No, tonight she was Chantel Johnson. A woman of class. A woman with dignity.

A woman so hot for the man sitting beside her that she was getting wet where she was pretty sure a real lady didn't.

THE WINE WAS GONE. When he glanced toward the wet bar in her room and thought about looking to see what it was stocked with, Colin knew it was time to go home. A man who grabbed too much in the moment usually lost the treasure in the long run.

His father used to say that. Colin didn't completely agree. Sometimes you had to grab a chance when you had it—but tonight he saw the wisdom in those words.

Standing, he pulled her up off the couch, keeping hold of her hand as he walked toward the door.

"Can I pick you up for the meeting tomorrow?" he asked. Like the lovesick pup he was rapidly becoming.

"I'd like that."

There was a new softness about her. Brought on by wine and the lateness of the night? By his company?

One that would be gone again when he came by for her the next day?

He didn't look as they passed her king-size bed with massive fluffed-up pillows and a beige-and-maroon comforter that would be as soft as it was luxurious. The details had been embedded in his brain from his first glance at the room.

"Is eleven-thirty okay?" He faced her at the door.

She stared up at him, her eyes open and speaking to him. "Yes. You'll bring Julie, too?"

"Yes." He couldn't pull his gaze from her lips. One kiss good-night… That's all he would ask, or allow. One kiss. To state intention. To be clear that they were more than friends.

A down payment on the future.

"I enjoyed myself tonight. Thanks for inviting me."

She'd have been on the list if she'd been in town when the invites went out. Lucky for him she hadn't been in town yet. "I'd like to be the one to accompany you, to be your exclusive escort, the entire time you're in town." The words hadn't been planned.

But more than hearing himself making a statement he'd never come close to making before—the whole exclusive thing—Colin's tension while he awaited her response took him most by surprise.

Those full, moist lips tilted in a tiny bit of a smile. "I'd like that," she said. But he hadn't needed the words. Her look had told him what he'd been waiting to hear.

Lowering his lips to hers was the next natural course of events. Colin probably couldn't have fought nature if he'd tried.

He didn't try.

CHAPTER SEVENTEEN

YOU HAVE TO keep him interested. The thought
scored across Chantel's mind as Colin's lips lowered toward hers. She wasn't just letting him kiss
her because she was hungry for the physical connection. She was serving those she was out to protect.

The action was justified.

It was the last coherent thought she could remember Harris having. His touch was not consuming. He didn't take or demand. He just touched his
lips to hers, almost tenderly.

Yet, to her battered senses, his kiss seemed to be
saying hello. Not good-night.

She increased the pressure of her lips against
his, opening her mouth. And when he responded,
she found his tongue with hers. She was aggressive. Too aggressive.

His arms wrapped around her, pulling her up
against his body so tightly she could feel the buttons of his coat pressing into her flesh. And the
hard length of him against her pelvis.

She slid her hands up his chest and around his
neck, never breaking contact with his lips, pulling

his head more firmly against her. Running her fingers through the thick hair she'd been wanting to touch for more than a week.

Shoving his tongue deeper into her mouth, he groaned. She stumbled backward but didn't fall. His arms held her up, and he moved until the backs of her knees were against the bed. His hand came around then, cupping her breast, and he broke their kiss to look her straight in the eye.

"I need you," he said. "To see you naked, to touch every inch of you and come inside you."

His words started an inferno raging through her. A sensation she didn't recognize. Couldn't control.

"Are you okay with that?" he asked while his thumb rubbed against her nipple, which had hardened beneath her dress and the thin piece of nylon bra.

Mesmerized—maybe as much by the intensity of his gaze as by the crazy way her body was reacting to his touch—she could only nod.

Pleasing him became paramount.

She'd never, ever even come close to feeling like he was making her feel. Like she was missing something elemental, something vital, something only he could give her. Getting it was the only thing that mattered.

She reached for the lapels of his jacket to hold herself upright. And then to shove them down over his shoulders. The heavy fabric dropped to the floor. She felt its weight on the top of one foot.

Adrenaline rushed through her, driving her to get what her body needed and to give him anything he wanted.

As she fumbled with his buttons, he unzipped her dress. Cool air met the heated flesh of her back, and she shivered.

His breath uneven, he slid the dress off her shoulders. Caressing her skin. And then stood there, watching, as slowly, she was able to get his buttons to give way. He wasn't rushing her. Wasn't letting impatience interfere.

He could have done it himself. But he didn't. And her flame shot up another notch.

Shaking, she struggled to hold on. And to find a way to let go. Tears sprang to her eyes for no apparent reason.

He froze. "What's wrong?"

"Nothing," she told him, working at the rest of those buttons.

"You're crying."

She shook her head and smiled. "I'm not a crier. Can't remember the last time I cried. I just… This… You're so… I don't know."

With a tender touch, he drew his fingers down her jaw from ear to chin. "I think I know," he told her. "It's the same for me."

"You're going to cry, too?" She chuckled, trying to find her center, to come back to a bit of herself. And freed the last of his buttons.

She was still shaking. But there was no stopping this…this…power that had a hold of her.

Colin set the pace. A slow, adoring, absorbing pace. Time passed, but she had no idea how little. Or how much. Noises sounded—the room's heat coming on, her breathing. His. The whisper of clothing leaving skin. Little sounds that weaved in and out of the sensations bombarding her. The taste of wine on his tongue as he kissed her again. The musky scent of his cologne mixing with sex.

It overwhelmed her. Deliciously.

With her still standing on the floor at the end of the mattress, he laid down before her. Completely naked. Open to her perusal. And peruse she did. From the smattering of dark hair across his chest, the small line of it drawn down his stomach, to the darker curls at the bed of his penis.

"Strip for me," he said, his gaze shaded as he looked up at her. His grin was devilish and fun and sexy.

Reaching behind her, she unclipped her bra, then slowly, one strap at a time, drew it down her arms and, finally, away from her breasts. They'd always seemed a little big to her. That night, exposed to him, they made her happy.

Her panties were next. She'd paid attention to them only because the lady in the secondhand shop where she'd found the designer clothes had told her that she'd need them so that panty lines didn't show when she wore certain dresses.

The black lace thong followed her bra to the floor.

"Come to me," Colin said, watching her intently, yet not making her feel as though she was on display. There was no discomfort in disrobing for him.

One knee at a time, Chantel climbed onto the end of the bed, making her way toward him.

"You really are the most incredibly beautiful woman." His whisper was broken and reverent. A sound Chantel knew she was never going to forget as long as she lived.

He gave her a glimpse of what he seemed to see. A slim blonde with curves in all the right places. A woman who turned men's heads. A woman worth wanting.

The insight changed forever her perception of herself.

In Colin's presence, she felt like that woman. When she was with him, the tough-girl tomboy she'd always been completely flew the coop.

HE DIDN'T INTEND to stay the night, didn't ever spend an entire night in a woman's bed. He preferred to avoid the potential for making awkward promises that he knew he couldn't keep.

That night taught Colin something about himself. Morning wasn't the problem. He'd been sleeping with women he didn't care deeply about. Having sex for physical release.

That night taught him that sex was far more than just a route to orgasm. As he slid his body inside

Chantel's, he became a part of her, solidifying the bond that was growing between them.

With her help, he'd gotten a condom on just before sliding home.

And even that had felt different.

In the past, he'd not only been practicing safe sex, he'd also been protecting both parties from unwanted pregnancies. With Chantel...

Thinking of her possibly carrying his baby... wasn't...horrible.

He fell asleep with her in his arms afterward. And woke her to make love a second and then a third time during the night.

A door closing in the hallway woke him just before five, and he knew it was time to go—to shower and be at the breakfast table on time.

Julie could think what she liked about him. It wasn't as if she thought he had no sex life.

But he didn't want anyone scrutinizing this relationship. What he had with Chantel was... untouchable.

Leaning over, he kissed her on the shoulder. And pulled back immediately when she sprang awake and out of the bed in one second flat. Reaching down to pull the sheet up and cover herself in the next second.

"I'm sorry." He held up both hands before getting out of the bed and reaching for his pants. Underwear could travel home in his pocket. He should never have stayed. Clearly he'd misread something...

"No." Chantel slumped down to the mattress, watching as he stepped into his pants. "I'm sorry. I…" Her eyebrows drew together as she shook her head. "I'm used to being on my own. Protecting myself…"

"Having a man kiss you awake isn't part of your normal routine," he said with a grin, starting to feel better.

"Exactly. A woman has to act first and ask questions later."

He was struck again with the idea that her past hadn't been as rosy as he'd first assumed. Chantel bore emotional scars.

He wanted to bear them with her.

"You're telling me that you aren't used to having a man in your bed." His shirt hung, unbuttoned, on his shoulders.

"That's right."

"Which means that I'm different…we're different…"

"Exactly." She still wasn't smiling, though.

He had to ask, "Do you regret last night?"

"No." Her answer held no hesitation or doubt. It was stated with the same straightforwardness he'd come to expect from her.

"Good," he told her, rounding the bed to pull her up to him. She let the sheet drop, leaving her bare breasts to press against his chest. He got hard. "I intend to do it again," he told her against her lips, pushing his thighs into hers. "Soon."

She nodded, looking at him wordlessly.

He wanted words. He needed to hear her confirm that they were in over their heads together.

"As often as we can during the time we have together," he added, just in case she was worried that he'd forgotten that her time in California was limited. Or maybe she was regretting that fact as much as he was?

She nodded again.

"So we're clear?" he pushed. "We're going to have sex again. Often."

For the third time, she nodded.

"Chantel? Are you here with me?" he asked when what he wanted to know was what demons he'd scared up with that kiss to her shoulder. Wanted her to tell him what had her so out of sorts. Uncharacteristically out of sorts. She was someone else entirely. A woman disturbed by something. Vulnerable in one sense, and yet…not seeming the least bit weak or afraid.

"Oh, yeah, I'm here," she said, her voice rough around the edges, less controlled than normal—confirming that he'd unnerved her far more than an unexpected kiss would have done.

He nodded. Deciding just to let it drop. To give her the space she so obviously needed. Just because she needed it.

"And you meant what you said about us being

exclusive during your time here?" he asked when he'd just told himself to let it go.

"Of course. You think you're the only one who wants that?"

Before he could answer her, she kissed him. Long. And hard. Taking ownership of him.

He wasn't particularly happy about being so vulnerable. But he kissed her back. Taking ownership of *her*.

The kiss was filled with passion. And more. It was the *more* that had his pulse clamoring. That compelled him to leave her to gather herself.

And to promise himself that if it was humanly possible for him to eradicate her demons, he'd do so. Or die trying.

"I have to go," he said with one last kiss.

Sadness filled her gaze for a second—or he was pretty sure that was the shadow that passed over her expression—and then she smiled and said, "Me, too."

Turning, she headed for the bathroom. She didn't hurry. As though she knew she obliterated every woman who'd ever come before her.

Just before the door shut behind her, she glanced at him over her shoulder. "Eleven thirty, right?" she asked.

"Yes, ma'am."

They were going to the library meeting together. And everywhere else, too.

They'd agreed to be exclusive.

And while he'd always imagined feeling a bit caged if he ever got to that point in a relationship, all Colin felt was…freedom.

CHAPTER EIGHTEEN

THE LIBRARY COMMITTEE meeting did not take place at the Morrison home on Saturday. While disappointed that she wasn't going to be able to see the home—a possible crime scene—disappointed that she wasn't going to be able to observe the overall environment in which Ryder Morrison was growing up, Chantel was even more worried about Leslie's absence from the wine tasting the night before.

They'd been raising money for Sunshine Children's League, one of Julie's—and Leslie's—personal causes.

It was possible that the boy who'd suddenly come down with the flu—preventing his parents from attending the event—had had enough of a recovery by the next morning to be left without his mother's care. Even more likely was the possibility that Leslie and James had family in the area to watch Ryder while his mother was away.

Chantel didn't think either option was the case.

They met at the new library building again, in a smaller room that now housed the cases that had been designated for a rare book collection that would be there permanently. While Leslie's face was unblemished and bearing no heavier than a normal dose of makeup, the woman had her hair styled differently. Instead of pulled into a twist at the back of her head—as it had been each of the other two times Chantel had seen her—her hair hung around her shoulders. Its thinness didn't make the style very becoming on the otherwise beautiful woman.

But it covered enough of her neck that, along with the high-necked sweater she was wearing, Chantel couldn't tell if she was hiding bruises.

She'd bet a year's salary that she was. Leslie was friendly and as outgoing as always. But her hands were fiddling with the folders on the table in front of her, and twice she'd dropped the napkin she'd picked up at the side table when she'd helped herself to coffee.

The gala was only three weeks away, and at the conclusion of member reports, Leslie filled them in on her week's progress toward the big event. Everyone got a copy of the script. They were to get any suggestions or opinions to Chantel by midweek.

Julie, sitting next to Chantel, seemed to be watching her friend more closely. But that could just be Chantel's imagination. She was extrasensitive to Julie at the moment.

Because of the rape.

Mostly.

And because she was feeling more certain than

ever that to help one of the women would help
the other…

Colin, who was far too gorgeous for Chantel's
good, sat, as before, on her other side, his hand on
her leg.

Reminding her that it would be elsewhere on her
body. Again. Soon. As they'd agreed.

She'd worn a sedate dark purple skirt and jacket
that she'd picked up that morning, along with a few
other things, on her way to have her nails done. She
couldn't see someone over and over without more
changes of clothes.

And he was taking advantage of the flesh her
skirt exposed.

His suit, gray today, didn't afford her the same
leniency. Even if she'd had the balls to reach for
him under the table.

Harris had them. Johnson didn't dare.

Julie reported that the guest list of accepted invitations had grown to beat their highest expecta-
tions. She glanced around the table as she spoke
and smiled when her gaze met Chantel's.

If she'd had any worries that Colin's sibling was
going to have a problem with her brother's preoc-
cupation with the new woman in town, Julie was
easily putting them to rest. She'd chattered from
the backseat of Colin's car all the way to the library. Mostly about the financial report she'd read
that morning from the wine tasting the night before. And her hopes that the league would be able

to grant her request for monies to fund a child-life specialist at the new Santa Raquel Children's Hospital.

She'd never said a word about Chantel and Colin's time together—not that Chantel would have expected her to do so. She had far too much decorum for that.

But if she'd had a problem with it, Chantel would expect to detect at least an edge about her.

The meeting didn't last long—half an hour at most.

Chantel kept a close eye out, but she didn't notice Patricia Reynolds paying any particular attention to either her or the Fairbankses. Mostly the woman seemed determined to get everyone's opinion on every single item on the menu for the gala—leaving Chantel starving for the lunch she was going to consume as soon as she got out of Johnson's clothes and back to her apartment.

Starting with two peanut butter and jelly sandwiches. And then as much of the quart of chocolate ice cream as she could manage. Enough to wash Colin's fire out of her body so she could be 100 percent present when she donned her badge and hit the streets for her shift that evening.

Julie turned to her just as Leslie adjourned the meeting. "I've made chicken salad this morning and cut up some fruit. Colin and I were hoping you'd join us for lunch."

"Please," Colin added, standing with his hand

on her shoulder. "I have to head to LA for a meeting this afternoon, but I'd like to have a meal with you first."

Her heart softened dangerously. Until her brain reminded her that Chantel being at home with Julie could possibly help the younger woman open up to her more easily. And more quickly.

"I'd like that," she said, and added, just to be safe, "Then I have to get to work, too." She stood, picking up the used but immaculate lavender Coach purse she'd also purchased that morning. "With all the time I spent on the script this week, I'm going to be writing straight through the weekend."

She noticed the long glance Colin gave her but pretended not to.

"Do you find that when you get into the book, it's best just to stay there?" Julie asked, loading her papers into the folder and then the small leather case she'd brought in with her. "I do," she continued before Chantel could answer. "Once it's flowing I just need to let it flow."

Thanking fate for another save, for being such a faithful partner on this venture, Chantel agreed wholeheartedly, and quite verbosely, with Colin's little sister.

"Julie…could you wait just a minute?" Leslie called out as they were about to exit the room. She'd been in conversation with Emily Longfellow, the woman who was in charge of all of the physical arrangements at the library for the big event.

Colin pulled Chantel out the door and into a little room across the hall while Julie went off to speak with her friend.

Was Leslie going to ask how the wine-tasting event went the night before? Apologize for missing it? Would she tell Julie the real reason for her absence?

Did Julie know if Leslie's husband beat her?

That he beat her. If Chantel was reading this all right.

"Did I hear you right? You plan to work tonight?"

"Yes. And tomorrow. And tomorrow night, too," she added. She was on shift the next day, starting a new rotation. She had no choice. She had to minimize complication where she could. Being available at his whim was impossible.

But she wanted the "exclusive" part.

It ensured her an "in" at any function that might also include the Morrisons and the society that would allow her to roam freely around Leslie's life without raising suspicion.

And the "in" that would allow her to find out who among them had raped Julie Fairbanks and not paid for the crime. Which would, hopefully, lead her to the mole in the Santa Raquel Police Department who put payoff money above the well-being of young women.

Leaning on his hand on the wall beside them, Colin asked, "Are you avoiding…"

"No." She couldn't lose him. Everything fell apart if she lost him. The Morrisons. Julie. Johnson...

Shaking her head at that last inane thought, she looked up at him. "I rarely work past midnight," she heard herself telling him. "If you don't mind the late hour, you're welcome to stop by after that."

She knew exactly what she was offering. She wanted to believe she knew why. She'd made a mistake and let things go way too far. But she couldn't back out now. Not without risking the entire assignment. She couldn't have him thinking that she had regrets.

Colin wasn't the type of man who begged. Unless he was certain he was going to get what he was after. One hint from her that she wasn't as interested as he was and he'd be out her door. Permanently...

She couldn't lose him.

He put his hands in his pockets, drawing her attention downward, and she grinned. "I guess that means I'll be seeing you?" she asked. Her body reacted to his in a way that shocked even Harris. She couldn't wait for the moment she opened that hotel room door to him...

"I'll be there," Colin said. "Order something chocolate from room service."

She was off at eleven and would bring a change of clothes with her to the station. Get out of her uniform in the backseat of her clunker, and then catch a cab to the resort. Unless there really did happen to be violence on her shift that evening.

She'd worked dozens of these events and mostly just got bored and waited for her dinner break. But there was always a first time.

In which case…she'd cross that bridge if she came to it. She'd call Colin with an excuse. And a promise to make it up to him.

Leslie Morrison got away with it—the lying excuses part. Allegedly.

She wasn't going to borrow trouble.

She had enough of it on her plate already.

COLIN PLANNED TO show Chantel around the mansion, being certain to include his private quarters—and skip his sister's—while Julie got lunch on the table. She'd been a little curt in her refusal to let Chantel help her, and he wanted to give his sister some space.

He also kind of liked the thought of having a picture of his very private space embedded in Chantel's mind.

"What's going on?" she asked as they stood in what had once been his father's law library but was now Colin's home office. "Did I do something to upset Julie?"

The genuine worry in her tone spoke to him more than it should have. He had it bad for her.

"No. She'd have canceled lunch if that was the case," he assured quickly. If Chantel was going to spend time with them, she needed to understand. "Ever since... Julie isn't good about handling personal tension. She can go head-to-head at a board table, but if it gets personal, she checks out. If she was upset with you, she'd more likely be bolted in her room right now, not getting lunch on the table."

A vision of the bolted lock Julie had insisted they have installed on her bedroom door—one that had a keyed lock that he could enter in case of emergency—sprang to mind. Giving him a second's guilt as he half disclosed the private information by his word choice.

Yet, he didn't feel as disloyal to his sister as he might have, which kind of disturbed him. He felt safe speaking with Chantel—certain that he could trust her. And he'd seen men fall, lose everything, for trusting a woman who drove his dick.

That wasn't him. He was too careful.

"So if it's not me, what's bothering her?"

Her gaze told him she wasn't going to let this go.

"I'm not sure," he said. But he had a good idea. The information just wasn't his to give.

"It must have been something Leslie said," Chantel continued, barely looking around the room where he'd spent so many of the important moments in his life. It was in this room that he'd told his father that he wanted to be a lawyer. It was also where he had learned of his mother's death.

He'd been sitting at that desk, working on a case and waiting up for Julie, the night she had come in ravaged and broken after Smyth had drugged and raped her.

"She was fine until she was in the boardroom alone with Leslie…" She sounded as though she was realizing the facts as she spoke. And she probably was. Julie hadn't been animated on the drive home, but she hadn't been obviously upset, either.

He'd known something was up. But had figured since she was keeping up appearances pretty well with Chantel, that it hadn't been a big deal.

Then Chantel had asked if she could help with lunch, and Julie had been curt and had immediately sent Colin a panicked look. She wanted to have lunch ready for him and Chantel. She needed him to get Chantel out of the room while she composed herself.

That look struck fear in his heart every single time he saw it.

Because the first time had been that god-awful night when he'd done nothing. Nothing. To protect his little sister.

"It's probably just something about one of their shared committees. Maybe Leslie made some calls looking for support for Julie's child-life funds and found out that Sunshine board members weren't going to vote in her favor."

He hoped to God that was all it was, but he didn't think so. That look wouldn't be in his sister's eyes.

"I just don't want her to think that she has to entertain me…" Chantel said.

Colin had promised himself he'd keep his hands off her. Until midnight. But she looked so genuinely worried about Julie, and he couldn't resist the urge to pull her to him. To kiss her tenderly. He wanted to thank her.

"Trust me," he ended up saying. "She wants you here. I think that, in a very different way, you're working your magic on her, too."

He sent up a small prayer to the heavens, maybe running it past the parents who'd left him in charge before he was ready, that he wasn't making a mistake where Chantel Johnson was concerned.

Trusting just wasn't his thing.

CHAPTER NINETEEN

LUNCH WAS AS she expected given the stereotypical perceptions she'd gained from her reach into society lifestyles. It wasn't Chantel's way to make conversation when there were real issues to be dealt with. Possible life-and-death situations needing attention.

Undercover work was frustrating as hell.

But the chicken salad was superb. And would have been even better if she could have helped herself to three times the amount she'd been served. Still, there was ice cream waiting for her at home. She'd be full before she went to work.

She planned to have a double burger and fries on break, whether Daniel felt like hamburgers or not. He could just stop twice if it came to that. She was having her burger...

As if thinking about the sensual pleasure derived from consuming fast food was somehow going to distract her desires away from the man whose knee had been touching hers under the table for the entire meal.

Johnson was out of control.

Chantel had made a mistake. She'd had sex with

an informer. And now more than ever she was going to do what she had to do to see that the assignment got done. Successfully.

She wasn't getting out until she was certain that Leslie and Ryder Morrison were safe. And until she'd brought everyone involved in Julie's rape—and hiding it—to justice. She also wasn't going to tell Wayne about her and Colin.

That would be stupid.

"I'm sorry, but I'm going to have to go," Colin said as he was finishing off the last piece of fruit on his plate. They'd spent twenty minutes at the table together and discussed the unseasonably warm weather, the lack of rain and the effect on the California water situation.

"You have to go already?" Julie asked, frowning at her brother. "I made strawberry shortcake."

One of Chantel's favorites. Next to chocolate ice cream.

"I'm already pushing it," he said, standing.

"That means I'll need to be going, too." Chantel gathered her things, welcoming the idea of a few hours free before work. She could change, eat and head in early. She wanted to look up the graduating class from the private school she'd heard Julie and Colin had attended. She was going to check out every male in the school, then cross-reference that list with functions Julie had attended, crossing off all boys whose families were also in attendance. Just because she'd turned down the chance for detective didn't mean she didn't have exemplary investigative skills.

"I can take you home."

Chantel wasn't sure who Julie's offer surprised more—Colin or herself. It wasn't as if the woman didn't drive. From what she'd heard, Julie traversed LA freeways like a pro, but…

She had to write. And…was supposed to have a few minutes alone with Colin in the car. Not that she needed them for anything…

But a few more minutes alone with Julie could produce meaningful information and save hours of name searching.

"I'm fine to go with Julie," she said, dropping her purse back to the chair next to her. "You're in a hurry, go ahead…" Strawberry shortcake sounded good.

With a second of hesitation, Colin stood there, looked between the two of them and nodded.

Good. He was going to go, and she could focus completely on the work at hand without wondering what might or might not happen during those few minutes she'd have had with him alone in the car.

He came closer. Leaned over. And planted a not-so-chaste—and definitely not-society-dinner-table—kiss on her lips. "I'll see you later." She heard the promise in the words and tingled all the way to her expensively shoed toes.

"See ya, sis." He grinned at an openmouthed Julie and was gone.

"HE SURE KNOWS how to make an exit," Julie said, shaking her head.

Chantel, hot and bothered and not at all comfortable, put her napkin on the table. She didn't need shortcake, after all. "I'm sorry about that," she said.

"What, the kiss? Don't apologize!" She sounded…almost happy. Then, her hands clasped together, she sobered. "I'm glad he's finally met someone who got through his walls of mistrust. Someone who makes him forget, at least for a few minutes, that I was hurt under his watch and he couldn't do anything about it."

TMI. Too much information. She didn't want it. Didn't need insight into his soul to get the job done.

She hung on to it, anyway. Tightly. Her heart hurting for the way she was deceiving him.

It was a major danger of going under, getting involved with a subject. She had to be able to wall off the tenderness to get the job done.

The job.

"What could he have done?"

"Absolutely nothing. I went to a party my parents would have allowed me to go to. It would have happened just the same if they'd both been alive and home waiting up for me."

More insight.

Colin had told her he'd taken his sister to the emergency room that night.

"He was waiting up for you, wasn't he? When you came in?"

Julie nodded.

Chantel needed to know who did it. Who was guilty of the crime that had irrevocably changed the lives of two very special people? Robbed at least one of them of the freedom to love openly. And the other of the ability to trust.

Julie wasn't running away. Hadn't left the table. Chantel waited. She couldn't risk pushing her away with an ill-timed question.

Waited and felt the ache growing in her heart. So maybe being undercover didn't mean you didn't feel. It just meant you were strong enough to do the job in spite of what you felt.

In spite of the fact that you were going to have to walk away from incredible joy.

The joy was only momentary, anyway. She knew that. Men like Colin, macho alpha males with that overdose of testosterone, men who were eaten alive by the fact that they hadn't been able to protect someone even when it would have been impossible—those kind of men didn't go for women who'd push them to the ground to protect them.

Men like Colin went for decorous women like Johnson.

"I heard today that the guy who raped me is going to be at the library function." Julie's voice didn't break, but it shook with emotional tremors.

Every nerve Chantel possessed was on alert.

"It's the first time he's openly responded with

acceptance to any function with which I'm directly involved," Julie continued.

The obvious effort it was costing her to speak—and the fact that she was doing it, anyway—brought the threat of tears to Chantel's eyes. She stiffened her backbone—not her tone of voice—and said, "You were in charge of the guest list."

"I know."

Wow. Maybe Julie was farther along in her healing than Colin thought. "And you invited him?"

"No. Neither did Leslie. But Patricia saw that they'd been left off. *She* invited them."

Shit.

"And they accepted."

"Yes."

Okay, they were dealing with something big here. Something that stunk. She didn't like it at all.

"Is that why Leslie called you back in this morning? To tell you?"

"Yes. Patricia had told her earlier. She said she'd noticed the oversight and corrected it quickly and quietly so no one would be embarrassed. She said she wouldn't have said anything if they'd been unable to attend, and they hadn't ever formally accepted the invitation, but now they have and since they were going to be there, they'd need place cards."

Julie was in charge of them.

"She knew Leslie would tell you."

"Yes."

Julie thought Patricia was on the committee because of her to watch her. Were they afraid she wasn't going to keep her vow of silence regarding the past?

And another unsavory thought occurred to her. Was Patricia there to make certain that Chantel didn't suspect anything?

Did that mean the commissioner knew about the cover-up? Knew there was a mole? Knew the mole?

Julie must think they knew the mole, or she wouldn't have thought Patricia was there to watch over her. Question was, did Julie know who the mole was?

Colin was sure Julie was being paranoid and would admit as much herself.

But what if Colin was wrong?

Wayne had said they had to be careful. That they shouldn't go to the commissioner until they had facts. Did he suspect the commissioner?

Did he know more than he was telling her?

"They're testing you," Chantel said, not because she was convinced of that yet, but because she had to know Julie's reaction to the possibility. She needed all of the information she could get because it might just end up being her against the world on this one.

It wasn't going to stop her. But she'd like to live through it.

"I think they are," Julie said, as though choosing her words carefully. "But if you asked Colin, he'd probably tell you that I'm just being paranoid."

"He seems to have your back, to believe in you—why would you think he'd blow you off on this one?"

Harris's words. Not Johnson's. She had to be more careful.

"He doesn't think Patricia knows anything about…that night."

"But you think she does."

"Not until she started showing up on all of my committees. And after this…I'm sure of it. They're pushing me. Forcing me to accept the fact that if I'm going to stay here, I have to live side by side with the man who raped me and not say a word."

Julie's voice wobbled. Her eyes filled with tears. But she blinked them back.

The entire Santa Raquel Police Department could be corrupt—if their leader was. She and other beat cops could be risking their lives every day, for very little pay, trusting their brothers to have their backs, when the only thing there was was power and greed. Back*stabbers*, not savers.

"Colin said that you and Leslie are friendly. She knows, doesn't she? About that night?"

Julie nodded. "She's the only one I've ever told."

Had Leslie said something to someone? Patricia, maybe? Thinking she was helping?

"Did you tell her before or after you signed an agreement never to speak of that night again?"

"Before. Colin didn't want us to sign them. He refused to sign one. Leslie and my mom weren't best friends or anything, but my mom told me once that if there was ever a time when I felt like I could trust only one woman in our circle, it should be Leslie. So I went to her and asked for her advice."

"She told you to sign it." Chantel didn't even need to ask. Leslie knew firsthand that there was no protection for domestic violence victims in their midst. And date rape could be considered under those auspices.

Julie nodded again, her lips pinched.

Taking a chance, Chantel reached out a hand, covering Julie's where they were clasped on the table. "Can you tell me who he is?" she asked. "I know your agreement says you can't, and you have no reason to trust me. But maybe, if you tell me, between Leslie and Colin and I, we can make certain the man gets nowhere near you that night."

Julie shook her head. "I can't go."

"Of course you can." Harris blurted it right out there. And Johnson tried to soften the response with, "You aren't alone, Julie. Not only is Colin here, but right now, I am, too. I'm a woman who's... been through things, too."

Not the same things. But some similar pain.

"I thought you probably had," Julie said. "You're...different. More touchable."

The real difference was that she wasn't one of them and wasn't doing such a great job pretending she was, since the two people who were spending time with her saw that she didn't quite fit in.

Which wasn't her biggest concern at the moment.

And she couldn't get off topic by discussing her own angst—either real or one she'd make up on the spot to fit her cover.

"You have to go, Julie," she said now, strictly for Julie's sake. "Because if you don't, they win. They've laid down the gauntlet. They're waiting to see what you're made of. If you show weakness now, they'll have won. And you'll either end up moving away from the home you love, or you'll live the rest of your life a shadow in your own world. You aren't the criminal here. You don't belong in prison—no matter how beautiful your cell might be."

When the other woman started to sob, Chantel broke off. She hadn't meant to go on so much. She hoped it hadn't been too far.

Squeezing the other woman's hands, she said, "I'll be there with you. Every step of the way. If you start to lose sight of your own strength, I'll loan you mine. We can do this…"

She believed that with every ounce of her being.

She got tears in her own eyes when, several minutes later, Julie nodded.

"You'll go?"

The younger woman nodded again. "I can't promise to stay. Or promise to stay out of the bathroom. I can't promise I won't embarrass you or myself or my brother, but..." She stopped and looked at Chantel with a warmth that touched her in places only Jill had ever touched.

That sacred best-friend place.

She forced herself not to look away. Or stiffen up. She'd lose her witness if she did that. Break the victim's trust.

"You've made such an impact on my brother. If he's willing to risk breaking down his walls, to fight through the demons and be open to a real relationship, then I owe it to him to do the same. It's my fault he's been locked inside himself for so long. I can't keep him there."

If it was possible to fall platonically in love, Chantel might have just done so.

Johnson had.

Harris had a job to do. "I'll need to know who he is," she said in Johnson's softer tones. "If I'm going to be able to help minimize contact."

"David Smyth." Julie's face twisted as though she'd tasted bile. "Jr.," she added.

She probably didn't notice that all of the color had left Chantel's face. She felt it go, followed by all warmth.

David Smyth Jr. Politician son of David Smyth Sr., a nationally known neurosurgeon—and close friend to Commissioner Paul Reynolds.

CHAPTER TWENTY

FOR THE FIRST time in his memory, Colin's mind was not 100 percent focused on the business discussion at hand as he played nine holes of golf that afternoon with one of his most lucrative clients.

He might just be on the verge of the best thing that ever happened to him—might be face-to-face with the woman meant to make his life complete. But he didn't believe in such things.

Not anymore. If he ever had.

Something akin to fear kept pecking at his heart.

He pulled out a nine iron. Popped his ball up onto the green. Picked up his bag and had a good five minutes to himself while he stood aside, watched his two opponents—a politician and his chief of staff—both take their shots from farther off and then walked toward the green.

Still, if Chantel was for real—if the feelings she'd ignited so swiftly, so fiercely, within him were real—he'd be a fool to get in his own way with a truckload of mistrust.

He had to give her a chance.

Even when every instinct within him was reminding him of the lessons he'd learned and the prices he wasn't ever going to pay again. It was a bitter pill of bile he'd had to swallow, again and again, as he'd realized that there was not one person on earth he could truly trust.

He'd realized that the only thing he could count on to see him through life's turmoil was power and money—as both were used against him and Julie in the name of justice. He'd earn the latter and wield the former with integrity. Because, in the end, he had to answer to himself.

But he'd never lose sight of the fact that he had to rely on himself and that his family had to be able to rely on him. He was never, ever going to put someone he cared for at risk. Or be sitting on the sidelines if they were at risk.

He knew there was nothing he could have done to prevent Julie's rape, but he never should have signed the papers, giving up her right to fight for herself. He never should have let *her* sign them.

His client's ball rolled within a couple of feet of his on the green. Some men would purposely miss the shot, taking a stroke to appease the client.

Colin made the shot. And increased his lead.

SHE ATE ICE CREAM. Went into work. Wayne was off. She'd known he would be and didn't call him in spite of the fact that she now had a doctor's name to give him. She needed time to think.

To talk to Julie again.

To see what Colin knew.

If, as she now suspected, the commissioner was in on the corruption that had allowed David Smyth to walk away from rape charges, any hint that the case was being reexamined could put both Colin and Julie in danger.

She had Leslie to look out for, too. In a crime that was ongoing. A further crime that could be prevented. James Morrison was also friends with the commissioner. She'd seen them together that first night, at the art auction.

If Julie's word that David Smyth had raped her, coupled with a medical report attesting to the same, hadn't been enough to get charges pressed, if strong evidence could just disappear, how was she ever going to hang a conviction on James Morrison?

No wonder his wife wouldn't speak up. She'd fear for her life.

Chantel saw no good way out. She also was not a quitter. Ever. The day she turned her back on people in need was the day she might as well be dead. Even if she couldn't help bring justice to Julie, for now, her best shot at getting any real information about the Morrison household would be through Julie.

Julie.

She couldn't get the woman, the determined and lost look in her eyes, or her brother out of her mind.

She couldn't put them at risk without their knowing. She'd have to come clean to do that. And lose what might be their only chance to find enough proof of violence to charge James Morrison, and then be ready to catch the commissioner trying to make the paperwork disappear.

She needed more information before she could do anything. Undercover work required patience.

Not her strongest suit.

But she'd be strong enough.

In the meantime, on her dinner break from the most boring detail of all time, she made a phone call while eating a double cheeseburger and fries—sitting alone in the cruiser while her partner enjoyed a Chinese dinner with two other cops. She pushed the first speed dial button on Harris's cheap smartphone.

"What's up? You coming for dinner tomorrow?" Max asked, picking up on the first ring. Which probably meant one or other of the kids had just fallen asleep on his shoulder and he hadn't wanted the phone to wake them. Max and Meri had dual rockers in the nursery and rocked them together every night that they could.

Chantel wasn't jealous of them. She just tended to forget bedtime more often than she should.

And they never called her out on it, but she always felt guilty when she realized the time.

"I'm sorry," she said now. Knowing that just as he didn't want the ringing phone to wake either Haley or Caleb, he also wouldn't talk much. She kind of liked that part. Her being able to do all the talking without him butting in, telling her what to do. Or what not to do.

"I did it again." She took a bite of burger. "I keep saying I won't and then I do." A fry followed the bite of burger. "You know that you and Meri and the kids mean everything to me. I just… I need to be more in tune." She was going to work on it.

Harder. "Just know that I'm truly sorry. Every single damn time I do this…"

Max wasn't good about letting her apologize. Or speak about her feelings. He just wanted to brush everything off and tell her it was all okay.

Which it was.

But sometimes you just needed to be able to get things off your chest. Guilt had a way of building up, and nothing good could come of that.

"I need a favor, Max."

"Anything." His soft tone was followed by some rustling. She figured he'd either put the child to bed or that Meri had taken him or her.

She felt a pang. Just because it felt so good to hold those babies.

Not because she didn't have any of her own. And, at the rate she was going, probably wouldn't.

"It's a biggie."

"I figured as much, or you wouldn't have called right now."

"Why do you say that?"

"You only call in the evening if it's really important."

So…maybe he was right. She didn't like to interrupt his and Meri's special time. Lord knew, she'd done enough of that when he'd been with Jill. Maybe that was part of the reason his marriage to Jill wasn't as close as it could have been.

"What's up?" he asked.

"Ten years ago a girl was raped. It was pretty brutal. She went to the emergency room here in Santa Raquel right afterward. A rape kit was done. Medical report stated that rape was obvious, even without the kit."

"What can I do? You need me to look at the report? Give expert witness testimony?"

"The report vanished, Max."

"What do you mean, vanished?"

"There's no record here. No record of charges being filed, either, but I know the girl made an official report. She was forced to make a deal, stating that the rape didn't happen. The report vanished, along with the medical evidence. But there might be a copy of it at the hospital. The doctor's name was Albertson—a female. I have no idea if she's still there, but you doctors are meticulous. She probably left a record someplace. Of course, it could have disappeared, too, for all I know. Unless she's still there and kept a private record."

"I don't want to know why you're looking at this again, do I?"

"Probably not."

"Is danger involved?"

"Possibly."

"But it would be less if I could find a copy of the report?"

If she didn't have the report, the commissioner wouldn't have as much reason to be concerned— assuming he was on to her before she was ready to go to the mayor. Or higher. Assuming he really was in on the corruption.

"Let's just say it could be much less messy and my chances of success would be much better."

"And if I don't help, there's no chance you're dropping this, is there?"

"You know me well enough to figure out the answer to that."

"I'll see what I can do."

"You're the best, Max…"

Daniel would be out soon.

She needed to thank Max for his time and finish her burger.

"You okay otherwise?" Max asked when she hung on the line.

"Of course. I'm always good. You know that."

But…

"Can I ask you something?" she said into the silence when he didn't do the polite thing and end the call.

"I'm still here, aren't I?"

"When you were married to Jill, were you happy?"

His hesitation was to be expected. It wasn't a

fair question. Not with Meri right there. Not with Meri in his life.

"Because of Meri, you mean? Because you know how completely she's the love of my life?"

"No…"

"It's a valid question, Chantel. Especially for you to ask. You were her best friend. And the answer is…sometimes. I loved Jill. You know that. I just…"

"Hated her job."

"I hated how helpless it made me feel. I hated knowing my wife, the woman who had sole possession of my heart, was putting herself in harm's way on a daily basis and there was nothing I could do to protect her."

"Except trust her, her training, her fellow officers, to do the protecting." It's what she'd need any man who was in love with her to do.

"How well did that work out?"

She'd walked right into that one. "So you're saying a female cop shouldn't ever get married because her job interferes with a man's natural instinct to protect?"

"No! This isn't about Jill at all, is it?"

"It's not about anyone. It's hypothetical."

"You've met someone."

"I have not." She was emphatic about that. "I'm far too busy right now to even think about meeting someone. In case you've forgotten, I'm currently working a full-time double with maintaining my regular shift and then doing this undercover thing."

But if she didn't give him something, he'd start drawing erroneous conclusions. Like maybe that her undercover work was getting to her. That she was falling for someone in the fake life she was leading. "I just... I'm almost thirty-three," she told him. "And starting to face that fact that I'm probably never going to have kids of my own."

Yeah, keep it about the kids. Max was a pediatrician. His whole life revolved around kids. His patients—and even more, the two he shared with Meri. He'd get the kid thing.

He got the kid thing. So much that he was still talking about her making whatever changes she needed to make so she didn't rob herself of the best thing life had to offer when she saw Daniel at the register inside the restaurant. Cramming the rest of her burger in her mouth, she told Max she had to go.

JULIE WAS LOCKED in her room when Colin stopped home to shower and change before meeting Luke Hudson, a law school friend. They talked about college, the law review they'd both been a part of. About sailing and golfing. And getting together again soon.

Neither of them had married, which was probably part of the reason they'd maintained close enough contact to meet for dinner at least once a month.

Luke asked about Julie. Colin said she was well.

As soon as dinner was over, he headed home to find out what had upset his sister at the library committee meeting earlier that day.

DINNER WAS OVER, and the cavalcade was out in front of a resort just down from where Johnson was staying. At her post across from Daniel, Chantel guarded the sidewalk at the left side of valet parking—an area cordoned off from resort guests that evening. The red carpet, which had seen the governor, his entourage and a couple of Hollywood's most successful darlings earlier that evening, was still laid out flat, waiting for those same shoe prints to traverse it one more time as they left the governor's birthday celebration. She wished they'd get on with it. It had to happen before Chantel would be free to hightail it back to the station, change and catch her cab to the Landau.

Johnson's phone, in the shirt pocket of her uniform, vibrated just above her nipple. Liquid heat bubbled for an instant in her midsection. Looking around, Chantel slid out the phone. Daniel and three other cops were talking quietly among themselves while keeping an eye on the secured area around them. She glanced at the text.

Jules said you know.

Had to be about Smyth.

Yes.

She typed with the thumb of the hand holding her phone. Her other hand rested just above her loaded holster, as it always did when she was on an assignment like this one. Just because danger had never happened on one of her babysitting watches didn't mean it never would.

Sharing that information puts her in danger of lawsuit. At the very least.

She read the text and looked around before responding.

I know.

Is your mother's name Pamela?

The question was so out of the blue she stared at it for a moment longer than she might have done.

And then she knew. Publishing in New York. The Johnsons. Pam was listed as publisher and CEO. He'd been checking up on her.

Because Julie had exposed herself, and Colin needed to know she was safe with Chantel? How far had he gone? Would he go?

No. My aunt.

She had to call her. To explain, in case he called. Had he already called?

She thought she heard a noise just off her left shoulder. Her heart had already been pounding. Adrenaline raced right along with it as she spun.

A body, dressed all in black, slid behind a pillar. Chantel quickly and quietly slid to the front of the same pillar, reached for her Taser gun and glanced to see if Daniel was watching.

He was not only aware, he'd moved into position across from the pillar. Signaled that he had his eye on the perp. A third officer appeared in Chantel's peripheral vision and, within seconds, everyone moved at once.

Thank God they had.

Five minutes later, when the governor appeared, the white, nineteen-year-old male was in handcuffs on the way to the station. The grenade he'd been holding, ready to lob at the state official, was on its way to the lab.

Daniel, who liked the limelight, was happy to make a statement to the press who'd been present in the wings, leaving Chantel to head back to the station in the backseat of another cruiser, with just enough time to get changed.

Lucky for her she was so invisible to her partner he'd never think to mention her part in the night's adventure.

Lucky for the governor that she'd been there when she had.

Which was why she did what she did.

Being known didn't matter. Making a difference in a positive way did.

CHAPTER TWENTY-ONE

HE WENT TO her because he had to. Colin didn't kid himself into thinking that he was only standing in the elevator at the Landau just before midnight on Saturday out of politeness.

No matter how much his life had started to fly out of control since Chantel Johnson had dropped into it, he was at least going to be honest with himself. He was addicted to her.

In less than two weeks' time.

His father had fallen for his mother the same way. Only the way he'd told the story, he'd announced to his father the night he'd met Colin's mother that he'd met the woman he was going to marry.

It was an age-old thing—guys being knocked for a loop the second they set eyes on their soul mates. Fodder for TV movies and country music.

He didn't believe in any of it.

But he knocked on the door of Room 12334 at five minutes to twelve with desire in his blood and an openness to possibility pushing at the rest of him.

When the door didn't immediately open, he took

a step back. Pursed his lips. Nodded his head and acknowledged the deep pounding of his heart.

There could be many reasons for her not to be there.

Some of them good ones.

Not so many that would also explain the lack of a phone call to save him the trip over here.

He knocked again. What was going on?

It was possible that she'd come to some harm and needed help.

Or wasn't feeling well.

It was possible she was hiding something from him. She'd appeared out of nowhere, with only a hard-to-come-by invitation as an introduction to a pretty close-knit society.

One in which anything or anyone could be bought.

Her name hadn't been registered on the guest registry.

Maybe the name she'd given him wasn't really hers.

Julie had trusted her with information that she'd sworn, under oath and by legal signature, not to share.

And what did they really know about Chantel Johnson? Other than the fact that both he and his sister had taken to her immediately—each in their own, completely different ways.

She had an aunt named Pamela who was in the publishing industry in New York.

Julie trusted her.

Colin trusted her more than he trusted most people.

And…

The door flew open. She stood there, an apology on her lips, looking gorgeous in black pants and a black-and-white jacket—stating professionalism as opposed to an evening out. Her blond hair, still full of body, hung around her shoulders and down her back. All he could think about was the way it had tickled his chest—and then other parts of him as she'd moved over his body the night before.

Had it only been a night ago? That incredible sex that seemed like eons past?

"I had to take a call," she was saying. He noticed her lips. And realized that she'd just said something about having been on the phone with her mother.

"It's two o'clock in the morning in New York," he said.

"I know. Which is why I had to pick up. Turns out she couldn't sleep and was missing me and knew that I'd still be up."

"You're a night person?" Hands in his pockets, he stood in the doorway, thinking that as much as she'd begun to consume his life, he should know something as simple as her sleeping habits.

He wanted everything—from social security number properly registered to Chantel Johnson on down.

"Always have been," she said, stepping back, inviting him in.

He accepted, keeping his suit coat on as he sauntered past the bed and over to the wet bar.

A couple of crystal decanters were there, one with bourbon, one Scotch. They'd be top-shelf. No question there.

He eyed the bourbon. There was no real need for his sour mood. Julie would only be in legal danger if Chantel Johnson betrayed her. And what reason could she have for doing that? His trust issues were the problem. He was letting them control him. "You want a drink?" he asked.

"I'd love one." She was watching him. The look in her eye reminding him of prey being circled. And he hated that he had that effect on her—making her feel cornered.

"What's your pleasure?" He waited to pour her drink before helping himself to a shot of bourbon.

"Scotch."

"With water?"

Her hesitation struck him, until she shrugged and said, "No, straight. And if that's unladylike, I'm sorry. In New York, I drink it straight."

More that he hadn't known about her. So much of it stretched between them, causing him discomfort.

He poured and handed the glass to her as she came over to the bar and slid up onto a stool. He yearned for the skirt she'd had on earlier. It would have allowed him to slide off her panties and take her. Right there.

Obliterate all thought from his mind.

He slid onto the stool next to her, facing the bar.

"What's wrong?" Her tone was soft, caring.

Looking into the small, gilt-edged mirror on the back wall behind the bar, he caught her studying him. He studied her right back.

And the world's grime started to drip away from him. The games and the lies. The compromises of integrity and justice.

She was one of the more direct women he'd dated and probably the most perceptive.

She had her hooks in him. And, God help him, he wanted them there.

"JULIE AND I'VE been carrying our secret alone for a lot of years."

She'd asked him what was wrong. He talked about secrets.

"Leslie Morrison knows."

"She told you that, too."

She was talking to his reflection in the mirror, and he hadn't turned around to face her. She wasn't sure why but played along.

"I asked."

"Leslie knew before we agreed not to speak of that night."

"You're so afraid of retribution? What can these men do to you except get some money out of you?"

"Take away the last vestige of respect that Julie has. Look at her, twenty-seven years old, alone in her room on a Saturday night. Every Saturday night. She doesn't date. She's a shadow of who she once was, even after ten years. Do you have any idea what it would do to her to have it all brought up again? To have to appear in court? To lose a case in court and be ordered to pay restitution to the Smyths for the brutality she suffered?"

Of course she didn't. Not even close. But she knew how it felt to have been fondled by her step-father and have her mother blame her for the creep's interest in her. He'd touched her breasts and...

Well, what mattered was that eventually Chantel had kneed him in the balls. When her mother had calmed down, she'd divorced the guy and done all she could to make it up to Chantel. But some scars didn't go away.

Ever.

"You have nothing to fear from me, Colin. I'm not going to hurt Julie. I want to help her."

The last statement was completely, 100 percent true. The former, that Julie wouldn't be hurt, she hoped would be true. She'd fight to the death to see criminals pay for their crimes. But she was neither jury nor judge. She was only the guy who got the thugs. It was up to others to take them to justice.

"Julie told me that she talked to Leslie back then because your mother told her that Leslie was the one woman she'd trust above all else."

"I didn't know that. But I know Mother trusted her."

Chantel was pretty much certain that the woman was lying to police. And medical personnel. And, by doing so, putting her and her son's lives at risk.

"You still think she's trustworthy?"

His shrug was frustratingly noncommittal. He sipped his bourbon and kept both hands around the glass.

She'd thought he was coming over for sex.

Off her mark again.

It wasn't that she'd been looking forward to another night of incredibly mind-blowing sex, but... she'd been curious to know if something like that could happen twice.

Had definitely been willing to find out.

But she was there for the job. Of course.

Maybe she was lucky he was there at all.

"You don't trust Leslie?" she pressed. Leslie Morrison was the reason she'd met Colin Fairbanks. She and Julie were the reason she was still there.

"I feel comfortable that Leslie has Julie's best interests at heart."

But... "You don't trust her?"

He looked at her then. "I don't trust anyone," he said. "Not even myself sometimes." His look grew more direct.

"You don't trust yourself with me, do you?"

"I'm uncomfortable with how fast things are growing between us."

She couldn't have him backing off. "We can slow down if you need to." Just as soon as he gave her definitive proof that Leslie Morrison was being abused.

And preferably after he made love with her one more time...

No. No! No! No!

They'd had sex. Out-of-this-world, best-there-ever-was sex. Love had had nothing to do with it...

"That's just it," he said, smiling for the first time since he'd come into the room that night. "I don't want to slow down. I want to speed up. Have you naked with me between your legs. Now. For the rest of tonight. And whatever tomorrows you have to give me."

Okay, fate. If you're still out there, I could use a little help here.

"I want that, too." The words must have been ordained. She had no idea why she uttered them. Or who uttered them. Harris? Johnson? Some power that had overtaken her senses?

"And it doesn't scare you?"

"It's completely unhinging me." A 100 percent honest response. She took her first sip of whiskey. Just a sip. Because she was Johnson. Any other night, feeling as she did, she'd have downed the shot.

Or gone straight for the ice cream instead.

He moved so slightly that she couldn't prove it was on purpose. His knee pressed against hers.

"Why do you think Julie talked to Leslie?" she blurted.

And then she was afraid she'd exposed herself, her true reason for being there, with the bald question.

"It's overwhelming, isn't it?" He was grinning now. "This need to know each other in the biblical sense and not let go. So much you're forced to bring up the bad just to get your mind off how great last night was and how much all you want to do is repeat it. Again and again."

Okay. Fine. "It is a bit," she allowed. He was going to know soon enough that he was having the effect on her that he thought he was.

"I think Julie talked to Leslie, and still does, exactly for the reason she told you she does. Because she listened to our mother's advice."

Not the answer she'd hoped for.

"Before Julie told me who'd done this to her, she made a comment, something about sensing that I'd been through something similar. It just made me wonder…you know, if Leslie has been…hurt, as well…especially considering how she thought the commissioner's wife was on the committee because of similarities between what happened to Julie in the past and someone else."

His eyebrows drew together, not with suspicion but with concern, as he shook his head. "You're referring to the rumors," he said. "The ones Julie alluded to in the car that first Saturday. About James hurting Leslie. Funny how, when something heinous happens, everyone is mum, but when someone points a finger at a good man, tongues can't wag fast or often enough."

"You're saying there's no truth to them?"

"Yes, that's what I'm saying."

"How do you know?"

"Because I've known James Morrison my entire life."

"You've known Smyth your whole life, too."

"Exactly."

He knew what the men were made of.

"You trust him, then? You trust James Morrison?"

He didn't go that far. And any idea Chantel might have been forming that she was wrong—that Leslie Morrison wasn't in any danger from her husband—disappeared.

"Like I said. I don't trust most people."

Colin had trust issues. She hadn't needed his confirmation to figure out that much. Still, he was there. Needing to be with her.

Giving her his trust—at least a modicum of it.

And more than she could remember needing anything personally, for herself, she needed to be worthy of his trust.

The feeling passed. As all of her personal feelings did. But the peculiar sense of hopelessness it left in its path didn't sit well with her.

Frustrated, Chantel took another sip of a drink she didn't really want. She was getting nowhere and losing the grip that would allow her to maintain the facade indefinitely.

"I actually didn't hear any rumors about the Morrisons," she told him. No, she'd gotten her information straight from the school counselor who'd told her about Ryder's collage reading. About the boy's timid denials of any wrongdoing in his home. From the emergency room medical reports, and from a sealed police record, denoting Morrison's murder of his younger brother. A record she could never, ever talk about to Colin. "Only what you and Julie mentioned obliquely in the car on the way home from the library meeting last week."

"Good to know," he said. "I've misjudged my fellow man."

"You didn't answer my original question, though."

"What's that?"

"Do you know if Leslie was ever…hurt? Like Julie thought I was?"

"Not for sure, I don't."

"But you have your suspicions?"

He hesitated. Emptied his glass. And then looked her in the eye. "I have my suspicions."

"You think she was raped?"

"I don't know any particulars. It's just something

Julie said one time when she was upset with me. Something about not understanding how it felt to be a woman who'd been overpowered. She implied that Leslie understood."

Chantel went cold. Adrenaline burned through her. "But you don't think her husband would hurt her?"

"Absolutely not. If anything, I think James does all he can to protect her. Probably because he knows she's more fragile than some. Like Julie."

Thoughts ran through her mind in beat with myriad feelings. Fear for the women unknowingly in her care. For any woman who, like her younger self, suffered at the hand of someone physically stronger. Chantel was the lucky one. She'd known how to fight back.

But she couldn't think about all that right now. She had to stay on track, stay in character. She needed to be Colin's girlfriend so that she could get her job done.

"What about you?" His look had turned tender. "Was my sister right in sensing that you've also been hurt?"

His words swamped her with a sudden need to have him protect her. Like he protected Julie. And thought James was protecting Leslie...

No. No! No! No!

"Not like that, I wasn't," she said softly, feeling, oddly, like she was turning traitor on herself. Her younger self. "But I lost my best friend to violence."

She hadn't meant to give him so much.

Or to lose so much of herself when he said, "Come here," so softly and pulled her down to the couch, to cradle her in his arms as though he really could protect her better than she could protect herself.

What scared her most was that for just a few minutes she wanted to let him try.

CHAPTER TWENTY-TWO

HE SPENT THE night with her. Woke up in her arms. And wanted to stay there. Conscious of how she'd been alarmed when he'd woken her the morning before, he just lay there, holding her.

Blond hair splayed across his arm. One of her legs was in between his. Her hand was resting on his thigh.

They were rougher than he'd expected, those hands of hers. He'd noticed the first time he'd held them. And again, each time she'd run them over his skin. They were strong, too. Sometime during the night, in between making love and dozing, he'd been aware of her hands on his shoulders, massaging him so well he'd awoken with delicious chills.

Not surprising, that strength. She was a writer who spent her days pounding keys. And the roughness—he liked that, too. Not only for the slightly raspy feel of her dragging them down his skin, but because of what those hands told him about her. She wasn't afraid to chip in and help out. To use her hands for more than adornment. Maybe she tended flowers. Or loved to cook and had her hands in water a lot.

Could be they were chafed from living in the cold of upstate New York? Though he knew from his mother and sister that lotion would take care of that malady.

She might paint. Julie, who was a writer, did. She grumbled about the turpentine taking a toll on her skin.

It could also be chocolate. He'd asked her to order some for the night before, though he hadn't realized until after their drink at the bar and a few minutes on the couch that she actually had done so. Fondue. To make up for the dessert they'd missed the night they'd gone out to dinner.

Her attachment to that night—their first official date, wanting to finish it—touched him. They'd reheated the chocolate in the microwave on the counter behind the bar.

And the things those fingers had done to his body with that chocolate—once it had cooled just enough for her to dip them...

Glancing from her hand to her mouth, remembering how her tongue had followed along behind her finger, licking and sucking the chocolate trail, he knew two things at once.

He was ready to make love to her again.

And she was awake. Watching him.

When their gazes met, her hand slid from his thigh to the hardness she had to have felt against her leg. Not the least bit embarrassed, Colin waited to see what she would do next.

Normally in charge of any physical relations he'd participated in, he wasn't sure how long he'd be able to lie there, unmoving, but driven by curiosity and some unknown need to let her do whatever she wanted to do, he kept his hands still.

She stroked him. Slowly, softly, at first—and then with more vigor. He didn't want this to be over so quickly. He wanted more of her. To share it with her. Reaching out a hand to stop her, he groaned instead.

He was too late.

IT WAS ALMOST eight the next time Chantel awoke. Colin had not only brought her to incredible climax with his hands, but he'd been ready to slip inside her by the time she'd finished and brought her to a second orgasm almost immediately.

She'd never known anyone like him. Reacted to anyone the way she reacted to him. She was in trouble. And after the night they'd just spent, the talking and making love, she couldn't keep lying to herself.

Crazy as it sounded, she was falling for Colin Fairbanks. Maybe even like Max fell for his Meri. In a way that was stronger than self.

Leave it up to her to do so in a way that would never bring her happiness. Colin would throw her out of his life as fast and as far as he could if he ever found out about her subterfuge. And if he didn't… she sure as hell couldn't pretend to be Johnson for the rest of her life. More than a night or two at the Landau would bankrupt her.

Even if, by some chance, he still wanted her around after he knew she'd broken his trust, they weren't going to work. He was an alpha male, a protector who, according to him, failed his little sister. And she was a cop.

And if that wasn't enough against her—if Chantel hadn't been so depressed she'd have chuckled to herself—she and Colin were nowhere near in the same league. She actually preferred her plain little apartment to the luxury of this room. Would much rather be in sweats and no makeup with her hair in a ponytail, in front of the TV with her feet on the coffee table, than walking on marble floors and sipping wine.

There was no future for them.

Knowing that didn't ease the ache in her heart that morning.

He stirred. They were both going to have to go. He had whatever it was rich rainmakers did on Sundays to tend to. And she was on shift at noon.

Still, she didn't lift her head from his chest. Or move her hands from where she'd fallen asleep holding him. His fingers threaded through her hair. Light little caresses, befitting of Chantel Johnson.

"I don't want to let you go." Her heart cried out to him. In Johnson's cultured voice.

"There's no need to rush on my account," he

rumbled against her ear. "I have brunch at eleven with a couple of investors brokering a deal, but it's local so I've got some time."

"I just…" She broke off, not knowing what to do. She rested her chin on her hands on top of his chest. "Promise me something…" She tried for low and sultry and sexy, when what she wanted to do was blurt out her fears and demand that he not hurt her any more than he had to. To tell him that he could trust her. Always. Except that she wasn't who she said she was.

She couldn't tell him. He was friends with Morrison and did not believe the man would ever hurt his wife. And she couldn't tell him what she knew about the man's past. Or his wife's medical records.

And he was a protector. He'd never be okay with his woman taking on the most powerful men on the Santa Raquel California coast. Most particularly after he'd seen what those men had done to his baby sister.

He'd never understand…

"What do you want me to promise you?" His gaze was half-lidded, and she had a feeling that while she was lying there angsting her heart out, he'd been dozing on and off.

"That if there ever comes a time when you're unsure about me, you give me the benefit of the doubt." She chose the words carefully. She knew it was dangerous to say them, to even hint at the possibility that there might come a time when he couldn't trust her, but she couldn't hold them back.

She was in over her head.

But she couldn't stop now. Not when she was getting somewhere. Getting close. Not when she didn't trust her own department to take the Smyth information and run with it. Not when she didn't know who she couldn't trust.

His hand stilled. "That sounds ominous."

Finally words came to her. "You don't trust people, Colin. You've said so, several times." Several times the night before, alone. "It's a bit daunting, to…care so much so quickly. Only to have you add in the fact that the guy you're suddenly besotted with isn't big on trusting, and you start to see the potential for disaster." She smiled to soften the words. To give them a Johnson-like quality.

"You're *besotted* with me?" He was grinning, too.

"I was, for a second there…." With a quick kiss, Chantel sat up. Taking the sheet with her, she started to stand. His hand on her elbow held her in place. She turned to look at him.

"I promise you that if I ever feel cause to doubt you, I will be cognizant of my challenges in the trust department and give you the benefit of the doubt."

The intense look in those deep blue eyes as he held her gaze unblinkingly spoke straight to Chantel's heart.

Yeah, she was in deep shit.

COLIN'S WAY, WHEN things felt like they were spiraling out of control, was to take action.

So he had trust issues—for good reasons. He also had instincts that were well honed, that had led him well time and time again over the past decade.

Promise me that if there ever comes a time when you're unsure about me, you give me the benefit of the doubt.

He'd made the promise. But wasn't sure, even as he'd done so, that he'd be able to keep it. He still wasn't sure.

He'd once trusted David Smyth Sr., as much as he'd trusted his own father. He'd had total faith in law enforcement. In the legal system that he now knew was as much about the best argument as it was about following the law. He'd trusted more than one woman with thoughts of a future together...

Promise me that if there ever comes a time when you're unsure about me, you give me the benefit of the doubt.

Why had she asked that of him? Had it really been as she'd said? That she was afraid of being so tied up with a man who had trust issues?

Or was she hiding something?

There was another glitch in the Japan deal. He got the call Sunday afternoon and would be on a flight later that night. Might be gone for a couple of days or more. His administrative assistant could clear his schedule.

Julie, who was used to his occasional and often unplanned absences, would be fine.

Chantel was the problem. He didn't want to lose a second of the time he had with her.

And he didn't want to leave town—feeling like his life was in an upheaval. He could call her—tell her he had to see her that afternoon. Get in a couple of hours with her after brunch before heading to the airport.

Or he could work toward making certain that information Julie had leaked, and the suppositions Chantel was consequently drawing, were not going to blow up in their faces, that the women would be protected while he was out of the country.

He chose the latter, of course, which was why he was sitting at a table at the country club, nursing a bottle of beer, with James Morrison across from him, doing the same.

James wasn't much of a drinker, something Colin had always liked about him. His unwillingness to give up self-control and awareness. Ever.

He'd asked the man, ten years his senior, how things were going, and had received a shrug in response.

"I have a difficult question to ask you," Colin said, leaning in to keep their conversation private. He'd chosen a table by the window, overlooking the tenth green and two tables away from the nearest customer in the half-filled room. But most of the men and women present knew one another—at least by sight and name—and Colin didn't want to appear as though he and James were open to anyone joining them.

Morrison's brow furrowed as he nodded.

"I need you to trust that I'm going somewhere with this question."

"Of course." James didn't hurry him or lose his sense of calm.

"It's come to my attention that Leslie has been… hurt…"

Morrison raised his hand, shaking his head. "Let me stop you right there," he said, his expression clearing. "You've heard the rumors, and while I respect that you've come to me rather than indulging in them—which I'd expect from you, by the way, to come to me rather than indulge—I'm also a bit surprised you'd have to ask."

"I'm not asking you if you abuse your wife, James." Colin needed to make that clear. "I put no credence in the rumors whatsoever and have done what I can to squelch them."

"I appreciate that." James sipped his beer, watching Colin.

"The answer to my question is none of my business, I understand that, but I have a good reason for asking. Has Leslie ever been…physically mistreated?"

James looked out the window. He remained silent for a long time. Too long. Then he looked Colin in the eye.

"Yes."

"Recently?"

Morrison's shrug bothered Colin. "She has accidents," he said slowly, picking at the label on his bottle. "She trips, knocks into things. Sometimes the damage is more serious than others."

Shaking his head, Colin said, "I don't understand. You're telling me Leslie's a klutz?"

"Only when she's feeling particularly low. It's all subconscious, but I'm given to understand that she does these things as a kind of self-inflicted punishment."

"But...why?"

Morrison folded his hands and looked outside again. Stared at the table and picked at the tablecloth.

Colin waited for the man to look at him, and then asked, "Why?" again.

"Because she blames herself for what happened to her in the past."

"What happened?"

"She was hurt. Bad." James didn't say any more, but Colin had a feeling that Leslie hadn't suffered as Julie had. Rape was an ugly thing, but people generally called it what it was. At least at times like these.

"She was beaten up?"

The man looked outside once more, his Adam's apple bulging as he swallowed. "Yes. More than once."

"By a man."

Morrison's eyes glistened. "Yes." The word was curt.

"One she knew."

"Yes."

"But not you."

"It was before we were married."

"Do you know who it was?"

Morrison shook his head.

He should let this go now. He had the information he'd been seeking. Confirmation that Chantel had been correct. Partially. Leslie had been hurt. But not by her husband. "Surely you asked."

"Of course I did. Many times. But she wouldn't tell me. She said I didn't need to know. That she wanted to put it all behind her."

"Could it have been her father?" Leslie's dad, a shipping magnate, had been through multiple divorces and was currently living in San Diego.

"No. He's a womanizer but a good man. A good father."

"Do you think it's someone you know? Is that why she won't tell you?"

"I hope to God not. And no, I don't think so. She was in LA at the time. My understanding is that it happened there."

The story had holes. A woman suffers physical abuse but won't say by who...

Colin's thoughts stopped him short. Julie was bound by law not to say.

But a woman who had "accidents" to punish herself for having been abused in her past? Who was he to judge? Julie blamed herself for what had happened to her that night at the party.

"You said you had a reason for asking," Morrison said. He took a long swig of beer and set his bottle down with a little more force than he had before.

"I'm going to tell you something, in the strictest confidence. Because I need your help...."

CHAPTER TWENTY-THREE

RIDING IN THE car with Daniel Lewis, wishing for once that he was a chatty guy, Chantel stared out the window—looking for trouble—struggling to keep her mind on the streets.

Johnson's phone vibrated, and she gave a start.

Her partner looked over at her.

She could look at her cell phone. He'd never know it was Johnson's. She waited until it vibrated a second time before she did so.

Colin had called and left a message. With her phone pressed to her ear, making sure to click the volume down so there was no chance Daniel would catch anything, she listened to her lover's voice.

He was leaving town again. Back to Japan. And needed to speak with her before he got on the plane at seven o'clock that evening.

She texted him right back, telling him that she was getting something to eat and would be in touch as soon as she was alone. Unanswered calls didn't sit well with him.

And a woman living in a hotel room being out to eat was believable. Expected. You could only eat so much room service.

"If you ever need any help, I'm here." Daniel's smoker's voice startled her. She looked over at him, not sure where he was coming from. Or what to say. Did she look helpless? He thought she was in trouble?

"I might not be the most pleasurable guy for you to be cooped up with all day, but I'm a good cop."

"I've never doubted that for a second. I trust you with my back. And I've got yours."

What was it with the guys in her life? Getting all emotional and gooey on her all of a sudden? Max with his protectiveness. Colin with his...well, everything. And now Daniel, too?

"Good cops know when their partners are moonlighting," Daniel continued, looking straight ahead now. "I'm not asking any questions. You'd tell me if I needed to know. I'm also completely sure that you're on the up-and-up. So just know, if you get in a spot and need help, you can call me. Day or night."

"Okay." She nodded. Looked at him. And then stared straight ahead, too, feeling a little less alone.

Not that she'd ever tell him so. Not in a million years. He'd probably ask for a new partner if she did.

COLIN WAS IN his room packing when his phone rang.

"Hey, that was quick," he said, catching sight of himself in his wardrobe mirror, hardly recognizing the young-looking guy grinning back at him. Weren't there usually more lines marring his forehead? He almost asked her what she'd had for dinner; he was so far gone he wanted to know everything about her.

"I'm still out. Picking up a salad."

Now that she mentioned it, he heard some noise in the background. Like she was outside. There were any number of build-your-own-salad places about town, most particularly in the upscale tourist section of the beach.

"You got my message. I have to go back to Japan. And it might be a little longer this time."

"Yes. I'm sorry to hear that." She sounded lonely already.

"Think of me tonight, when you crawl into that great big bed…"

"I'm afraid I have no choice in the matter. It was already happening before you spent the past two nights in it. I severely doubt I'll ever be in it without thinking of you now."

He grinned some more. And then sobered. "I'll text you as often as I can."

"Good."

"I have a favor to ask, Chantel."

"Of course. You know I'm here for you. What do you need?" God, it felt great having a woman he could count on, having anyone he could count on to help ease the guilt of leaving his responsibilities behind every time he left town.

"I need you to look in on Julie," he said. "With all that's been happening—her worry about Patricia on her committees, and now Smyth going to the library event—I don't want her holed up alone in the house for days. I asked her to come to Japan with me, but she adamantly refused."

"Does Leslie know you're leaving?"

"Her husband does." He'd told Morrison some of what was going on. Not Smyth's name. Or the exact nature of the harm that had come to Julie ten years before. Only that his sister had been in danger at one point. He'd asked the other man to be on alert in case Julie needed some real protection and told him to call their private security service, not the cops, if something materialized. He'd also asked him to keep an eye out for Chantel, to take care of her if she needed anything. "Julie knows she can call him if she needs anything. Leslie will also be getting a text from someone in my office if I'm going to be missing the next library committee meeting."

It was scheduled for the following Thursday evening. They were going to be finalizing all the details for the big night.

"We aren't going to have much time to practice our parts for the murder mystery, but if you've read the script yet, you'll see that there's not much."

The script. Shit. He'd left his copy at the office. He'd taken it with him on Saturday when he'd gone into work because he'd left it in the car after the meeting. Completely unlike him. "My copy's at the office."

"Like I said, it's not much. We can ad-lib most of it. And we're still almost three weeks away. I'll go over it with you when you get back."

He liked the sound of that. "Over a pot of chocolate fondue?" he asked, wishing he didn't have to leave that night.

"Of course. You owe me a body drawing…"

Picturing exactly how he'd do that, Colin turned away from the mirror. A man his age shouldn't be looking that sappy.

"In the meantime, of course I'll stay in touch with Julie. I would have, anyway. I like her."

"You two are becoming friends."

"Yes."

"I'm glad."

He kept her on the line for another five minutes—teasing her, getting himself too hot under the zipper in the process.

And when he finally rang off, he was actually starting to believe that life—his life—could be more than just monetarily successful.

THOUGH SHE HADN'T expected to, Chantel slept well Sunday night. She was in her own bed—in underwear, as she always slept—with the television she'd mounted on the wall across from her bed streaming sitcoms softly in the distance. When she awoke, they talked her back to sleep.

Probably helped that after two nights of extreme lovemaking, not to mention working two jobs, she was exhausted.

On the noon-to-eight shift through Wednesday, she could have been fully back into a normal routine—have a real chance to convince herself that what she felt for Colin Fairbanks had been an aberration—if not for the need to check on Julie. But the need fit her purpose, too. Visiting with Julie, at Colin's behest, gave her the perfect excuse to hang out with her and steer the topic back to Leslie Morrison. To get Julie to trust her enough to tell her what she knew about Leslie's battering.

Because one thing was quite clear to Chantel, most particularly after hearing that Colin was in enough with the other man that he'd already told him he was leaving town after only having found out an hour or so before. Whether Colin truly believed in the other man's innocence where the rumors circulating about his wife were concerned or merely believed the justifications Morrison must surely be giving him, was immaterial to Chantel.

She wanted the truth. The man needed to be stopped.

A little hampered by her work schedule, she nevertheless called Julie Monday morning, hoping to find some time to get together for breakfast the following morning. Julie suggested that Chantel might want to come watch a movie with her that evening. When Chantel told her that she'd planned to work on her book until at least eight, Julie suggested that she spend the night at the mansion. That way they could enjoy a glass of wine. Watch a movie or not. And have breakfast together in the morning.

Remembering that breakfast with Colin was part of Julie's normal routine, Chantel agreed immediately—mentally calculating the logistics of getting out of her police uniform, into Johnson's clothes, packing a bag of Johnson's things and driving Johnson's rental car over to Colin's house by nine. She'd have to pick up a Johnson-type overnight bag on her way into work and hightail it to the resort as soon as she was off shift.

With the new pseudo understanding between her and Daniel, she could pretty much plan to be off on time. He'd handle whatever might run them over shift if he thought she was dealing with her other "thing."

Yes, it was all going to work. Was falling into place perfectly.

With renewed energy, she worked out in the poor excuse for a gym in her apartment complex, showered, dressed in jeans, boots and a T-shirt, pulled on her denim jacket and headed into the station a couple of hours early to check in with Wayne and help with whatever research she could.

She just wasn't sure yet if she was going to tell him their rapist's name. She wanted to. Trusted *him*. But didn't know for sure that he'd know if someone else they'd trusted was lying to them.

Maybe Colin's paranoia was wearing off on her. Maybe he wasn't paranoid at all, and the man who oversaw the entire Santa Raquel police force, a man both she and Wayne trusted with their lives, really was bad.

She knew better than to keep anything from her partner. Most particularly on her first undercover assignment. But when she saw Wayne later that morning, she didn't say a word.

IT WAS ALMOST five when Chantel's cell phone rang. Harris's phone. Johnson's had received a couple of texts from Colin. He'd arrived in Japan. And he missed her.

She'd read and returned them both. She missed him, too. And would be spending the night at his house—a girls' night with Julie.

He texted back telling her that he'd already texted his sister and insisted that Chantel sleep in his bed.

So he could imagine her there, she was sure. The pervert. But she'd be doing the same thing—lying on his sheets, smelling him, wishing...

When she saw Max's name on her caller ID, she told Daniel she had to take a pee break and then called Max back immediately.

"What's up?"

"Dr. Albertson's gone, but I found someone else who talked to me," he told her. "Someone who doesn't want to be mentioned."

"Another doctor?"

"Perhaps."

She needed to know what he had, so she chose to let the informant particulars go for the moment.

"Albertson took a job in San Diego shortly after that night," Max said. "My source said it was a sudden move. Albertson kept insisting she'd met someone and had put in for a transfer, but my source never completely believed her. In any case, Albertson left her one file. Said to keep it just in case. But not to do anything with it unless either Julie or Colin Fairbanks came asking for it."

"Which they never would."

"No, but I did."

"You aren't either of them. Why'd this person think to tell you about it?"

"Because I knew about a rape, and because this person is in the emergency room. And has seen some things that are bothersome."

Chantel's nerves started churning until she really did have to pee. "What things?"

"This person hears details and says that there have been at least three other cases in the past ten years that all have a similar, very bothersome situation."

"He's done it more than once. Julie isn't his only victim."

"The paperwork Albertson left was in a sealed envelope. My source was sworn not to open it. Ever. Of course, my source did open it. She needed to know what she was holding on to, or she wasn't going to hold it. She knew they were dealing with powerful people and didn't want to get herself in trouble. At least not without knowing why."

"She."

"Let it go, Chantel."

For now. She might need testimony. And to get her hands on that report, which could come later.

"She told me that all three victims were drugged in the same way. A unique cocktail combination with aspirin added." Max delineated each component in medical terms. Again, something she could get later. "And all three were violated in the same way."

She wanted to ask more but didn't. Colin had said Julie had been brutalized. She didn't need to impinge any further on Julie's privacy. She had the details she needed.

"The rapes were similarly situated in ways that are unique enough to leave a signature." She pulled out the point that was important to her investigation.

"That's my conclusion. And my source's, as well. And, Chantel...the most recent was less than a year ago."

Mind spinning, Chantel held her stomach, leaning back against the gas station bathroom wall. "He has to be stopped."

"I know. But you're dealing with some powerful people here, Chantel. Three victims and no charges have ever been filed. Someone's willing to do what it takes to see that nothing is done."

"Your source checked on that?"

"If your suspect had other charges against him, you'd have known that."

He had her there. "And if I don't do something, he's just going to keep on, and there will be a lot more than three victims for us to talk about. For that matter, there probably are more. We only know of the ones who've gone to the Santa Raquel hospital for help. But what I also know is that the next one will be on my head."

Which brought another link to Julie's and Leslie's cases. Now they both presented current danger.

"I hate your job."

"I know."

"Be careful, my friend."

"I will. And, Max? Thanks."

She rang off before he could suggest, again, that she get a desk job.

USUALLY ONE TO sit back and let the business at hand take its course—using his father's advice not to grab at the first chance but rather to build business relationships that would last a lifetime—Colin drove his clients, and their potential Japanese business partners, to work until everyone was almost too tired to think. He had someone call for a meal catered in. And he still didn't stop. He'd already pushed powerful men to work through the night.

It was Monday night at home. And Tuesday morning in Japan. And he was starting to question what in the hell he was doing.

Strong, lasting business deals, decisions of that magnitude, weren't to be made through pressure or exhaustion. Some people did business that way. Successfully, even. If all they wanted to do was take the money and run.

Now Colin just wanted to run. By the time he'd spent one full day away from home, his instincts were screaming at him to get back there.

In one sense, it was as though the night Julie was raped was happening all over again. He was working, focusing on the deal in front of him, with his sister on his mind.

That night he'd been waiting for her to get home.

Because he hadn't wanted her to go to the party in the first place? The thought rose unbidden. The Smyths had been close family friends for years. They had all spent Christmas together! But there'd been something almost unsettling to him in the way young David had looked that night as he'd picked Julie up. A strange energy about him.

One Colin hadn't acted on. Or allowed himself to dwell on since.

Smyth had looked Colin in the eye. Been perfectly respectful. He hadn't smelled of drugs or alcohol. There'd been no reason not to let his sister go to the party in the company of so close a family friend. One sanctioned by the friendships their parents had formed with and through them over the years.

Part of the problem had been that Colin hadn't been able to put a name to what he'd been feeling.

Or been old enough to discern it.

Colin had put it down to teenage energy the night of his first big party. He'd let his sister go and had felt uncomfortable the rest of the night.

He was feeling the same kind of discomfort as he sat at a board table in Japan, trying his damnedest to get the work done so he could be on a plane back home.

Only the possibility that he was letting his emotions get to him, get in the way—that his unrest was derived from the fact that he wanted to be in Chantel's bed because he had no idea how long he'd have to convince her to stay—had him finally backing off and agreeing to a traditional Japanese breakfast with their hosts before heading to his hotel for some rest.

CHAPTER TWENTY-FOUR

SHE'D MEANT TO handle Julie with kid gloves. Because Colin did. Because he'd want her to. Because she now knew far more about the nature of the horror the other woman had suffered and couldn't imagine living with those kinds of memories.

But somehow, sitting with Julie over a glass of wine on the huge, soft leather sofa with reclining everything in a place she called the rec room, facing the largest television she'd ever seen in real life, Chantel allowed herself to follow the course of action Harris placed upon her.

They'd never gotten around to turning on the television to figure out what girlie movie they were going to stream in the soundproof room. Julie talked about her work, about the possibility of starting to send out query letters. She'd shown Chantel a few pages of finished art with calligraphy lettering.

They talked about literary agents. And in the end, Chantel promised to contact her family the next day, to see what they could do.

She'd already called her mother—had been on the phone with her the second night Colin had shown up at her hotel room—to ask her to get in touch with the sister she hadn't had much to do with for years. To let her know that if anyone called for a Chantel Johnson, it was her. And not to say she was a cop, just that she worked at the very small publishing operation—as she had for a brief stint when she was a teenager.

And then had to assure her mother that she'd only changed her name and hadn't gotten married. She'd said she'd explain later.

Her mother, who spent her life with the guilt for what had happened to Chantel growing up, had agreed to do as she asked. She'd texted Chantel the next day to tell her that she'd spoken with her sister, no one had called and Aunt Pam was happy to do whatever Chantel needed.

She also asked that Chantel give her a call.

So now she would.

But first...

"I need to speak with you, Julie," she said. An idea had been forming since the second she'd gotten off the phone with Max. She knew what she had to do.

She just wasn't sure about all of the details yet. She had ideas. Good ones. A solid plan. One that would work.

But she needed help. At the very least, she'd need someone to control the lights at the library the night of the gala. Someone who would blend in as a member of the elite crowd without raising any suspicions.

Ideally, she wanted someone who could have her back enough to get help if something went wrong. Someone who was in on the plan.

Someone who might have to testify in court...

But she was getting way ahead of herself. How much did she say? Where did the subterfuge and reality collide? Or coexist?

Could she trust Julie with the truth?

She had to be the absolute worst undercover officer of all time....

"Something's wrong, isn't it?" Julie's frightened tone brought her back to the moment—and the realization that her silent introspection was scaring the younger woman. "You heard something about Colin..."

"No!" She covered Julie's hand with her own and then sat back. "No. I mean, yes, I've heard from him. About half an hour ago actually. And he's fine. Having breakfast and wishing he was on a plane home."

Because he wanted to be in his bed with her that night. She opted not to share that part.

"He misses you already, huh?" Julie asked, an impish smile replacing the fear of seconds before.

"He misses you, too," she said to cover her embarrassment. She wished things were different, that she could just be open with Julie, tell her everything, like she'd always done with Jill.

"He might, but not enough to want to rush home," she said drily. And then, with a less teasing grin, she said, "What was it you needed to speak with me about?"

"I want you to help me with something. What I'm going to ask isn't going to be easy. But I believe all the way down to my soul that it's vitally important."

"If you think it's that important, then, of course. I'll do whatever I can."

Chantel nodded. And started with first things first. "You know Leslie Morrison pretty well, don't you?"

"Yes. But you know that already."

"If you told her something and asked her to keep it to herself, would you trust her not to tell your brother, her husband, anyone?"

"Absolutely." Julie paused, and then said, "There's a bond between women who've been... mistreated. A level of trust that runs pretty deep."

Julie seemed to be including her in that bond. Chantel didn't want to accept it. She hadn't been hurt as badly as Julie had been, as she expected Leslie had been. But...

Being included in that bond would help her help them...

She'd been about to ask about including Leslie in her plan. Having the evening's organizer on board could greatly escalate her chance of success. Most particularly considering that she was going to need to change the script. She thought she'd have to work up to the other point she wanted to bring up—getting Julie to confide in her about Leslie's home life.

Instead, she'd been handed the "in" she'd needed. Fate again.

"And you know for certain that Leslie has been mistreated."

Julie nodded. Then she jumped up to grab a couple of throw pillows off a chair and sat back down, hugging one to her chest. Her glass of wine sat, mostly untouched, in a built-in holder in the arm of the couch. "I think you have, too," she told Chantel. "I don't mean to pry, but we've done all this talking about me and I don't think I'm the only one who knows what we're talking about."

Whatever Chantel might have said stuck in her throat.

"My brother tends to think that I'm the only one who's ever been raped," she said, seeming to be able to talk more easily about her ordeal just in the ten days she'd known her. "He likes our world to revolve around me. He can't seem to understand that sometimes his hovering just makes things harder. He makes me feel like a freak, like something's wrong with me. I'm not the only one here who matters." Her voice gained conviction at the end.

Chantel had to give her something, but telling her about her stepfather's behavior didn't seem like it was going to cut it.

She hadn't suffered as Julie had. She hadn't been raped. Not even close. She'd been neglected. The state had charged her mother with that on one occasion, between divorces. She'd been dating a lot and forgot to come home sometimes. She'd been touched. She hadn't been raped.

Rape was something she couldn't lie about. Most particularly not to a woman who had been.

"I watched my best friend die." She heard the words before she'd made any conscious choice to say them. "We were out," on a call. Jill and her partner had been first responders. Chantel and her partner had arrived on the scene in time to watch every detail of those last few seconds...

"A thug on the street..." A perp Jill's partner had approached for a drug collar. "He pushed her down on the pavement right in front of me..." After she'd lunged for his gun just as he was getting a shot off at Jill's partner. Her partner hadn't been harmed. "He held her down with a boot on her chest. And while she was lying there on her back, looking up at him, he shot her right between the eyes."

Jill's partner shot him, too. But not in time. Chantel, who'd been running up to the scene among tourists and other pedestrians, had her gun in her hand but hadn't been able to get a clear shot off in time, either.

"Was he arrested?" Julie's eyes were wide and filled with compassion.

"No." He was dead. Nothing to arrest. But she knew what she had to do to get Julie's cooperation. Develop trust with your subject, she remembered from one of her investigative classes. Find a rapport. If his brother died, yours did, too. Your goal is to save lives. And in order to do that you have to get the confession. Or the information.

"And this is kind of what I wanted to talk to you about," she said, hating what she was doing even as she said the words. "It eats at me, Julie. Every day. That he didn't ever have to pay for what he did. I lie awake at night, or most often wake up in the middle of it, and all I can see is Jill lying there, with his foot on her chest, trying to get up. Looking at his gun. And that bullet hitting her..."

Tears came from somewhere, blinding Chantel to the vision that did still haunt her dreams. It would debilitate her nights, too, if not for the sitcoms she'd trained herself to concentrate on so she could sleep.

She didn't just have water in her eyes. It spilled down her cheeks. In rivulets.

Something was happening to her. Something she didn't understand. Something that scared her to death.

She was crying like a baby, which she hadn't done even as she'd said her final goodbyes to the only person in the world she'd truly loved.

COLIN WAS BACK in his hotel room, with a promise to be showered and at the board table with his clients by two that afternoon, when he got Julie's text.

Chantel's asleep. She told me about her friend's murder and was pretty upset. Her phone keeps going off. I assume it's you texting her. I've got this. Let her be.

His baby sister had his lover's back.

Colin crawled into bed without brushing his teeth and fell immediately to sleep.

JULIE WOKE CHANTEL up to get her into Colin's bed. It felt strange, crawling beneath his king-size sheet, laying her head on his pillow. But with his sister right there, pulling the covers up to her chin, she felt completely safe.

She thought about finding a remote to turn on the television mounted to the wall opposite his bed, too, but she was asleep before she did anything more than think.

She didn't wake up again until morning.

COMPLETELY DISORIENTED AND out of sorts, Chantel showered in Colin's bathroom. Her bag was there, waiting for her—Julie obviously had brought it in the night before. She donned a pair of Johnson's designer jeans and a black silk contoured blouse and slipped into black wedge sandals. Got through the painfully awkward process of putting on makeup. Fluffed the hair she'd covered with a shower cap so she didn't have to deal with drying it and found her way to the dining room she'd eaten in once before.

Julie was already there, sitting with a cup of coffee and a drawing pad.

"I am so sorry," Chantel said. "I swear to you, I didn't have anything to drink before I came here last night…"

Waving a hand in the air, Julie smiled at her. "Don't," she said. "You have nothing to apologize for."

"But…"

"Forget it." Julie stood as Chantel dropped down to the seat she'd occupied the last time she'd been there, for brunch with Colin and Julie after Saturday's library meeting. Just three days before?

How could three days seem like more than a lifetime?

"Do you realize that last night was the first time in ten years that a friend leaned on me?" Julie asked. She'd stopped in the doorway between the kitchen and the breakfast room behind it.

She couldn't remember the last time she'd leaned on anyone.

Well, yes, she could actually. It had been the night before Jill had been killed. A night she hadn't thought about in years—maybe since her friend had died. Odd that she'd wiped it out of her memory. It hadn't been anything earth-shattering—just her lamenting about never finding a man like Max, one who loved her in spite of her job. And about wanting kids of her own…

Jill, being Jill, had hugged her. And told her that

she'd have all the kids she wanted. She just had to put the thought out to the universe...

"I have no idea what came over me," she said now. "I...didn't even cry at her funeral." She stared at Julie as though the other woman would have some explanation for Chantel's bizarre behavior the night before.

She'd cried herself to sleep in Julie's arms. The memory was embarrassing beyond words.

Disheartening.

Frightening.

And...nice. Which made not one whit of sense to her.

She had to move past it—accept that it happened, learn from it and make certain it never happened again.

"I just... I'm glad it was me you picked to share your grief with," Julie said and left the room before Chantel could figure out what to do with that.

COLIN WAS IN meetings when he got the text from Chantel.

I swear to God I had nothing to drink, and I don't even take aspirin or acetaminophen for headaches. No clue why I fell apart on your sister last night. I hope I didn't do any damage. She seems fine. Please advise.

Probably one of the oddest texts he'd ever received.

The one from Julie came in while he was reading Chantel's.

She's up and at the table. I just left her to get breakfast from the oven. I made my quiche. Ha! Be jealous, you know you love it! She's uncomfortable, but seems much better this morning. You made a good choice, bro. I approve!

Bro? She hadn't called him that since she was about...fifteen. Which had been the year their mother died.

Excusing himself from the table, he stepped out into the hall and answered Julie first.

Thanks, Jules. You're the best. And save some quiche for me. Love you.

Chantel was a bit more difficult.

After several tries, he ended up with, You're fine. Welcome to the family. Even if it's only temporary. Next time you sleep in my bed, I expect to be in it. Please advise.

He waited a couple of long minutes.

And didn't receive a response back.

CHAPTER TWENTY-FIVE

"I FEEL GUILTY, being spoiled like this," Chantel said as Julie put a plate of quiche and a bowl of fresh fruit on the table in front of her. "I would have been happy to help."

"So would our housekeeper," Julie said. "Her name's Louisa, by the way. I'm sure you'll be meeting her soon. Anyway, I thought it was important that she was home to fix breakfast for her kids and see them off to school before coming here, so I do breakfast and she has dinner ready before she leaves. We fend for ourselves if either of us is here for lunch."

"I still could have helped." Chantel made a mean pancake. She liked them with chocolate ice cream on top instead of syrup, but she could adapt.

"I love to cook," Julie told her. "So did my mom. She cooked most of our meals when I was growing up, much to Daddy's chagrin. I look forward to my mornings in the kitchen." She grinned as she took her seat.

And Chantel wished for about the millionth time that she'd met Julie on the street or in school. Any-place where they could have been real friends.

The woman had spunk. And a spirit that, while damaged, was stronger than just about any she'd ever encountered, including her own. And Jill's.

In another life, Julie would have made a great cop.

"Last night, you said you had something to talk to me about," Julie said, as though she'd read Chantel's mind.

She and Jill used to do that. Know what the other was thinking.

This was getting weird.

Then she remembered where she'd been heading when she'd derailed the night before.

"I know how it feels to have someone get away with a horrible crime," she said, taking a bite of delicious broccoli quiche minus her usual appetite.

Surely that wasn't going to change, too, the random thought popped up. She liked eating. It brought her pleasure.

And...back to topic. Jill's killer had died before he could be brought to justice. That bugged Chantel. He'd made her suffer. He should have had to suffer, too.

"You do, too," she said, testing Julie's waters.

Julie nodded, without looking broken.

"So...as I was working on the script for the library event, something occurred to me and I can't let go of it. You said David Smyth was going to be there."

"With his wife, yes."

"He's married?"

"For six years," Julie said. "They have a couple of kids now. A boy and a girl."

A little girl. Whose father was a rapist. A memory flashed before her eyes. The touch of a hand against her breast. Groping. Stealing away all innocence. And faith in her mother, too. How could a woman trust anyone to look after her if her own stepfather could do such a thing?

Did Smyth's wife know? Was he rough with her, too? The questions rose up in a black cloud before her mind's eye.

Julie's fork had stilled.

Chantel was going to have to tread carefully here. "We have to stop him."

She saw Julie's hand start to shake, heard the clatter as the utensil fell to her plate.

He's still hurting people. He has more victims. She couldn't tell Julie any of that. Johnson had no way of knowing it.

"I know you can't say anything, Julie. I'm not asking you to be directly involved." Not yet, anyway. Not unless a prosecutor needed her testimony. But that was a bridge she might never have to cross.

Julie wrapped her arms around her shoulders; she seemed to be shrinking in on herself.

Then Chantel was a kid again. Telling Jill that her mother had just blamed her for what her stepfather had done. Begging her friend to let her spend the night at her house. She couldn't go back home to face those two.

"You have to take your power back," she said aloud. Exactly what Jill had said to her that night.

Chantel had stayed not only that night with Jill, but several after that, as well. Defying her parents and even the truant officer—a fake, she later found out—who came looking for her, she'd hidden in Jill's bedroom until that day her mother had visited Jill's mother, begging to see Chantel. Her mother had known where she was all along, which was why she'd never reported her missing or had the police looking for her.

That day, her mother had shown her the divorce papers she'd filed and begged her forgiveness. The ex was giving her everything—walking away with nothing—as long as no charges were filed. He still denied the whole thing.

Chantel had done what her mother asked. She'd settled with "everything" and had gone home.

"How do I do that?" Julie's pleading words broke Chantel away from the painful memories. "He took my power. And then, by signing that agreement, I gave him the rest of it."

Now wasn't the time to tell Julie that no legal agreement that took away a victim's rights to defend herself in a court of law would be binding in court. Colin would know that. It could only keep them from speaking to anyone other than an attorney, the court or other legal officer pursuant to the case.

It was Colin and Julie who'd given up on pressing charges. They still had that right. They just didn't have any evidence, any grounds against which they could file charges. Any hope of getting past a grand jury, let alone to court.

Colin would be well aware of all of that, too.

"I want to try to trap him into getting caught." Chantel knew a second of real fear when she heard herself say the words out loud. "I'm confident I can do it. But I'd need some help. And the most important part is, no one can know, including your brother. If you think you can't do it, or can't do it without telling him, I need you to be honest with me and I'll let the whole thing drop."

She wouldn't. She couldn't. But she also wasn't going to have Julie blowing her out of the water before she'd had her chance. She wasn't going to let Julie shoot herself in the foot again.

But there was the minor problem of needing help...

Shaking her head, Julie said, "I don't understand."

Of course not. How could she? "I've said as much as I'm going to until I know whether or not you can keep this to yourself. I don't want to come between you and Colin—ever. And if your loyalty needs to be with him, I understand."

"What about *your* loyalty? He really cares about you, and I thought…"

Whoa. This whole conversation had just taken a very wrong turn. "I *do* care about him!" Chantel said, infusing more truth than she wanted to know existed into the response. "More than I've ever… cared about…any man before in my life." The absolute truth.

More than she cared about Max.

She couldn't go there right then.

"But sometimes a woman just has to do things for herself," she said now, words coming to her that were completely unplanned. She tried to get back on track. "You know your brother, Julie. He's a protector. A doer. Like you said last night, he's made his whole life about keeping you safe."

"And now you, too."

"I think it's too early yet for that, but you seem pretty certain." Which was good; it would work in her favor.

And could it be true? Was she more than just a passing fling for him, in spite of the fact that she'd told him she'd be gone soon?

For a split second her heart soared.

"If Colin knew I was planning anything that involves David Smyth, he'd do everything he could to stop me," she said now.

She had to know if she had Julie's trust. For her. And then to get her to let her help with Leslie, too. Julie had admitted the night before that she knew

Leslie had been hurt. A little bit more, and she'd have Julie telling her who'd hurt Leslie. If she could help Julie believe that something good could come of breaking her friend's trust.

"He says that the only thing we can count on is that money can buy anything," Julie said softly. "The Smyths have more of it than we do."

"My plan...if it fails, will mean no one is the wiser. They won't even know we tried. If I succeed, we'll have him dead to rights in front of everyone. I just need a chance to try, and I'll need a little help behind the scenes to make it happen."

It was a damned good plan.

"I'd love a chance to show you—and show me, too—that money and brute force don't always win. That sometimes right wins. That there is justice. And that even though we're women, we can be as powerful as anyone else."

Another Jill throwback, one they'd based their lives on.

Until Jill had gone overboard and thought she could take care of everyone else, too.

Growing cold, Chantel sat there. Was she Jill? Thinking she had all the power and could save everyone?

Jill had tackled a known drug perp who'd been holding a loaded gun.

Was Chantel's plan as reckless?

No. And Jill hadn't been reckless. She'd saved

her partner's life. It was the oath they'd taken—to protect at all cost.

And Chantel would do the same.

"What's your plan?"

Once again Julie's words saved her from the craziness—the unwanted memories—that were invading her brain.

"What about Colin?"

"I won't tell him. I'm not agreeing to help, either, but I won't tell him."

"You're sure? If you don't feel good about that, let me know. It's fine. I just… I need this chance, Julie, and I wanted to offer it to you, too, but don't take it if…"

"It won't be the first secret I've kept from my brother, Chantel." Julie's words held a hint of the dry humor Chantel had glimpsed in her a time or two. Chantel wanted to meet Julie's former self, the one Colin hinted at. She nodded.

"What Smyth did to you. It probably wasn't the only time…"

"Believe me, I've thought about that."

She had the go-ahead. But she held back.

"The thing is…until I do this, there's not going to be any chance for me to pursue anything with Colin," she said, when she'd meant to begin laying out the plan. "I…can't believe how much he's come to mean to me in such a short time, but I'm not…ready…for a relationship. Not like what seems to be happening between us. Last night made that pretty clear."

She wanted to be talking Johnson rhetoric. And was afraid that she was not.

But she couldn't let any of it stop her.

"I understand." Julie actually smiled. "He can be a bit overpowering. But he's really a big pushover, once you know how to handle him."

"You feel strong when you're with him, don't you?"

Julie's nod was slow but sure. "I always have. He brings out the best in me."

And in her, too?

Was she going to lose the best thing she'd ever had—the best thing she ever would have—before she'd even had it for real?

"But I have to feel strong in myself. To have the kind of courage you do—enough to move across the country all on my own, because it's the right thing for me. Or to be able to attend a fundraiser, regardless of who's present, because I care about the cause. Without having a panic attack." She wasn't grinning now.

And so, without further soul-searching, Chantel told Julie about her plan to rewrite the script.

"The new rewrite already has the hostess, me, being a flirt and the host, Colin, being overly interested in money. Leslie had said she wanted things beefed up with more suspicion, and that seemed the obvious venue to take."

At least it must have to whomever Wayne had retained to rewrite the script.

"I plan to make a private aside or two to David Smyth early on. Enough to get him going. What I plan to add, is to have me be murdered during the evening—a surprise thing. I'll have it done in that small room upstairs that's being turned into a reserved studying room. Everyone will come up to look at the body and look for clues. I'll be lying there, dead. After we know that junior has seen me, a call will go out, gathering everyone downstairs in the main room for a big announcement. The dead bodies will remain in place, as already planned, but everyone else, including Colin, will be in the drawing room. The big announcement won't even be known to Colin. Someone will have to read it."

She'd been thinking Leslie would be good for that part.

"Before the announcement is read, all the lights in the library will go out. No one will know if that's for real or not. They'll come back on in a moment or two. My hope is that junior will take that opportunity to sneak out of the room and head back upstairs to where I'm still lying there dead. If he gets caught, he's just looking for clues." She was profiling. Deliberately taunting the rapist with a temptation that should be hard for him to resist. Counting on him to take her bait. She'd seen it happen enough to know the ploy worked more often than most would expect.

"I'll have a camera set up in the room. He comes in. Comes on to me. I tell him to get lost. He gets mad and tries to force me. Then we've got him on film. I scream. Everyone rushes upstairs to see what's going on. He gets caught," she hastened to add. "I'll scream before it gets any further than that."

Julie wasn't shaking her head. "What do you plan to do with the video?"

Julie would never believe they could go to the police with it.

"Play it right there, if I have to. I'm hoping the mob will lynch him as soon as they see what he was trying to do. At the very least, his wife will see him for what he is."

"And Colin?" The look on Julie's face was more shrewd than Chantel would have liked.

"What about him?"

"You expect him just to sit back and be content with a lynch mob when he sees the man who raped his sister going after his girlfriend?"

His girlfriend. She sat there, nonplussed. How *had* she expected Colin would react?

"You're forcing him to take action," Julie said, and Chantel couldn't tell what his sister thought of that. "You're doing this to help him, too. And that's why you don't want him to know what's going on. Not just because you know there's no way he'd ever agree to it, but because you want him to have the chance—in his own eyes—to make this right.

You know he won't refuse to go after David to the fullest extent of the law."

Maybe Johnson could have had the thought a time or two if she'd let herself bring Colin into the mix.

So was Julie going to refuse to help her, after all? Because she'd seen something Chantel hadn't been willing to look at? The fact that she was playing God, manipulating Colin into coming to terms with the past so the he could be free to embrace the future.

Or at least trust himself a little more. And not be so damned obsessive about protecting the world all by his testosterone-driven self.

"You don't have to help me," she reminded Julie, who'd picked up her fork and begun eating again.

Knowing that it would be a sin to let such great food go to waste, Chantel joined her.

"I want to help you more now than ever," Julie said over her second bite. "I'd give just about anything to be able to undo the choice Colin and I made ten years ago. Sometimes I think signing away our rights has hurt us more than the rape did."

It was going to work. She was going to be able to make this work!

"Obviously, I can be in charge of the lights going out," Julie said. "If David doesn't leave the first time, I turn them out again. The new breaker box is on the wall just outside the windows in the main room. It's not like anyone would think it strange if odd little agoraphobic Julie slips away…"

"No one calls you that."

"Not to my face." She shrugged. "Doesn't matter, anyway. What matters is finding someone to call everyone down for the announcement. And to keep them there long enough for David to do his worst."

That's where Leslie came in. If…

"That's why you asked me about Leslie last night, isn't it? Because you needed a third and she and I are close?"

"Yes." No beating around the bush.

"And you wanted to know if we could trust her to help us without saying anything to anyone."

Well, yes, but… "I was thinking, if she's been… hurt…too, then she'd be more able to go all the way with this."

"She wasn't raped, if that's what you mean."

Chantel hadn't thought she was. "But she's been physically abused."

"Yes."

And there it was.

"By who?" She asked the case-solving question. All that would be left would be getting someone to testify to the truth.

"I don't know," Julie told her.

"Have you asked?"

"Yes."

"And she won't tell you."

"She says it's best for me if I don't know."

She couldn't believe that Julie, as she now knew her, would have accepted that answer.

"You buy that? That it's best for you to not know?"

"What I think is that it wouldn't matter if I did. What I am certain of is that nothing would be done about it. That's what Leslie said, too."

"And you believe her?"

"I did until this morning."

"You think you can convince her to believe differently, too?"

"I know she'll agree to help us. What have we got to lose? The worst that can happen is that David Smyth doesn't take our bait, your mystery is solved—just make sure Colin isn't the one who did it, please—and we all go home with no one the wiser."

"Exactly. Colin can't be the one. I have to make sure I've got him well and truly occupied someplace else the entire time this is going on."

She couldn't deny his effect on her.

"I'm thinking that instead of having him in the main hall hearing the announcement with everyone else, I'll stick him in the room with the old safe in it—guarding the family riches. Guests will be able to find him there to ask him questions and he'll have preset answers to give them. Answers that will lead them to the real killer—if they pay attention, if they find a letter that will be hidden in another part of the house. And a knife that's going to be planted in a bedroom where one of the dead bodies is found."

"Who's going to be playing the original two dead bodies?"

"That's already been left to Leslie to figure out."

"She's going to help us," Julie said with an energy about her that seemed different. Or maybe just wishful thinking on Chantel's part. Maybe guilt at using the other woman, lying to her about who she was and what she was doing there, was driving her to see things that weren't there.

"She'll have no problem keeping our secret. She's had a lot of practice."

She'd left Chantel another perfect opening, one she had to take. "Who do you think is hurting her?"

"Same person her son's school thought was hurting her. Not that anyone did anything about it but sweep it under the proverbial rug. It's her husband, Chantel. It has to be."

She had confirmation of her truth.

But she wasn't nearly as happy about that as she'd thought she'd be.

CHAPTER TWENTY-SIX

COLIN DIDN'T TRUST HAPPINESS.

Chantel Johnson had swept in and nothing made sense anymore. He didn't recognize himself. He'd go out to eat. Order his usual. And think that it tasted better than he remembered. He heard himself laughing and thought it sounded strange. Julie hadn't locked herself in her room since he'd been home from Japan—almost a whole week now. He noticed the way the roses smelled when Julie had them in a vase on the table in the dining room.

Sex was...like he was still a teenager. Only a hell of a lot better at it.

And at work—he'd found himself seeing sincerity in people. Taking them at face value.

And he knew better than that.

What was worse, when he was at work, any time he was apart from Chantel, he longed for her with the stuff poems were made of.

And none of it made him happy. With every day that passed, he grew more and more uncomfortable.

If he didn't know better, he'd think he was falling in love.

In his worst moments, he knew he was.

And yet...he still didn't trust her. Not completely.

He believed in her, though. Believed she meant well and knew she had Julie's best interests at heart as she talked her sister into attending the library gala in spite of the fact that David Smyth Jr. was going to be there. He was forever indebted to her.

"You ever think about having kids?" he asked her one Monday, five days before their murder mystery debut. He'd read the script and hadn't been thrilled about the flirtiness of her character, but he'd agreed that it, coupled with his greedy obsession with the valuables locked in the safe, added greater depth to the plot—and would, therefore, make for a much more successful evening.

"Every once in a while," she said, answering his question about kids as she gazed out at the ocean.

They were on his boat—a small, fifty-foot yacht—anchored far enough offshore to be in a world of their own but close enough to be back to shore for an early night. She'd brought a bag and was staying at his place until morning. She stood at the rail on the back deck, watching the sun set.

She'd worn a jacket, as he'd advised, but only had it buttoned up halfway. Her blond hair lifted off her shoulders now and then as a small breeze picked up. Colin was pressed up against her back, holding her.

Didn't matter what the woman was doing. How she looked. Where they were. He wanted her.

Lately he'd been thinking about wanting kids with her, too.

"How about you?" She turned her head to look at him over her shoulder. "You're so good with Julie, so patient. You'd make a great dad."

He didn't think so. "I haven't given it all that much thought," he said out loud.

"Well, you must have thought of it some, since you brought it up."

They weren't drinking. While the boat was fully engine equipped, it was also valuable and always prey to the whims of the ocean. He didn't consume alcohol when he was captaining it.

"I guess I have thought about it," he said now. Dusk had fallen. "Just never in terms of doing something about it."

As though he was thinking about it now? They were spending pretty much every night together— though sometimes not meeting up until late—but that was because their time was limited. She'd be leaving. Why was he talking about kids as though they had some kind of future together?

Because he wanted one?

He'd told himself, in the beginning, that he'd cross that bridge when they came to it.

Surely he wasn't thinking they'd come to it.

His thoughts skittered through the night. Bouncing off the truths he wasn't ready to see?

"I don't think I'd be good at parenting," he told

her. Just so she'd know he wasn't moving in that direction on purpose.

"You'd be great at it," she told him without hesitation. Which made him a bit angry. For no good reason.

"I'm always going to see danger and do whatever it takes to prevent it from happening. To their detriment."

It's what he'd done with Julie. Instead of building her up, giving her the strength to face a tough court battle, he'd agreed to take the safest way out and sign those damned papers.

"A parent's job is to see the dangers and prevent them," she said with a note of bitterness to her voice that he hadn't heard before.

And he thought about what Julie had said about the night the two of them had spent together. About how Chantel had cried over the death of her friend.

But what would that have to do with parents?

"You sound as though you're speaking from experience."

He'd tried, several times, to talk to her about that night she'd spent with Julie. She'd distracted him with sex. Every single time.

And he'd let her.

Because…they were only together for a while. She was leaving.

Even though he wasn't happy feeling out of control, these had been the happiest weeks of his life…

"My stepfather tried to have sex with me when I was fourteen."

The words fell so baldly, so unemotionally, on the wind, he was left feeling as though he was watching from afar. Seeing a woman in a movie.

Until he felt the rage. The need to find the guy and wrap his fingers around his neck…

"You said 'tried.'" He focused on the facts.

"He came into my room and pulled me up out of my desk chair. It wasn't late, but my mother had a migraine and was in their room, asleep."

Money, privilege, didn't mean safety. It didn't mean trust. To the contrary. Money gave you the power to do whatever you wanted and get away with it.

He hadn't realized her parents were divorced or that her mother had remarried.

And didn't like the feeling of not knowing such an elemental thing about her. Even after their almost four weeks together.

He couldn't stand there and let an unknown man walk into fourteen-year-old Chantel's room and do nothing about it. He wasn't made that way…

"I tried to scream, but he had his hand over my mouth before I could get more than a squeak out. He ripped my blouse open."

She was facing the ocean. Colin wanted to pull her more tightly to him, to keep her safe from the evil that lurked everywhere, but he let his arms drop as he stepped up to the rail beside her.

He understood now why she was able to reach Julie when he could not. They were kindred souls.

And he felt helpless again. As helpless as he'd felt the night his baby sister came home to him completely broken.

"He grabbed me. And it hurt," Chantel said in that same strong monotone. "He turned me around and told me what he was going to do to me. I've never been as angry as I was in that minute." She turned her head to look at him. "I didn't think, I just spun around so fast he lost his grip. I hurled my knee up as hard as I could and ran for my mother."

There was more. He could see it in her eyes. "Mom didn't believe me at first. Not until I didn't come home for days and the bastard showed no signs of caring that I was gone. Then she realized that when he'd told her I'd hit on him, he'd been the one who was lying. She'd believed him at first. Believed that I'd hit on him. You'd never betray your child, Colin. You'd be a parent your child could always count on. In the end, that's all that matters."

He wasn't sure she was right—that protection was all that mattered—but he wanted to believe she was.

Wanted everything about her to be true. Including his love for her.

SHE HAD TO get out. The words were a litany to Chantel as she worked her shifts Tuesday and Wednesday. The stuff with her stepfather...she couldn't believe she'd told Colin. Couldn't believe she actually remembered in such detail. Or that she felt so...strongly...about it.

She and Daniel were on days through Thursday. She had Friday, Saturday and Sunday off. Long enough to get through the gala.

Have a day to deal with the fallout.

And be back to work on Monday.

Her time with Colin was coming to a close one way or another. Whether she and Julie and Leslie were successful Saturday night or not, she couldn't keep pretending.

She'd never told anyone, not even Jill, the full extent of what had happened that night in her bedroom—how close she'd come to being another statistic. Why in the hell she'd poured it all out to Colin, she had no idea.

They'd been on his boat for a romantic dinner. But his talk about not being a good dad had reminded her what Julie had said about saving Colin from himself by giving him a chance to put Smyth away instead of signing away his right to do so.

She'd had to show him what a bad parent looked like. He didn't bear even the remotest resemblance.

They'd had dinner. And sex.

Later that night, after sharing a nightcap with Julie, they'd made love again, in his bed. She'd fallen asleep in his arms.

She hadn't woken up once all night long.

She was in too deep.

She'd awoken the next morning, had breakfast with Julie and Colin and then rushed to the resort to switch cars and get home to her apartment to scrub off the makeup, get her hair up into its ponytail, don old jeans and her work boots and get to the station.

She'd told Wayne that she had confirmation that Morrison was beating his wife. And had come clean with him about the news she'd heard from Max and discussed the plan that was in place for Saturday night.

He didn't like her involving Leslie and Julie—two untrained civilians, not to mention victims—but when she'd remained adamant to the good it would do both of them to regain some personal honor, as well as the fact that there was no way anyone from outside their society was going to gain entrance that night without raising questions that could sabotage the entire operation—even the caterer was family—he'd finally conceded.

And, as she pointed out, if the plan worked, two hundred or more people, including the police commissioner, would be present.

And if it didn't, no one except the four of them would know there'd even been a plan.

In the meantime, working so closely with Leslie was exactly what she'd been aiming for before beginning the undercover assignment. She was winning Leslie's trust. If they were successful in bringing Smyth to justice, then she had every hope of convincing Leslie to trust the system to bring justice to her husband, as well.

If it didn't, she and Leslie would have forged the friendship she needed to get inside the woman's house, into her home life and find the evidence she needed to make it happen.

It was all coming to a head. And then a close.

She told herself she was glad.

CHAPTER TWENTY-SEVEN

DINNER WAS BEING served at round tables set for six in the main lobby of the new Santa Raquel Public Library. Linen tablecloths, fresh flowers, Waterford china and sterling silver were all part of the gala affair.

Chafing dishes were on every table, allowing the patrons to serve themselves.

An hour before the doors would open, Colin surveyed the room. Everything looked perfect.

Julie and Leslie were in a room upstairs with Chantel, helping her get into costume. Some sexy outfit he had yet to see.

He'd dressed down for the evening in an old tweed jacket borrowed from a college theater department—so he'd been told—and brown pants bought off the rack and not tailored to his form. He was ready to play the part of down-on-his-luck, avaricious and greedy heir to the castle.

His sister came downstairs first.

"You look beautiful," he told her, watching as she came toward him, her head held high. In a dark blue, strapless gown that hugged her slimness, she was wearing a diamond brooch their mother had left her.

"I *feel* beautiful."

He didn't know that he'd ever heard her say such a thing. But he was more and more open to the surprises she had in store for him.

A seventeen-year-old-kid had left him. He was eager to get to know the twenty-seven-year-old woman who was emerging.

"Leslie will be down in a minute," she told him. "She and Chantel had some last-minute things to go over."

"That surprise twist you three have been planning," he said, grinning. They'd been like giddy kids, plotting to take their guests by surprise. They'd insisted that he be kept in the dark as well, because it played into the evening's unraveling.

He knew who'd "done it," of course. Just not exactly how the winner was going to reach that conclusion. There were several possible ways. The beauty of the evening was that no one would know until it happened.

Much like his own life was turning out. He didn't know until it happened what was coming, but he was beginning to look forward to the possibilities.

"I'm thinking about asking Chantel to marry me." He didn't need Julie's permission. Nor did he doubt her approval.

He was just caught up in her smile. In the miracle of having Julie fully alive again, even if just in bits and pieces. In the knowledge that Chantel would be sleeping in his bed that night.

And wanting her place there to be permanent.

He was embracing the concept of trust, if not fully indulging in it himself.

"What do you think?" he asked his little sister, who was standing there gaping at him.

"I… Not before tonight's performance, right?" she asked. Inanely, he thought. It wasn't like anything more than money rested on the night's entertainment. The real event taking place was Julie's first face-to-face appearance with David Smyth. And Leslie and Chantel's support that was going to be with her all the way.

"Of course not before tonight's performance," he told her with a grin. And then, when understanding dawned, he added, "I'm not going to distract your new best friend away from you when you need her most. Or any time you need her."

"Maybe you should sometime." Her response was more of the completely unexpected.

"What does that mean?"

"I mean that if you're going to spend your whole life putting me first, not only above yourself but above anyone you fall in love with, you're probably not going to be as happy as you deserve to be."

Where had that come from?

"Did Chantel…?"

"No!" Julie interrupted him. "She didn't. I have eyes, Colin. Not only that, I've been at the other end of your unblinking ones for ten years. Let me go, just a little. It's not only okay, it's healthy. That's all I'm saying."

He nodded. Said okay. But he didn't understand. Not really.

The way things had been going lately, he wasn't sure he would ever again have complete understanding. Of anything.

CHANTEL HAD THE seating chart memorized. She and Colin had already eaten and were in place at the front door, greeting everyone who came in, giving them their first clues for the evening. And directing them toward their tables. Julie would be seated with Leslie and her husband toward the front of the room. The Smyths, who were at the commissioner's table, were on the opposite side of the room, toward the back.

She and Wayne still didn't know how deeply involved the commissioner was with the David Smyth cover-up, but they had determined that, with Chantel's plan, it didn't much matter. That was the beauty of it. Even if he was in over his head, he'd still have to hold the man until he was arrested if he was caught molesting a woman in front of their entire crowd.

Most particularly since he'd know that the woman in question was one of his own.

But if he wasn't in that deep, if he was the man she'd honored and respected above all else this past year, then he would not only help her take down Smyth Jr. but by so doing should be able to help her convince Leslie to come forward and tell the truth about what her husband was doing to her. Help her see that at some point James Morrison was most likely going to turn his fists on their son, too.

"You as ready as I am for this to be finished?" Colin leaned over to whisper after he'd given a long spiel about the pure gold pen and pencil set that were among all of the things he was soon to inherit.

Batting her eyes at him, Chantel leaned forward far enough for him to see down the cleavage of her low-cut, short black dress and whispered back. "I'm ready to see if that gold pen of yours means as much to you as this does."

She was playing a part. And nervous as hell.

The Smyths had yet to arrive. He'd seen them many times over the years, spoken to them, treated them cordially, but that didn't mean he'd be happy about introducing them to Chantel. She got that.

Brett Ackerman, founder of The Lemonade Stand—the unique women's shelter that had provided Meri with a safe haven during the weeks she'd been on the run—was going to be there that night with his wife, Ella, the charge nurse in the neonatal intensive care unit at the new Santa Raquel Children's Hospital. They hadn't been sure they'd be able to make it because Ella was expecting their first child any minute, but she'd been adamant that if she hadn't delivered yet, she wanted to be there.

A member of the High Risk team herself, she was on sabbatical from it only until after her son was born.

Though they knew nothing of the evening's operation, they knew Chantel was undercover on a missive from the team. And, as they greeted her as if just meeting her for the first time, they managed to give her hand an extra squeeze.

Their presence calmed nerves she hadn't expected to have or planned for.

She'd have liked to have had Max and Meri there. Unfortunately, they weren't in the multimillionaire league.

As it turned out, the meeting between her and both David Smyth Jr. and Sr. was mostly uneventful. They'd come in with at least ten other people directly in front of them, and Colin was busy with the first few couples when the Smyths walked past his little grouping to seek her out.

Deliberately avoiding him? Probably.

She was glad they'd shown him the respect of letting him know he intimidated them that much.

She played her part with the father, making a comment about how handsome he looked that evening.

When David took her hand, holding it a bit longer than his father had, she leaned forward and whispered in his ear, telling him, in the obviously made-up accent she'd adopted for her character that evening, that he was exactly what she'd go for if she were free to go.

He looked surprised. And then grinned. She grinned right back.

She knew that he was taking her bait.

LESLIE GAVE THE official start to the evening as soon as the last guests had arrived. With a little over two hundred people in the room, she was using a PA system and, in an impressively dramatic voice, informed everyone that just that afternoon, when they'd come to prepare for the evening's entertainment, two bodies had been found on the premises—one in a bedroom and one elsewhere. She asked for everybody's help in finding the murderer or murderers. She gave an official introduction to Chantel and Colin, the alleged heirs to the mansion, followed by a few guidelines that would rule the evening.

A reward was being offered to the first person or persons who solved the crime—an exotic vacation for two.

Over dinner, Colin and Chantel made their way around the room, leaning over to whisper things in their guests' ears. Clues—some true, some completely bogus—for each one alone. It was up to them if they shared information among themselves. The evening would likely end sooner if they did, but she and Colin were careful to not give too many different clues to anyone sitting at the same table.

Since Julie and Leslie had been in charge of assigning seats based on who would be more likely to pair up, they were pretty safe in their dissemination. No two people got the same information.

Chantel had offered to take the Smyth table. She hit the commissioner up first. The secret she gave him was that she hoped he enjoyed his evening. She was a little nervous about the operation she was conducting that evening without his knowledge.

Moving around the table, she took more time with all of the men than she did with the ladies. And told David Smyth that she hoped she'd see him upstairs, alone, later.

She had a similar message for the other tables. That she'd like to see someone upstairs later. She told men at some tables, women at others.

Entrapment wasn't going to be an out for Smyth. She was going to have him dead to rights, in front of everyone he knew. An entire society would have to turn a blind eye to his criminal activities this time.

She'd had a call from Wayne that afternoon. He was busy trying to track down other Smyth victims, talking to people who worked in the emergency room and researching known associates for anything that raised a flag. They had no idea who Max's informant was and had no warrant to otherwise access emergency room information, and so far he'd had no luck but she was confident that once Smyth got caught, others would come forward.

Her stomach was in knots as she and Colin helped the caterers deliver dessert trays to each of the thirty-four tables. As soon as the guests rose to start their sleuthing around the mansion, she had to head upstairs. Her murder was going to be one of the first things on the agenda. They couldn't take a chance that someone would solve the mystery before the night's events had a chance to play out.

Nor did they want everyone dispersed before Leslie could make the announcement that there'd been another death upstairs, telling everyone they might want to view that crime scene, as well. She wasn't going to say who'd been killed. There'd been some changes to her original plan, but she was still satisfied that it would work.

This was at Chantel's insistence, with Wayne's input, to avoid any hint of entrapment.

Colin was bound to hear about it—as guests visited him in the study with the safe. Which was why he'd been told that there was a surprise twist to the evening.

Confident that the plan was going to work, that they'd thought of and arranged for every eventuality, Chantel made her way upstairs as soon as she'd delivered her last dessert tray.

She'd chosen the room with care. It was far enough away from the night's events, from any other clues, to give Smyth the feeling of safety. Yet had an old antique air duct and heating register that would allow her voice to travel, and be heard, when she screamed. The room was empty—as were most of the upstairs rooms. Pulling her gun from her thigh holster, cocking it to put a bullet in the chamber so it was ready to go, she put it back.

She was overreacting. She knew that. Smyth's only violence happened when his victims were nearly comatose. He was a coward. She could take him hand-to-hand.

But she was a cop on assignment. And always had a gun with her.

Even in the hotel room with Colin. And at his house. Tucked away in a compartment at the bottom of her cosmetic bag when she couldn't wear it on her person.

The room was good. The camera in place. The gun was good.

Pulling up her skirt a little, she lay down and opened her mouth.

And then remembered that she'd forgotten to pop the packet of fake blood Leslie had brought for her with the rest of the props from the community college theater department.

Sitting up, she grabbed it from just inside her holster and squirted a bit on her thigh and chest. What was left, she sprayed on the newly laid laminate wood floor.

And then, as preplanned, she screamed.

CHAPTER TWENTY-EIGHT

COLIN PLAYED HIS PART. But as thirty minutes passed, as more people visited him, clearly enjoying themselves, when he should have felt satisfaction that the work was paying off, that the venture was successful and the library would be certain to receive over and above the projected donations, he grew increasingly unsettled.

Chantel had been murdered. That was the big secret. From what he'd heard, there'd been a scream and then Leslie had called them all together in the main room to make the announcement. He didn't understand how the maneuver added anything to the night's adventure. Were people supposed to think that whoever had killed the first two perps was still among them?

Still murdering?

He didn't like it. Too much tension could result in panic.

Instinct told him to leave his post immediately. To investigate.

His new outlook on life urged him to take a deep breath. To trust the women in his life to know what they were doing. Julie and Chantel were both writers.

Who was he to question artistic license?

When David Smyth Sr. entered his room, he was ready to bolt and kick ass. Not necessarily in that order.

The elder Smyth was traveling the mansion with his wife, along with Paul and Patricia Reynolds, but entered the room alone as the other three were stopped by mutual friends just outside the door of the study.

"I'm glad I have a minute alone with you, son," said the man who'd once been his father's best friend.

"Don't call me son." Colin wanted to take the words back the second they were uttered. He was exposing himself. Something he'd sworn he would never do in front of that man.

Smyth bowed his head. "I apologize."

What kind of game was the bastard playing?

"I just wanted to tell you that you've found a good woman. That I know your father would approve. That I miss him every day of my life. And I regret every day of my life the position my son put me in. I hope that someday, when you have children of your own, you'll understand."

Feeling the pulse beat at his temple, in time with the heat suffusing his entire head, Colin gritted his teeth.

"I was glad to see your sister here tonight. I can't tell you the number of nights I walk my house, unable to sleep, with her pain on my conscience."

Colin wanted to tell the man to rot in his hell. He thought he might have, but the others joined him before he got the words out of his clenched jaws.

Then he just played his part.

As always. He could count on himself for that.

CHANTEL HAD NO idea how two hundred people, in twos and fives, could all visit a room, gape at a prone body on the floor, look around at the rest of the nothingness and be gone within half an hour.

What she did know was that as she lay there, peering at them all through the arm she'd thrown over her eyes—to give her a way to observe surreptitiously—was that David Smyth Jr. had had a gleam in his eye as he'd stood with his wife, listening to her chatter about the evidence in the room. The two of them had been traveling alone, and at first, Chantel had worried that her plan was going to fail. If David's wife had no one else to talk to, he might not come up here alone...

But then another couple joined them. A woman David's wife was obviously fond of. When the woman, her husband and David's wife all left the room, he paused, stared at her thigh and she knew that her plan was going to succeed. Because David Smyth Jr. wanted it to. She'd issued her invitation earlier, and he would have found a way to keep it even if she hadn't made it easy for him.

Video chip was on and in place. The cop was on duty.

And justice would be done.

THREE PEOPLE WERE in the room with Colin when the lights went out. He'd been told to expect the moment, and he played along—pretending to be alarmed, wondering what was going on. The idea to lose the lights, momentarily, had been Julie's— to add suspense to the evening.

He hadn't been sure of causing panic in the dark, but when Chantel and Leslie had agreed with Julie, he'd gone along with it. He'd do just about anything to encourage Julie's self-confidence. She was there. Taking part.

Thankful for the miracle, he made certain to instill calm in the three people he had with him and hoped to hell the evening's guests played along as expected.

Commissioner Reynolds was there. While Colin had no personal respect for the man, he did believe he was a great cop who wouldn't want mayhem and panic to break out among his peers. Colin could always hope that the man's presence would invite a feeling of safety among the guests.

But he didn't like being trapped in one room. Didn't like Chantel and Julie out among the masses—masses that included the Smyth family—without him. He wasn't comfortable sitting in the dark doing nothing.

And he most definitely wanted the evening done.

THE LIGHTS WENT OUT. Chantel lay in the dark. On full alert.

She couldn't stop Junior from anything he might do until the lights came on and the camera caught him in the act, couldn't render her second scream until everyone could see well enough to rush up and find out what was going on.

Until she heard enough people milling around outside her door to know there would be enough of a crowd finding him in the act to raise enough of a stink that more of them would come to see for themselves what scandal was taking place.

She wasn't particularly a friend of the dark. She liked sitcoms to share the dark with her.

She waited.

No one came to her room.

No one was there.

And the lights turned back on.

Shit.

Where in the hell was he?

The scumbag had to act true to character. Just one more time.

She was not going to let him get away.

The lights went out again.

And Chantel willed the monster to come find her.

THE SECOND TIME the lights went out Colin went for the door. Six people were in the hallway, five were in his room.

Most were chatting. About who done it. And about their kids, too.

He was overreacting, thinking only he could save the day.

Julie's words from earlier that evening came back to him.

I've been at the other end of your unblinking eyes for ten years. Let me go, just a little. It's not only okay, it's healthy. That's all I'm saying...

He'd been holding his sister captive with his need to protect her. He'd let her go to a party, and she'd been raped. But he had to let her do this. And Chantel, too.

So he tried, but he wondered if maybe, just maybe, she had it all wrong.

SHE HEARD THE door shut before she realized she wasn't alone. He was one-up on her. She couldn't afford a second.

Her gun between her thighs was small comfort. Shooting Smyth would get her nothing but charged with attempted murder. Or, more likely, murder. Because if she shot she wasn't going to miss.

She had no way of knowing for sure that it was Smyth who'd joined her. In the dark, the small peephole she had in the crook of her arm gave her nothing.

And then she smelled it. The same musky cinnamon smell he'd reeked of when she'd first met him that evening. She was never going to like cologne again. Or maybe she'd love it, because it gave her the impetus she needed.

She was going to get this man. Put him down. For life.

For all of the lives he'd taken…

"Finally, I've got you all to myself," he murmured. If she hadn't already recognized his scent, she'd have known his voice.

While her skin crawled, or maybe Johnson's skin did, Chantel welcomed the adrenaline that surged through her.

"You know I'm not really dead," she said, losing the high-pitched ditzy voice she'd used earlier in the evening.

"Of course. You want a drink? I brought one for me, too."

He handed her the glass in the dark. Sitting up, Chantel took it. "What is it?" she asked. Because a reasonable woman would.

"Drink it, you'll like it," he told her.

She pretended to sip, then tipped the glass under her arm, letting enough of the liquid drip to the floor.

Thanks to Max, she knew what was in her glass. The mixture that Smyth could find in any bar and that, with a simple aspirin added, would render her incapable of fighting him but keep her conscious enough to remember every single thing he did to her.

Just as Julie remembered. And every one of his other victims did.

Because David Smyth Jr. was not only a rapist, he was one who needed to know that his women remembered him and knew that they couldn't beat him.

He wasn't going to touch her until he thought she'd had enough of the drink to serve his purpose.

Julie would be turning on the lights again any second.

"Drink," he said. He was close now. Too close. He'd see her if she didn't sip.

Desperate, she pulled down the top of her dress. Bending forward, she emptied the glass. And lifted herself up, exposing herself to the fiend's gluttonous gaze.

"All done," she said, slurring her words just enough to give him pause. She dropped her glass. It didn't spill a drop.

"Come to Papa…" Junior's voice sounded victorious, and Chantel braced herself for his touch.

Come on, Julie. Turn on the lights.

His hand planted itself on her exposed breast. Chantel moved lethargically. Fell down to the floor and rolled over onto her stomach. She couldn't let him that close again. No one touched her breasts without her permission.

Ever.

She couldn't let him find her gun.

Her mind knew. Her body felt a little...weak. He'd touched her. Intimately. Roughly. As her stepfather had. She knew the touch of a man intent on rape.

And she was afraid of what she'd done.

LEAVING GUESTS WITH their mouths open, Colin pushed past them and into the main room, looking for Julie, and Chantel and Leslie. This had to stop.

Money for the library be damned.

Lights out with Smyths in the house was not acceptable. He wouldn't put it past Smyth Jr. to have turned them off himself.

He couldn't find his sister. Or Chantel.

He knew the worst had happened.

He was going to kill him.

Shoving a couple of his clients and their wives out of the way, he headed for the main room, the podium where Leslie had announced the unexpected murder. She had to be close by.

No one was there.

Just as he was turning to leave, he heard her voice—or thought it was her voice.

She sounded drunk. Her freneticism fueled his, and he stormed forward into the room off from the dining area—the room where the caterers had set up for the evening.

"Oh, God, James, I've made a horrible mistake.

I let Julie go out there and now she hasn't come back. The lights aren't back on and…"

"Leslie." The voice was harsh.

"It's him, James. Chantel…she set a trap…for Julie's sake…but it's him. For me, too."

Colin was close enough to see them now. Leslie, like a rag doll, being held up by the upper arms in her husband's hands.

"What do you mean, for you, too? Who are we talking about? Leslie, talk to me."

Morrison shook her so hard Colin felt his own teeth rattle.

He thought of the rumors he'd heard. About James hurting his wife.

"David Smyth Jr.," Leslie said. "He's the one who hurt me. He raped me, James. He was a kid. Told me he needed a ride…my dad knew his dad. I believed him. And he raped me…"

Colin froze. He knew Smyth had to be stopped. It wasn't just Julie; it wasn't a one-time thing that got out of control because of the alcohol like everyone had said.

"I'm so sorry I didn't tell you, but I couldn't, don't you see? What it would have done to you to not be able to do anything about it. And then he… poor Julie. It's my fault, James. All my fault. I was afraid to say anything, and then he hurt Julie, too."

Leslie was slumping down to the floor, in spite of James's attempt to hold her up. Colin's gut wrenched for the woman, for his friend, but he couldn't help them. Not then.

"Where is he?" he demanded, not recognizing the harsh tone of his voice. He had to get whatever he could out of Leslie before she became completely hysterical. Or passed out.

She must have been drinking. The pressure, knowing Julie and Smyth were going to be together that night, had gotten to her...

"She was supposed to scream," Leslie said. Which made no sense.

"Where's Julie?" Colin was upon them now, his hand at Leslie's back as she crumpled against her husband, who'd slid down to the floor with her.

"It's not Julie. It's Chantel."

"I'm right here, Colin." Julie's voice sounded behind him. "I tried to get the breaker back on, but it's stuck..."

"Where's Chantel?" he barked like a madman.

"Upstairs. I'll take you." Julie grabbed his hand, glancing back at Leslie with James. "Get the lights," she said just as a soul-destroying, nerve-breaking scream rent the air. Coming from upstairs.

Julie said something. It sounded like, "Oh, good." And then, "Hurry."

Colin ran.

CHAPTER TWENTY-NINE

CHANTEL HADN'T WANTED to scream so soon. But she wasn't going to be raped for the job. Why the lights didn't come back on, she didn't know. The chances of the camera she'd planted along the floorboards getting enough footage in the dark were slim.

But she couldn't let it go this far.

Smyth had his hands on her. Running them along her sides. Groping her.

She moved away, fought him, and he smacked her down to the floor. She hit her head. But she kept her legs squeezed shut against her gun. She didn't have enough evidence to end this yet. Not until someone saw them.

He'd covered her mouth when she'd screamed and now was talking. Dirty talk, like when she was fourteen. Her mind started to freeze him out. Freeze *them* out. To shut down. She had to hold it together. Hone in on her goal. He thought the scream was all part of the night's acting, that Leslie was calling another meeting downstairs. He thought that gave him time.

It excited him—all the murder-mystery tension. He was telling her what he was going to do to her.

Her video chip might not be getting picture, but it would record sound.

She asked him, in a perfectly calm tone, if he knew how to do the things he was saying he was going to do. Told him he was nothing more than a daddy's boy who wished he were a man. She laughed at him.

The effort sent a sharp pain through her head.

Nearly slobbering with his disgusting passion, he told her about another night, another woman, as he continued to squeeze her butt. He told her she'd know soon enough that she didn't get to choose whether or not she allowed him to do what he said he was going to do. He was going to show her.

He gave her details. She remembered a desperate spin around, a fourteen-year-old knee that fate had placed in just the right spot for her...

Sound was good.

Like the sound coming from outside the room—footsteps storming up the stairs, voices in the hall asking what was going on.

More footsteps.

And just after the door burst open, the lights came back on.

"Get up, you bastard. I'm going to kill your sorry ass." Colin burst into the room, reaching for Junior.

Telling the video he was going to be a murderer.

Not Colin. He was the good guy.

Still thinking about that, Chantel realized that David Smyth Jr. was reaching for his ankle. Recognized the holster beneath his raised pant leg. He had a gun! She'd miscalculated.

"Police! Freeze!" she said, all Harris as she sprang up, dizzy but capable, grabbing her gun and running straight into Colin, knocking him back just as she got a shot off.

Junior's gun fell to the floor.

And so did Chantel.

"You were amazing."

Colin heard his sister gushing. Didn't disagree with her.

But he couldn't look at the woman she was talking to, either.

Police! Freeze! As if in a bad movie, the moment kept replaying itself in his mind. Chantel was a *cop*?

A cop!

One who'd shoved him aside like he was of no consequence and then shot at another human being.

A cop. Who worked for Commissioner Reynolds.

A cop. And a liar.

She'd betrayed him—worked him—knowing that he was a man who didn't trust easily.

"I can't believe you're really a cop…" Julie had said the words half a dozen times at least. In a far different echo than Colin's thoughts were repeating them. "Even with a head injury, you pulled your gun—I can't believe you had a gun strapped on beneath that dress you were wearing—and shot his hand before he could pull the trigger. Colin would have been dead…"

Julie's voice broke again. She'd been crying on and off for the past hour. Reliving the night, and another night, as well. Ridding herself of years' worth of pent-up anguish, Colin figured.

"I just did my job." Chantel's words were slightly slurred. And not at all cultured. She'd been given something to help with her headache. They'd taken her straight in for tests the second the ambulance had arrived and already had the results back. There were no brain bleeds. The swelling was only surface. Other than a mammoth headache, she was going to be fine.

"I'm sorry I had to lie to you. To both of you. I had to do my job."

He got the message, whether Julie did or not.

She hadn't been in love with him; he'd been part of the job.

Even as he had the thought, Colin recognized that it wasn't completely true. But he clung to it, anyway. Because he could.

Because it was easier.

She's a cop!

Chantel…Harris, he now knew, was in a hospital bed. Just for the night. Under direct order from Commissioner Reynolds. Her boss.

She was being held for observation.

He still couldn't believe she'd planned the whole thing. The woman who'd lain so sweetly in his bed over the past weeks had purposely put herself alone in a room with Julie's rapist.

To avenge his sister and all women like her. Because it was her job to do so. She was a cop.

Her intelligence had missed the fact that Leslie Morrison had been one of Smyth's victims, though. And apparently the fact that Junior wore a loaded ankle holster.

And then there'd been the breaker glitch. Old breakers had a tendency to stick or snap. Thankfully, the one at the old Estrada mansion had merely stuck. As soon as James had reached the breaker box, he'd managed to get the lights back on in the building.

"I understand why you lied," Julie said, holding Chantel's hand from the side of her bed where she'd been sitting for the past fifteen minutes. "You had a job to do. Besides, you were just there to help Leslie. What you did for me...you didn't have to. You did that because you cared. How could I possibly be upset about that?"

His sister didn't get it. Chantel had played them both. Used them both. In order to help them.

Because it was her job. Didn't have to mean she'd cared.

She'd gone to bed with him.

For the job?

Women did it all the time.

She'd shoved him aside like a sack of potatoes and saved his life.

Not that he wasn't perfectly capable of having saved it himself...

He'd been thinking about asking her to marry him before she finished her book and had to leave.

She wasn't a writer.

She wasn't leaving.

She's a cop!

Colin was content to have Julie there—sitting with...the cop. It kept him from having to step up. Or sit closer. His sister seemed to have taken her life back.

And was certainly taking the night's events in stride. But then, she'd had a heads-up on most of it.

Except the part where the woman they'd taken into their confidence, their home, had been an undercover cop. Playing a part.

But Julie was better. She'd faced Smyth and survived. She'd had the satisfaction of watching him be put in handcuffs.

He had his sister back, which made all of the confusion and betrayal worth it to Colin. He just couldn't pretend to have personal feelings for the stranger in the hospital bed.

"How's Leslie?" Chantel asked, looking over Julie's shoulder to where he was sitting against the wall. "Did I hear that James called?"

"He did. The doctor's been to see her, and she's sedated. But James seemed to think that she was going to be fine. Better than fine. He thinks that tonight was a turning point for her."

Chantel nodded.

"I feel horrible thinking that he was the one who was hurting her," Julie said. Colin had told her about Leslie's self-sabotaging accidents.

"I thought so, too," Chantel told her, her eyes drifting shut. Colin was glad to know that she'd been wrong about something.

And that he'd been right all along.

LIKING THE TOUCH of Julie's hand against hers, Chantel drifted in and out a little bit. It had been a long night. Much more tense than she'd expected as she'd lain there alone in the darkened room and knew that the entire operation was up to her.

And that no one had her back.

She'd been in danger before. Risked her life before. She'd witnessed death and destruction, blood and horrible tragedy. She'd pulled mangled bodies out of smashed cars.

But lying there, knowing that if something happened to her, Colin would never forgive himself—because she was there to help his sister and because he seemed to blame himself for everything that happened to anyone he cared about—she'd had a moment when she'd wanted to stop the whole thing.

He hadn't looked at her since she'd declared herself just before shooting the gun out of Junior's hand.

She'd known she was going to lose him.

She just hadn't realized how badly it was going

to hurt. How could you hurt over something you'd never had to begin with?

Colin had been falling in love with Johnson. Not Harris.

Her door opened. Probably someone else coming in to draw blood or look in her eyes, check the machine holding her IV drip or...

She looked up to tell whoever it was that she was fine, that she didn't need anything and would probably get more rest at home if they'd just let her out of there....

"I told Wayne not to call you," she said, looking at the ashen face of her best friend in the world.

"I knew better," a voice said from behind Max. *Wayne.*

"After all we went through." Meri's voice came next, softly, as she followed her husband and Wayne through the door. "We're a team. Family," she said. "Of course he'd call us."

Aware of Julie's fingers leaving hers, Chantel sat forward to return Meri's hug and Max's. Wayne gave her a soft punch on the shoulder.

"If I'd known what you were planning to do, I'd never have helped you," Max said, frowning down at her.

"Yes, you would have," she told him, all trace of Johnson's highfalutin tone gone now. "And as you can see, I'm perfectly fine."

She loved that they were there. But she wanted

them gone. Colin was standing now, and she didn't want him to leave.

Meri turned as Chantel looked in Colin's direction. "Oh!" she said, as though just noticing him. Julie had already left Chantel's side by the time Meri had made it into the room.

"Colin, Julie, this is Max, Meri and, in case you didn't figure it out, my partner on this assignment, Detective Wayne Stanton. Everyone, meet Colin and Julie Fairbanks."

The guys shook hands. Politeness all around. Meri took Julie's hand in between both of hers. "I heard you helped Chantel tonight…"

Meri wouldn't have been told about Julie's rape. That was all yet to come. What was going to be done about Smyth's past crimes.

"Max and Meri are my closest friends," she said, looking directly at Colin. She wanted him to care. To look at her real life and have it matter to him.

He nodded politely, looking toward the door.

"He's a pediatrician," she continued and added, "His first wife was my best friend, Jill."

Julie came forward, took a seat on the end of Chantel's bed. Claiming ownership? Chantel wanted to think so. But knew she wasn't thinking all that clearly. "The friend you told me about? Who was murdered?"

She nodded. And hoped Julie wouldn't blame her for the parts she'd left out.

"And you were there?"

The fact that Julie asked the question told her she didn't know what to believe. What parts of what Chantel had told her were true. "Of course. Everything I told you about that day was true. I just didn't tell you I was in uniform. Or that Jill had lunged for the guy with the gun because he was about to shoot her partner."

Colin visibly pulled back, and she knew she'd lost him. She could have withheld that last detail. But there was going to be no more hiding.

She wasn't good at it.

And he didn't deserve it.

"You said you all became family over what happened," Julie said then, looking at Wayne and Meri and Max, who were all standing on the opposite side of her bed, between her and the door.

Colin remained standing in the corner—clearly ready to go. But he wouldn't leave without Julie.

Meri smiled and nodded at Julie. "My ex-husband, who was a former Las Vegas detective, was after me. I had to leave Max and our young son to protect them from him."

"She went rogue and thought she could take on the fiend on her own," Chantel said drily, laying her head back against the pillow as it grew heavier.

"Max knew, though," Meri said, and the look she gave her husband cut through to Chantel's heart again. As it had the day they'd been in that same hospital, with Meri in the bed, after they'd found her stumbling half-dead outside the home where her ex-husband had beaten her. "He called Chantel, who called Wayne, and the three of them didn't give up until they found me."

Glancing at Colin, Chantel looked for any sign that he was proud of her, that he cared at all.

He was studying Max. And Wayne.

"Is Maria with the kids?" Chantel asked, referring to Wayne's wife. It had to be close to midnight.

"Yes, and we aren't going to stay long," Max said with a glance over his shoulder, and then a raised eyebrow to Chantel.

"Not now that we know you aren't here alone," Meri added and with a grin turned to include Colin. "I understand now why you were asking me all those questions when you were over for dinner..."

Questions about being two people at once. About keeping her distance. Keeping her life straight.

"Chantel and my brother are seeing each other," Julie said, her chin in the air. But she wasn't looking at Chantel's guests. She was looking straight at Colin.

He excused himself and left the room.

CHAPTER THIRTY

COLIN WAS ON the golf course Sunday morning when Julie texted him to let him know that she was headed to the hospital to get Chantel and take her home.

He thanked her for letting him know. Because he always liked to know where she was. And then concentrated on his shot. Focused. Kept his eye on the ball. Swung.

And took a penalty for hitting it in the water.

JULIE CHATTERED ALL the way home from the hospital. She explained that Colin wanted to be there to pick up Chantel, too, but that he'd had a business meeting he couldn't avoid.

He was playing golf. He'd already told Chantel about the game he'd scheduled with a business owner he was courting for the firm.

Even if things had been good between them, she wouldn't have expected him to cancel. She was perfectly fine. She shouldn't even have stayed at the hospital overnight except that she'd been too tired to argue about it.

Asking Julie to drop her at the Landau so that she

could collect her things, and her car—the department was arranging for the rental car to be picked up there—she thanked her for the ride and agreed to meet her for lunch the next day.

She teared up when Julie gave her an unexpected hug when she went to open her car door and get out.

This whole bump-on-the-head thing was really messing with her.

COLIN HAD NO intention of seeing Chantel Harris again. She'd done her job. He was grateful. Would have his assistant send her some candy or something along with a thank-you card and a check to cover the time she'd spent undercover without pay.

Wayne had filled him in on a few more of the details of the job after Colin had left her hospital room the night before to give them all privacy.

She'd had a job to do and she'd done it. Just as he would have done.

David Smyth Jr. was already in jail, having had his hand wound tended to in the emergency room the night before. Word was he was going to be staying there. Colin couldn't ask for anything more.

And in the years to come, when he thought of Chantel, it would be with supreme gratitude for what she'd done for them.

Yes. He had it all neatly tied up and was ready to pack it all away to sit in the back of his memory bank, gathering dust.

The only reason he'd asked Julie for more detail about Chantel's friend's death, on the way home the night before, was because they'd all been talking about it in the hospital room. Max had been married to the woman who'd died.

He couldn't imagine being him.

But as he put his clubs in his trunk and looked out to the ocean, deciding a Sunday afternoon sailing his yacht was just what he needed, he was suddenly struck with a vision on the incoming tide. Chantel at fourteen, fighting off a lecherous man she'd trusted.

She'd learned young how to take care of herself.

As had he.

And that there was no one else going to do it for her. That those she should be able to trust most weren't trustworthy.

As had he.

She was a rock.

Until she was in his arms. Then she'd been a grown-up version of that fourteen-year-old girl. Just before her stepfather had walked into her room and closed the door.

He had no proof of that. Just as he'd had no proof that he couldn't completely trust her all these weeks.

But he'd been right then.

And knew he was right now.

Just as he knew that he could never, ever be like

her friend Max. He couldn't sit at home, knowing she was out there…in danger…and do nothing.

He just wasn't that man.

THE CAPTAIN HAD told Chantel to take as many days off as she wanted. By Sunday afternoon, she was ready to come back, and she called to tell him so.

He said she needed at a least week. She'd had no vacation since she'd been there and had been working two jobs for almost a month. Plus, she'd taken a fairly substantial bump to the head.

She said she'd be in as scheduled the next day.

He compromised with Wednesday.

Pissed, but knowing she was only going to hurt her cause if she argued, she hung up. Then she changed into black leggings and a short-sleeved Lycra shirt and went to the complex gym to work out.

A girl could only eat so much chocolate ice cream.

THE BOAT DIDN'T make it out of the harbor. Or even away from the dock. Colin boarded her. Did the pre-sail checks. He looked at the back deck and was reminded of Chantel Johnson standing there.

Remembered how much she'd meant to him.

And sat down. Feeling the boat bob on the water.

He'd fallen in love with a fantasy.

Johnson wasn't going to be easy to forget.

Two hours was about all she could do with only a treadmill and free weights to work with. With a soaked towel around her neck, Chantel headed back to her apartment in the cool afternoon sunshine.

Normally, on duty or not, she'd have noticed the man standing on the sidewalk outside her front door before she was almost upon him.

But nothing about her felt normal.

She only noticed him when she was about six yards away. In light gray chino pants and a short-sleeved light-colored shirt, he stood on cracked pavement and watched her approach.

She wanted to turn around and go the other way. And couldn't slow her feet down.

Heart beating, she watched him right back. When she drew close enough, she looked him in the eye. "You want to come in?" she said.

Her place was an embarrassment compared to what he was used to. But it was neat. Clean. And she could afford the rent.

"Yes."

He didn't ask how she was. Didn't comment on her sweaty state.

He looked over her body in the revealing work-out clothes. And her heart skipped a beat.

If she'd meant to drive him crazy with desire for a woman who didn't exist, by excusing herself to the shower the second they got inside the door of her tiny apartment, she'd succeeded.

Colin sat on her brown tweed sofa, acknowledging to himself that he liked the way things were arranged on the entertainment center across from him.

"I just had to stop by." He was ready the second she came out of the bedroom, which was only feet away from where he was sitting. "To make certain that you were okay, and to thank you again…"

She'd left the bedroom door open when she'd gone in to shower. He was fairly certain some of the heat he was feeling was the steam.

A fresh soapy scent came with her into the room.

"You smell like Johnson." He hadn't meant to say the words out loud. But he was still a bit off his game.

"She smelled like me."

In sweats and a T-shirt, with her hair in a ponytail and no makeup, she curled up on the opposite end of the sofa, tucking bare feet in between the cushions.

It touched him…the way she tucked those toes. He'd kissed those toes.

"I'd offer you a glass of wine, or a beer, but I don't have any."

"You got Scotch?" She'd said in New York she drank Scotch. Had that been Chantel Harris? Or make-believe?

"Yeah, but I save it for...well, anyway, I don't drink on Sunday afternoons."

"Are you being deliberately difficult?"

She didn't even blink. "I don't think so."

"I fell in love with a fantasy." There. It was done. He could move on now.

"Yeah." Johnson would have said, "Yes," with those same lips.

His penis was growing, just like it had the first second he'd laid eyes on Johnson.

"So what was real?"

She shook her head, the swinging ponytail distracting him. He wasn't sure if he liked it or not.

"I'm not sure what you mean."

"We spent four weeks together. Was anything you told me during that time real?"

Frowning, she picked at her fingernail. If he wasn't mistaken, she was trying to get it to come off. "I only lied to you when I absolutely had to, Colin."

"That doesn't answer my question."

"I guess because you haven't asked it in a way that tells me what you want to know."

"Did you feel...anything...between us?"

"Beyond great sex, you mean? That's what you're asking, isn't it? You want to know if, when I slept with you, I prostituted myself for the job?" Her tone was unfamiliar. Harsh.

The fourteen-year-old girl after her stepfather had entered her room.

"No. I was there. You weren't faking." And maybe that was why he was with her now. He sure as hell couldn't figure out another reason. "I want to know if, when you said you'd like to be exclusive with me, you were saying it because of the job or because of me."

"Both."

He wasn't sure what to do with that answer. Or even why he'd felt compelled to ask the question.

He remembered that first night they'd made love, before it had gone that far. They'd been sitting on the couch, and she'd started to cry...

"Those tears, they couldn't have belonged to Johnson," he said aloud.

Chantel stared at him hard. "What are you doing, Colin? Why are you here? What do you want from me?" Rapid-fire questions issued as a challenge.

"I can't just walk away."

"I'm not rich. I hate makeup. I live in a one-bedroom apartment and work for a living."

"I like your apartment." It reminded him of her hotel room. Which was a ludicrous thought, until he realized that what he looked for in that room was anything that spoke of her, and what had stood out to him was her neatness.

The apartment wasn't much larger than her hotel room had been and was just as neat.

"It feels good, sitting here," he said when she remained silent. She wasn't kicking him out.

Johnson would have been too polite to do so. But

Harris? He had a feeling she'd have him out on his ear in seconds if that was what she wanted.

"Julie's not going to let you go," he warned her. "You have a friend for life there."

"So does she." Chantel didn't miss a beat. "I already told her so."

He was in way over his head.

"If I asked you out again, would you go?"

"I work second shift a lot."

His heart started to pound blood to his nether region in a rush. "When's your next day off?" He ignored the at-work part. For now. He was just trying to understand something.

"I'm on mandatory leave until Wednesday." The way she ran her tongue over her lips was not a mistake. It couldn't be.

"You want to have dinner with me tonight?"

"I can't do the whole Johnson dress-up thing." Crossing her arms, she pushed her breasts upward between them. Consciously?

Through narrowed eyes he watched her, not sure what in the hell he was doing. Not sure what she was doing, either.

Those eyes…he'd watched them move behind closed lids as she'd slept. Had wondered what she was dreaming. Hoped that if it was good, it was about him.

Two nights ago that body had been in his bed. And while it had been fantastic, there'd been no fantasy there. It had been very real.

"Can I spend the night here tonight?" It was a bold move.

Harris seemed to need them. Or maybe it was just that he did.

"I haven't changed my sheets in almost a month."

He got her drift. She was the housekeeper here.

"You haven't slept in them much, either." She'd either been at the hotel or in his bed. He knew because he'd been with her.

"I'm not going to be a rich man's plaything."

"I don't see myself ever being married to a cop. One more night. That's all I'm asking. To say good-bye."

"At least we understand each other."

He nodded. So did she. And then she asked what he wanted on his pizza.

He didn't dare tell her he had no idea.

CHAPTER THIRTY-ONE

HE WAS HER "MAX." Chantel had known that weeks ago. He wasn't going to stay with her. She knew that, too.

And understood.

Just like she couldn't be Johnson for him.

But he was her happiness. And she was going to hope that they'd always at least be friends.

He stayed at her place Sunday night. In a mixture of Johnson's clothes and her own—she left her hiking boots at home—with her hair down, the fake nails off, but a little bit of makeup on, Chantel spent Monday night with Julie and Colin.

Just one more night. To ease out of things and into friendship.

They talked about David Smyth Jr. and about Leslie's shocking revelation, which had been kind of lost in all of the drama of Saturday night's shooting and arrest.

"James told me something, today," Colin said as the three of them sat over a game of cards that Chantel and Jill used to play with some of the other recruits.

He was looking at Chantel but not with a lover's

gaze. And she knew it was beginning—the real-life part. She drew. Played a couple of cards and had to discard without making much progress. "What's that?"

"He checked with Paul Reynolds and found out that his sealed juvenile record had been accessed."

Julie's gaze darted between the two of them. It was her turn. She wasn't taking it.

"We were investigating a potentially dangerous, high-risk situation, Colin. It was not only well within our rights, but if we hadn't done so, if we'd blown off the reports that were coming in and something had happened to either Ryder or Leslie…" She was spitting her words out. She wished a little more of Johnson's decorum had worn off on her.

"Hey." He held up his free hand. "We are all extremely glad that you went to the lengths you did."

"You have no idea," Julie said. "I no longer have to live with the fact that the bastard got away with what he did to me. I'm going to be free to attend all of the social functions I'd love to go to. But you also just gave me back a huge sense of security I hadn't even realized I'd lost. I feel like I can trust the police again. I know that I am protected…"

"Never doubt that we are extremely grateful to you. Or think that we aren't aware of the sacrifices you made…"

She wished Julie would just take her turn and that Colin would, too. But since they didn't, Harris just blurted right out, "It's fine, you two, really.

Now either let it go, or I'm out of here." Were they being friendly because they thought they owed her?

She'd gather her things and leave. She wasn't a charity case. She didn't need handouts. Of money *or* friendship. Colin had already written her a check to cover the time she'd been undercover. She'd ripped it up and thrown it back at him.

He'd had a good dose of Harris then.

Julie's horrified expression made Chantel ashamed of herself.

"I only brought it up because I wanted to tell you that he told me about what was in that report," Colin said, switching her attention to him. "He said he's actually relieved to have me know, to have someone know, after keeping his secret all these years."

"What's in the report?" Julie asked. And then said, "Oh, wait, you can't tell me, right? Either one of you?" She looked at Chantel. "Because you're a cop." And then at Colin. "And James swore you to secrecy." She took her turn.

Colin nodded. And said to Chantel, "He said that the pressure of the false allegations from Ryder's school was really getting to him. Because what happened in the past…was a total accident. A couple of kids playing. He's lived not only with the guilt of that his entire life, but with the knowledge that he could hurt someone. He's always taken such extra care to be gentle with Ryder and Leslie, and yet it seemed to be blowing up in his face, anyway…"

He played every card in his hand, drew more then turned three in a row from his pile and finally discarded.

"Did he tell Leslie?" Chantel asked.

"Not yet. But he's going to as soon as she's feeling better."

Leslie had been sedated Saturday night. And was still, by Tuesday, feeling a bit under the weather. She'd been all alone with her secret for so many years, having to see the Smyths without letting on what David Jr. had done to her.

But she'd known who his father's friends were. She'd known that it would be his word against hers. She'd been humiliated and embarrassed. And afraid what people would think of her.

Later, after Julie had told her what he'd done to *her*, and she'd seen him get away with it, she'd known she did the right thing to remain quiet. And yet, had felt the guilt of her silence in terms of Julie's rape. Leslie also knew that if she told James, he'd lose his mind over not being able to do anything about it. And she'd been afraid of what he would do.

She was going to be getting help for her "accidents." The hope being that now that she'd finally told the truth about what had happened, she could begin to see that it hadn't been her fault. And that she could stop punishing herself.

Plus, she was joining one of the counseling groups at The Lemonade Stand.

The alarms sent up by Ryder's collage had a three-fold effect. First, he'd overheard his mother having a breakdown one night with his dad and knew she'd been hurt in a really bad way at some point. Second, he'd heard his father mention getting his baseball bat out again—and had been reminded of the fact that his father would never play ball with him. And then third, he'd been frightened by all of the accidents his mother kept having. Which had come out when the family had gone to a therapist together the day before.

It was Chantel's turn. She cleared her pile. Won the game. And asked Colin and Julie how they felt about chocolate ice cream.

COLIN PRETENDED THAT life was as per usual on Wednesday. He got up. Alone. Got dressed. Had breakfast with his sister. Drove to the office and went to work. He participated in meetings. Had a lengthy lunch that netted him a new million-dollar account. He went to a court hearing and closed on a seven-figure real-estate deal.

And every five minutes or so he glanced at his smart watch. Not to keep track of upcoming appointments. Or the time. But to see if he'd had a text from Chantel. Or *about* Chantel.

He didn't hear from her at all that day, or that night, either.

Nor on Thursday.

As a friend, the least she could have done was

let him know that she was safely home from her first couple of days back on the job.

Or had he now been relegated to one of those people who'd one day, out of the blue, get a call telling him someone he'd once known had been killed?

When Paul Reynolds showed up on his caller ID late Thursday afternoon, his heart stopped. Was he getting that call already? The one he was going to prevent by not marrying her?

"Paul? What's up?" he asked, motioning his assistant out of his office with the door closed behind her.

"I'd like a meeting with you, if at all possible," the commissioner said.

"Has something happened to Chantel?"

"What? No." A pause on the line followed. "No, I'm sorry, Colin. I failed to see how this might appear. As far as I know, she's on the street doing her job. She's one our most exemplary officers, by the way." He went on to give Chantel a glowing review that Colin didn't need to hear.

He didn't *want* to hear it. He would rather not think of her on the job.

"I need a meeting with you on another matter," Paul said. "Today, if possible."

He'd had his last scheduled appointment for the day.

"Name the time and place," he said and then agreed to meet the commissioner at a beach bar half an hour down the coast.

He knew what that meant.

COLIN HAD SAID he couldn't be in a relationship with a cop. She knew he'd meant it. Still, she'd thought he'd call—at least once—to make sure she was still alive. She thought about texting him. About a hundred times a day. But she didn't want to rub it in that she was out on the streets risking her life without him there to protect her.

She'd had her off-duty weapon in plain view in her apartment. Had it concealed in her purse at his house, but he'd known it was there. He'd seen her put it there, and he hadn't said a word about it. Period. Hadn't asked how many times she'd had to shoot it during the line of duty.

Hadn't asked her if she'd ever killed someone.

She hadn't. But she knew she wouldn't hesitate to do so if she had to. As she prepared to go on shift Thursday afternoon, Wayne stopped by and told her the captain wanted to see her.

Following him to the interrogation room where the three of them had met before she'd gone under, she felt like she'd come full circle.

Everything had changed in the past five weeks.

And nothing had.

"Sit down, Chantel," Captain Reagan said. Wayne was already doing so. The captain, in a suit and tie, like Wayne, sat last.

"I wanted to give you an update on David Smyth Jr.," the captain began.

She nodded and heard how, after speaking with his counsel, he'd agreed to plead guilty to fourteen counts of rape—with a mandatory prison sentence of not less than twenty-five years, and could be as much as seventy-five, depending on further investigation and a decision from the court.

"Wow," she said, starting to smile. "So no one will have to testify?"

"That's correct."

"But…" Something else was going on. She saw the look Wayne exchanged with the captain, and her stomach dropped.

"In exchange for that, for the fact that he's going away—to a minimum security prison for people of money, and to do so without a trial that would necessitate victim testimony and could cost the state up to a million dollars or more—this stays out of the press. Victims aren't named. His wife and kids and family are protected from the scandal…"

Right. Fine. Get to it. The guys knew she didn't give a hoot about what kind of prison he was in as long as he was in it. And that she also would be fine with this happening in a way that ensured his family—also innocent victims of his crimes—would not have to suffer.

"And they want you and Wayne to let the rest of this drop."

"What does that mean?"

"We're aware that you know of the deal made between the Smyths, and the Fairbankses, involving certain representatives of this department."

Wayne gave her one glance. A pleading look.

And she understood.

"You want me to ignore the fact that Paul Reynolds was party to letting a rapist live among his own friends? That he let the man continue to harass and brutalize possible wives and daughters of his friends?"

"He didn't know, Chantel," Wayne said. "I mean, he knew about the situation with Julie. He'd been told it had started out mutual, and then when Julie didn't like it, it went bad. That, at the most, it was excessive force on a date. The commissioner wasn't even present when they went to Julie and made the offer to let it drop and save her reputation. He was presented with a done deal. And saw no reason to ruin a promising young man's career, to drag a young girl's reputation through the mud, because of a date gone bad. He had no idea there were others."

"There were medical records," Chantel said. "Details that make me sick to my stomach. You want me to believe that he didn't know about them? They just disappeared all by themselves?"

"He says he didn't know," Captain Reagan said, his face as serious as she'd ever seen it.

"They're willing to offer you any job you want in the department, Chantel. You've more than proven yourself. You'd already passed the investigators' exam before you transferred up here. You name your job, and it's yours."

For three days she'd been trying to push away the idea of moving to a desk job. She was good at investigating. And maybe if Julie's case had come across her desk, she'd have been able to see to it that her friend received justice. One day back on the job and she already knew that she wasn't going to be able to be in a relationship with Colin and work the street.

Not just because he was shutting her out, but because he hadn't called.

She couldn't work the job because all day yesterday she'd been aware of that fact that, if she got hurt, it would hurt Colin. As much or more than Max had been hurt when Jill had died.

Maybe even as much as he'd hurt when Meri had been missing.

She couldn't do that to him.

The truth was, she wasn't even sure she wanted to do it to herself. She was almost thirty-three years old. She'd lived a lot of her life—most of it—with only a best friend for family.

For the first time since she was fourteen, she was beginning to feel like part of a family. She didn't want to risk losing that by dying on the job.

She just might have too much to live for.

"And David Smyth Sr…he gets off even though he helped his son get away with rape?"

"He didn't know, either, Chantel. He'd been told exactly what the commissioner was told. Other than that, he was present during the negotiations with Julie and Colin."

"He threatened and blackmailed them," she said.

"He thought he was protecting his son from the horrible consequences of a date gone very wrong."

"It was a party. Not a date."

"Julie was David's date for the party."

She might have known that. She couldn't remember at the moment. Couldn't think. And it didn't really matter if she'd been his date or not. Or even if they'd been at a party. What mattered was justice for Julie.

"James Morrison has already agreed to let this go," Reagan said next. "It's best for Leslie's recovery if they just move forward."

"The commissioner's a good guy, Chantel," Wayne said. "Something like this…it would ruin his life. And Patricia's, too."

But what about the lives that were ruined because he'd believed a friend and turned a blind eye to all of this? Someone had allowed those charges to not just be dropped, but to disappear out of the system as though they'd never been filed.

Someone had destroyed the medical report sent over by Dr. Albertson—who'd left the hospital soon after that.

And a cop was on a fishing boat in Florida, too.

"Someone went to a lot of work to conceal tracks for something that no one thought was more than a date gone bad," she said aloud.

"Think about what you're doing, Chantel."

She was thinking. But she didn't need to. Her gut had already made her decision for her.

"I'm not a person who can benefit my own skin at the cost of others," she said. "We don't even know how many victims Smyth has. Nor do we know who they are or what *they* want. We have no idea the extent of damage that was done, the lives that were irrevocably changed, because the commissioner didn't do his job."

"Think of all your fellow officers, Chantel. The ones who come to work every day and give everything to the job. You try to make a stink here, it's going to make every one of us smell."

Wayne was clearly going to sign. Morrison was on board. Colin and Julie had already agreed, ten years before, to remain silent.

Chantel didn't have a chance in hell of accomplishing anything here but getting herself fired.

"I'm sorry," she said, standing. "I took an oath. I watched my friend die for that oath. I've been willing every single day to die for that oath. I am not going to tarnish that by agreeing to this. I'm sorry."

They'd find a reason to get rid of her. She didn't doubt that. Just as she knew that she'd move on. Just as she'd moved out of New York. She couldn't work for a corrupt leader, nor could she let this go.

She'd do everything in her power to expose what had happened in Santa Raquel without hurting the victims any more than was necessary. Because if the corruption didn't stop, nor would the number of its victims stop growing.

And if she failed?

There were police departments everywhere.
She cared about the job.
So someplace she'd get it done.

CHAPTER THIRTY-TWO

"So you see, Colin, all we need is an assurance of your continued cooperation and this should all be behind us."

"Morrison's already signed on?" Colin had ordered a bourbon straight but hadn't taken a sip of it.

"You're getting what you wanted. David Smyth Jr. will be behind bars for a very long time. Julie won't have to testify. She's back in society with no one knowing what happened to her. Smyth's wife and kids are protected…"

"Your job is protected," Colin added. "And Patricia is saved from humiliation and a possible change in fortune."

The man's brow furrowed. "I'm not proud of turning a blind eye to what happened ten years ago, Colin. You have to know I truly believed it was a date gone bad."

"But you didn't look at the facts, Paul, did you? And let me save you from a lie here. Because if you'd even looked at the doctor's emergency room report, you'd have known it was more than that."

He stopped short of describing Julie's injuries to the other man. But only to protect his sister.

"Julie would want you to let this go." Paul hit him where it counted most, as men of power usually did. "She's got her life back. Let her have it."

He'd like to think he'd learned a thing or two in ten years. But Colin was tempted to swallow the bile in his throat and do as the commissioner asked.

"You have my word that anything you want, or need, anytime—I'm your man."

He'd be one of the most powerful men in the area. Powerful men could get a lot of good done.

"What happens to Chantel?"

"She's being offered the job of her choice within the department. She's a great cop. And will make a great leader within the force, too. I look forward to many years of having her on my team."

"She's agreed to that?"

"I'm sure she has. They were meeting with her this afternoon. I'd have heard if there was a problem."

Johnson might have agreed to the deal. To protect others.

He had to believe that Reynolds was bluffing on that one.

Harris would never agree to it. She knew that hiding, pretending that pain didn't exist, hurt more than anything else.

If she'd been a woman who would take a deal, she'd never have fought for Julie in the first place.

She'd had his back even when he hadn't known she had it. His and Julie's. She'd risked her life for them.

And who had *her* back?

Ever?

"I'm sorry, Paul, but I can't do as you're asking. Julie and I have already spoken about going public with this. And if Chantel wants to pursue the matter, she will have our full support."

Paul Reynolds stood so quickly he knocked the table onto two legs. It teetered and fell back to place. "You'll regret this."

"Possibly. But I don't think so. I'm willing to consider another deal with you, Paul. One I'm sure I can get Chantel to agree to."

"And that is?"

"You resign. For whatever reason you deem appropriate. Pack up your things and go quietly, and you go with your reputation intact."

Paul's thrumming fingers on the table was the tell he'd needed. "And one other thing," he said, doing not half-bad on the fly.

"What's that?"

"I'll want the names of anyone else in the Santa Raquel Police Department who had any involvement in allowing criminals to run free." He was thinking like Harris.

And he didn't hate the feeling.

"I'm not going to…"

"Think about it, Paul. Julie and I plan to have something ready for the press by the end of the week."

"Give me through the weekend. I need to speak with Patricia."

Colin stood. Held out his hand. When Paul shook it, he knew he'd won. The commissioner would be a fool to refuse him. He came from money and had enough of it from the investments he'd inherited to live in style for the rest of his life. He also was in a perfect position to crawl farther up the political ladder—as long as there was no scandal attached to him.

"Oh, and one other thing, Paul," he said as the two of them were walking out together.

"Yes?"

"It's about Patricia. Just out of curiosity, why was she suddenly showing up on every committee Julie was on?"

He had the man dead to rights then.

"Because you two were worried that, with the new information surfacing about the Morrisons, Julie and Leslie together might decide to revisit the past?"

"I'll make an announcement and give you those names by Sunday," Paul said and strode away.

CHANTEL WAS SITTING with Wayne in the interrogation room, listening to him talk about all of the reasons why she needed to rethink her position, when Captain Reagan came back to the door.

"Chantel? There's someone here to see you."

"Who is it?" she asked, but the captain had already turned away. He was not happy with her. Yet she had the impression that he wasn't all that unhappy with her, either. Captain Reagan was a good man. Maybe she'd have an ally in him somewhere down the road.

Still in uniform, though she'd been off shift more than an hour, she rose. Wayne made good points. She respected him.

But she wasn't going to change her mind.

She also had no idea what she *was* going to do. Taking down the police commissioner without any help was not going to be easy.

Neither had kneeing a man two hundred pounds heavier than her been easy. But she'd done it.

Heading out front to the lobby, she saw Colin before he saw her. And almost turned back. She could send out word that she was busy. Didn't feel well. Change and escape out the back.

She was Harris, not Johnson. She didn't run from trouble.

So she boldly walked right up to him—uniform, holster, Taser gun, hiking boots and all.

"You wanted to see me?"

He stepped back. Looked her up and down. And then grinned. "I could get used to that," he said.

He leaned forward, his mouth to her ear. "In my bedroom. Especially if you bring the handcuffs."

She wanted to slap him. But then she saw the seriousness in his gaze.

"What's going on?" she asked. People were starting to notice her standing there with a man who was clearly not one of them. They may or may not recognize him, but Colin spoke wealth from the top of his expensively cut hair down to the handmade leather shoes.

"Two things," he said. "First, I hear you had an offer from the commissioner."

Wow. They didn't waste any time pulling their punches.

"I turned him down."

Colin grinned again. "I rather thought you might," he said. "I came here straight from my meeting with him because I wanted you to be the first to know." He leaned in again. "And unfortunately, for the moment, you can be the only one who knows, but I can trust you to keep a secret."

"What is it?" She pulled back to look him in the eye. Would the man ever stop confusing her?

"He's going to resign, Chantel. He's making the announcement on Sunday. Right after he delivers, to my office, the list of names of everyone in this department who's been involved in making deals."

Her mouth dropped open.

He closed it for her.

"People are staring," he said softly enough that

no one could hear. But she looked around, and he was right. A small crowd was beginning to form, Wayne right there with them.

"I didn't plan it this way, but I have to say I'm not sorry to have them here, seeing that you trust them with your life and let them trust you with theirs..."

Now he was talking nonsense. Was he jealous of her fellow officers?

Before she could ask, he went down on one knee and took hold of her hand.

"Chantel Harris, I'd meant to do this when you were still Johnson, Saturday night after the gala, but you went and shot someone, and, well..."

People were closing in on them. She was sweating like a pig.

"Will you marry me?"

"You don't want to be married to a cop." She was going to ask for a desk job. Because she didn't trust herself not to hesitate in the face of danger, and she didn't want to hurt Colin and Julie.

"I'm not sure I'll be any good at it," he said. "But I definitely want to be married to you. And you're a cop."

Everyone was staring at her. Waiting.

"I don't like the idea of you putting yourself in harm's way," he said. "But what I've come to see is that you're damned good at what you do, Chantel. And you're well trained. I guess what I'm trying to say is that I trust you to keep yourself safe."

He trusted her. *And* he was giving her the freedom to protect herself.

"Help me out here, Chantel. I've had zero practice at this. You've been tough a long time. Can you meet me halfway? Let me share the job of having your back?"

Tears sprang to her eyes and spilled over as her chest started to rumble. "Oh, my God," she said, the words ending on a sob before she stopped herself by holding her breath. He stood. She stared up at him. He got something about her she hadn't. Not until that moment.

She'd learned early on that she couldn't count on anyone to watch out for her. The job was hers alone. So she'd done what she could to be up to the task.

It was always about the job.

Because it was through the job that she felt safe living life.

Colin pulled her up against him as she forced herself to take deep breaths against the tears that were squeezing past her resolve to hold them in check. He held her, giving her time to calm herself.

"Does that mean she's saying yes?" she heard someone ask.

"Yes." She recognized that voice. It was Wayne's, with a peculiar note, like he was celebrating or something, and it gave her the impetus to look up at Colin.

"Yeah," she said loudly. Boldly. Harris style. "I

will marry you, Colin Fairbanks. And yes, I will share my back with you."

He kissed her then. Like he had when they were all alone in her posh hotel room. And she returned the kiss.

Not giving a rat's ass about the whoops and hollers going on all around them.

* * * * *

LARGER-PRINT BOOKS!

HARLEQUIN

Presents®

GET 2 FREE LARGER-PRINT NOVELS PLUS 2 FREE GIFTS!

PASSION
GUARANTEED
SEDUCTION

YES! Please send me 2 FREE LARGER-PRINT Harlequin Presents® novels and my 2 FREE gifts (gifts are worth about $10). After receiving them, if I don't wish to receive any more books, I can return the shipping statement marked "cancel." If I don't cancel, I will receive 6 brand-new novels every month and be billed just $5.30 per book in the U.S. or $5.74 per book in Canada. That's a saving of at least 12% off the cover price! It's quite a bargain! Shipping and handling is just 50¢ per book in the U.S. and 75¢ per book in Canada.* I understand that accepting the 2 free books and gifts places me under no obligation to buy anything. I can always return a shipment and cancel at any time. Even if I never buy another book, the two free books and gifts are mine to keep forever.

176/376 HDN GHVY

Name	(PLEASE PRINT)	
Address		Apt. #
City	State/Prov.	Zip/Postal Code

Signature (if under 18, a parent or guardian must sign)

Mail to the **Reader Service**:
IN U.S.A.: P.O. Box 1867, Buffalo, NY 14240-1867
IN CANADA: P.O. Box 609, Fort Erie, Ontario L2A 5X3

**Are you a subscriber to Harlequin Presents® books
and want to receive the larger-print edition?
Call 1-800-873-8635 today or visit us at www.ReaderService.com.**

* Terms and prices subject to change without notice. Prices do not include applicable taxes. Sales tax applicable in N.Y. Canadian residents will be charged applicable taxes. Offer not valid in Quebec. This offer is limited to one order per household. Not valid for current subscribers to Harlequin Presents Larger-Print books. All orders subject to credit approval. Credit or debit balances in a customer's account(s) may be offset by any other outstanding balance owed by or to the customer. Please allow 4 to 6 weeks for delivery. Offer available while quantities last.

Your Privacy—The Reader Service is committed to protecting your privacy. Our Privacy Policy is available online at www.ReaderService.com or upon request from the Reader Service.

We make a portion of our mailing list available to reputable third parties that offer products we believe may interest you. If you prefer that we not exchange your name with third parties, or if you wish to clarify or modify your communication preferences, please visit us at www.ReaderService.com/consumerchoice or write to us at Reader Service Preference Service, P.O. Box 9062, Buffalo, NY 14240-9062. Include your complete name and address.

HPLP15